To D.

STEPPING
UP

DAVE PALMER

Thank you for the support.

All the best

[signature] x.

Stepping Up

Copyright 2025 Dave Palmer

ISBN: 978-1-7385451-3-1

Also available as an eBook

Editing by: Louise Harnby
www.harnby.co/fiction-editing

www.davepalmerauthor.co.uk

website by Marcell Media
www.marcellmedia.co.uk

Printed by Expresta in Europe

DEDICATION

My wonderful family and friends for all their marvellous support and encouragement.

A particular shoutout to my darling wife Rachael, my daughter Louise Clay and my dear friend Marcus for their unwavering belief in this project.

And as usual, my brilliant editor, Louise Harnby.

1

Today's the Day

The late-summer morning sunshine poured through the window of Jack Clay's Camden hotel room. And it wasn't welcome. He felt like crap. Hardly a surprise given the massive amounts of alcohol and cocaine he'd consumed over the past few days. Binges took their toll. He knew it, and he was paying for it.

The thunderous snoring coming from the bed opposite only added to the assault. Jack sat up and stared the source of the cacophony. Callum McCormack. His best friend ... and his best man. Or at least he would be later today. The man had a quite extraordinary ability to sleep through anything and everything. Always had done. Jack envied him.

But right now, the more pressing issue was his bladder. He dragged himself off the bed, and made his way over to the bathroom, scratching his balls on the way. After answering natures call, he glanced in the bathroom mirror. The sight reflected there wasn't a pretty one. Thank fuck Lorraine couldn't see him right now. She'd have lost it if she knew what a state he was in. This was her big day and he'd promised her he wouldn't get rat-arsed the night before. Had she really believed that shit? Surely not.

Jack laughed. Fucking Callum – it was all his fault. They'd been at it until four this morning. But, after all, that was what best friends were for, wasn't it? Taking responsibility for when you disgraced yourself. Good old Callum.

Still, he did need to get himself straightened out, and sharpish. The Fitzpatrick brothers – two other long-time friends and business associates – were due to pick him and Callum up in the lobby at midday. The wedding was at 1.00 pm, and it was already just after eleven. It wouldn't do to keep John Junior and Liam waiting.

Jack splashed water over his face and winced as he patted his cheeks dry, his still recovering finger catching in the towel. A reminder of what he'd been through in the past few months, like he needed one. Things hadn't been easy. The injuries from the Yardie's machete and knife attack were healing nicely but his finger still throbbed like hell. And the pain was still unbearable when he accidentally knocked his hand on something. He'd been extremely lucky that they'd even managed to save it, although sometimes he wished they hadn't. During one of his recent and seemingly endless visits to the physio, he'd asked them to cut if off. They had refused. While he appreciated their attempt to get the finger's function back to some degree of normality, some days it felt like the cost of achieving that was too much. Thanks to that deranged, machete-wielding killer, St Georges hospital in Tooting hospital had become almost a second home over the past two months.

He'd had no choice but to grab the weapon. If he hadn't grabbed it, the Yardie would have severed more than a finger. But the attack had cut clean through his tendons – because, yeah, machetes were really fucking sharp – and despite the remarkable work of a wonderful surgeon, that finger's tendons were now slightly shorter than previously, which meant he still had limited mobility, particularly when it came to opening and closing his hand. That the damage had been done to his dominant left hand didn't help either. After all the physiotherapy, he still found it hard to hold a spoon properly or even sign his name on anything.

Still, no use crying over spilled milk. It could have been worse. 'Jack Clay's still here,' he said, grinning into the mirror, 'and he's about to marry the girl of his dreams. So fuck you, Chambers.'

He went back into the bedroom, and found Callum stirring. Laughed and said, 'Morning, wanker. I don't know who looks worse – you or that dump I've just had in there.'

'Piss off, you prick,' Callum said. He smiled and sat up in the bed. 'What time is it anyway?'

'Time you got up, dickhead. We need to be at the church in less than two hours, and the boys are picking us up at twelve. You've got sixty minutes to get your shit together.'

'Fuck me,' Callum said. 'Is it eleven already?'

'I'm afraid so, son.'

'God, I feel like shit,' Callum said, yawning like a hippo. 'Talking of which, Jesus H Christ, mate, what the fuck is that smell?'

Jack just laughed and headed towards the door. 'I'll go and get us some proper coffee from reception, but I'd give that toilet ten minutes or so if I were you.'

2

What's to Worry About?

Tommy Spillane's youngest daughter was pregnant, and it showed.

His wife, Peggy, had told him not to worry. 'You'll be amazed at what we can do with the right dress and a little bit of magic. No one will know the difference.'

'They will when the baby pops out less than five months from now,' Tommy said, leaning back against the kitchen counter and shaking his head.

'How about we worry about that when we have to, my darling?' Peggy waved an admonishing finger in front of his face, but her smile was broad. 'For now, let's just make sure we give these two young people the wedding they deserve. And that means you concerning yourself with making sure our daughter has everything she needs.'

Tommy rolled his eyes and laughed. His childhood sweetheart knew best, always had, and in moments like these he didn't think he could love her any more. And she was right – of course she was. What was he getting so worked up about? He had a fantastic wife who was a wonderful mother. Money wasn't a worry. And he'd given his family a lovely new home. At the end of the day it all came down to family – that's what

Peggy was always reminding him. So when it came to his girls, what they wanted was what they got. Simple as that really.

Less simple was the investigation into Tommy's business affairs. The brutal murders of Mickey Grover and that Sweeney police inspector Paul Summers only two months ago had brought down some serious heat on him and his organisation. The killing of a working police officer, crooked or not, never went down well with the establishment and was usually avoided at all costs.

Those bloodthirsty Parkhurst brothers – they'd really done a number on him this time. At least one was dead; that was something. Shame it hadn't been the other one though. Harry Parkhurst, the brains behind the South London mob, had survived the shootout that had taken place while the brothers were in the process of escaping after killing two men in the sleepy little district of Hythe in Kent. Grover had been a grass and wouldn't be missed or mourned by anyone but his mother. But Summers? Now that was a different kettle of fish. Tommy suspected that Summers's guvnor, that bitch Chief Inspector Sandra Bates, knew he'd been bent. Not that the filth would ever reveal it, if the statements in the media that had appeared following the bastard's death were anything to go by. They'd expressed complete and utter shock that a good, honest and hardworking police officer, one who'd simply been looking after a key witness in a murder case, had been so cruelly cut down while attending to his duties.

Tommy still didn't know whether to laugh or puke.

And Harry Parkhurst could be a problem. He could make life difficult for Tommy. He had nothing to lose now, did he? Because it was Harry and his now-dead twin, Jimmy, who'd been instrumental in arranging some retribution for Tommy via their psychotic nephew Danny Mason back in the day, and more recently with the Saunders and Green murders. It was a worry, no doubt about it. Bates, the investigating officer, had already made it clear that she was looking into three other murders that she believed Tommy had been involved in. Indeed, she'd promised him that she wouldn't stop until she'd found the evidence she needed to ensure she got another day in court with him.

Stupid bitch. Bitter as fuck, that much was clear. Like an obsession. She still hadn't got over that fact that he'd walked away from the Old Bailey a free man several months earlier, when he'd been acquitted of the murder of a Sussex businessman. That lunatic Mason had recorded Giles Anderson's brutal end, while implicating Tommy as the one who'd ordered the hit. But Tommy had been exonerated. And that was that. He couldn't be retried for that at least.

Darren Davies was a different matter. Another obsession of the chief inspector's. Darren had once been Tommy's trusted lieutenant. And then, back in the late eighties, the man had betrayed him. He'd been arrested for drug supply and had climbed into bed with another gangster, one Billy Saunders, which had ended up with Tommy doing a six-year stretch. Saunders and his friend Karl Green had tried to be a couple of clever fuckers, thinking that with Tommy locked up they'd gain access to his drug supply in North London. It hadn't worked, of course. His trusted friend and long-time associate Albie Spires had made sure of that.

Tommy had no regrets about killing Darren. As far as he was concerned, Darren had got what he deserved. Back in the early days, violence and murder had been an everyday part of Tommy's world. Sometimes he missed those days. Taking personal responsibility for Darren's demise had made him happy. In fact, he'd rather enjoyed caving the bastard's head in with a baseball bat at the firm's lockup unit over in Kings Cross.

It had been an unusual move on Tommy's part. Usually, he arranged for others to do his dirty work. Like with Billy Saunders and Karl Green. It had been the Parkhurst brothers and their psychotic nephew, Mason, who'd been tasked with getting their hands dirty. That, too, was still a live investigation now that the police had found Mason's body in Spain, and Tommy was seriously worried. Mason might have left evidence behind before his own murder and burial at the Parkhurst's villa over there. And on top of that, Saunders came from a well-known Traveller family over in Wandsworth. His brother Charlie had sworn to avenge his brother's killing, and had put out the offer of a substantial reward for any information leading to the identification of the perp.

The whole mess made Tommy shudder. If Harry Parkhurst gave him up, it would lead to a war that Tommy didn't think he could win, despite having Jack, Callum and others like John Fitzpatrick and his sons on his books.

Of course, there was always Ronnie Fisher. Now there was a man no one wanted to cross. He was a psychopath, and couldn't be relied on when it came to delicate matters. Tommy used him only when extreme violence was required. The man was as loyal as an old dog. All Tommy usually had to do was utter his name and the problem would go away. So, yeah, a very useful man, but only in very special circumstances. Which wasn't what was required at the moment. It wouldn't end well for any of them if violence and mayhem were in play, particularly not with the wedding and Tommy's first grandchild on the way.

And anyway, there was nothing Tommy could do about Harry Parkhurst at the moment. He was banged up in one of Her Majesty's most secure prisons, the infamous Belmarsh. A category-A establishment usually reserved for Britain's most dangerous criminals, and, if some of the reports were true, staffed by Britain's most dangerous prison guards. Which meant that, for the time being at least, Harry was untouchable.

Whereas Charlie Saunders wasn't. Charlie was having it good. Tommy knew so because he'd done some business with Charlie and his family. Thanks to Tommy, they'd increased their income substantially over the past year or so and were now turning over six kilos of Tommy's cocaine each week. The kind of business not to be sniffed at. Tommy chuckled at his little joke.

Then again, there were a lot of skeletons in that cupboard, too many for Tommy's liking. Perhaps Charlie Saunders needed to go. Something to think about. Particularly because he'd heard rumblings from that side of London that things had spiralled out of control. Eastern European and Jamaican Yardie gangs were an even bigger force to be reckoned with. They were taking over huge swathes of London. He was used to that, of course. On this side of the water, the Turkish mafia had taken a huge step up the ladder in drug distribution and street dealing. It didn't bother him that much because they specialised in heroin and crack cocaine, and Tommy had vowed never to get involved with that side of this murky business. Cocaine was one thing, and mostly used in a recreational way. Heroin and crack – different matter. Two drugs that had given birth to a living, breathing monster, not just on the streets of London but around the country. Crime had gone through the roof, perpetrated by those addicted to it. Even old ladies were being mugged for their pensions. It made Tommy sick to the stomach.

Tommy had warned his trusted lieutenants – Jack, John Fitzpatrick Senior and Callum – never to get involved with it. Jack and Callum had agreed and vowed never to, despite the huge profits to be had from their supply.

He didn't have to tell Ronnie Fisher. John was a different matter.

3

Old Dinosaurs, Young Mavericks

John Fitzpatrick and Tommy went back a long way. As in four decades' worth of long way. Right back to the sixties. John had his own firm – or 'family' – that controlled drug distribution in Islington, Camden Town, Stoke Newington and other areas of North London, operating under the Spillane banner. Though a staunch ally of Tommy's empire, he'd made it clear to the Tommy that he thought the old-school way of doing things was becoming obsolete.

The disrespect that incoming operators had for men like him and Tommy was unprecedented. Back in the old days, they'd have been dealt with quickly – and as painfully as possible.

But not now. Tommy Spillane had gone soft. That part he'd kept to himself.

All those little fuckers were laughing at them, but all Tommy could say was 'Times are changing, John boy. Maybe it's time we moved over and let the youngsters have their time.'

Well, fuck that. It was all very well Tommy saying that from his bloody ivory tower. He'd earned his money and could afford to retire if that's what he wanted. But John? No, he had bills to pay.

And, let's face it, habits to feed.

It had been ten years since he'd lost his wife. Ten years since he'd gone off the rails in no small way. Ten years of feeling lonely and craving the company of a woman. No mean feat for a man in his sixties. And so he'd taken to making regular visits to high-class prostitutes up town, then more recently the lower end of things in Kings Cross. It was costing him a bloody fortune, especially as his taste in girls had changed somewhat over the years. The younger the better, which cost a lot more than the usual. As did his now out-of-control drug use.

There'd been a time when he could handle the drugs, but these days it was affecting his ability to make sound judgements. Big time. He hid his best to hide it, but the façade was crumbling. He'd never made a secret of his dreams of grandeur and thirst for power to those who knew him best, but more and more, most people he still mixed with just laughed it off, putting it down to his heavy drinking – another thing that had escalated recently. It had got to the point where he could tell that people thought he was being a bit of a pain in the arse when he was indulging, and his relationships with those who'd once been unwaveringly loyal to him were starting to diminish somewhat. And it wasn't so much the drinking or the casual use of recreational drugs that was the real problem. It was because the crack had changed him. He knew it had. Freebasing had made him unpredictable. And that got people's teeth on edge, made them worried, made them not trust him.

At first it was just a few times a month. He'd been curious, had let himself be drawn into it. Now his use was heavy. He'd disappear for days on end. His two sons, John Junior and Liam, still had no idea – he hoped – but others had surely spotted the signs. It wasn't good. If Tommy found out about the crack, he'd be finished. If Tommy found about the young girls, Tommy would finish him. End of. The big sleep. The man was old school and had daughters of his own. No way would he tolerate that.

The changes on the streets were clear as day. All over North London, maverick groups of young men from all walks of life, with no allegiance to anyone, were dealing their wares all around him. It was blatant. They didn't even bother trying to hide it. And, yeah, so he supplied most of the cocaine to some of these fellas – large lumps that they'd cut and distribute – but these boys were always looking for a way to maximise their profits. Every fucking gang was looking to undercut him – the South London Yardies, the North London Albanians and Turks. And so while their profits were up, his had diminished substantially these past few years. Plus, without the old-school hierarchy, it was only a matter of time before all hell broke loose between these rival gangs, and old dinosaurs like him and Tommy were pushed aside. They simply didn't have the clout anymore.

That young upstart Jack Clay was part of the problem too. He was marrying Tommy's daughter, and Tommy was using Jack more and more and pushing John aside, giving John no option but to look for ways to bring a bit more cash in while good old Tommy moved into his new palace, barking out strict instructions not to mess with heroin or this new crack epidemic that had crept over the water from America like a snowstorm. How the fuck dare he?

No, just no. John wanted a piece of the action. And no one, not even Tommy Spillane, got to tell him shit while sitting in his newly acquired mansion and order someone like John as to how to earn his living. The old man needed to open his eyes and take a good look at what was really happening on the streets around him.

So John was going to do what he felt was best for him and his family, and fuck Tommy Spillane. It wasn't like he had the muscle either. Oh, yeah, he had Jack and Callum and maybe a few others, but that was about it really, wasn't it? John and his boys could manage them if they needed too. Once upon a time, Liam and John Junior had been thick as thieves with Jack and Callum. A formidable foursome who'd stuck together whenever there was trouble. Few people had dared to mess with them. But of late there'd been dissent. Liam and John Junior were second-generation Irish boys. Fighting was in their blood and they didn't like being ordered around by anyone. They had ambition, too, and were fed up with the restrictions imposed on them by Jack, now Tommy's right-hand man. Once a partner in crime, Jack now kept a close eye on their activities. He'd been their equal; now it felt like he was their boss. It made them wary of him of course – he was tough, fearless, relentless – but they weren't scared of him. Or Callum for that matter.

But maybe the most important advantage that John had was his relationship with Ronnie Fisher. They went back years. They were tight. And Ronnie had confided in John, said that Tommy was using him less and less.

Which meant mad, bad Ronnie was an ally.

What more did you need?

4

Next Move

Tommy was thinking. And thinking a bit more. In two hours, his daughter would tie the knot, but that was a small thing, a pleasant distraction. Right now, it was dissent he was contemplating. They thought he didn't – John Senior, Jack, Callum, Ronnie, all of 'em – but that was no bad thing. Sometimes it was best to keep your cards close to your chest about such matters. That way, they didn't see you coming.

He'd heard the rumour – that he was hiding away in his ivory tower. But some of those spreading them were out of touch or out of the loop. He was still doing the rounds of his manor, mostly at weekends and usually alone, before it became too lively. During those rounds, he'd spend some time with old school buddies, several of whom ran pubs and clubs around Camden and Islington that Tommy had a controlling interest in. Tommy supplied most of them with fruit machines, which brought in a tidy income. Very few people knew about that, and that's just the way he liked it. Cash was king.

John Fitzpatrick and his sons had an inkling that he was involved in certain establishments but had no firm evidence. Indeed, not even Jack knew about these interests.

Although that would need to change. Tommy had high hopes for Jack, especially now that he was going to become part of the family and there was a child on the way. Tommy would need to bring him in closer, not so much for Jack's sake but for the child's and any of Tommy's future grandchildren. A legacy – that was what this was about. Creating a legacy.

Those trips to the pubs and clubs were critical. The landlords and their friends had a wealth of information to impart about what was happening in the North London establishments where most of Tommy's cocaine was distributed by a small army of foot soldiers. It was Albie who'd done the work of controlling all that in the past. But Albie was gone. Mowed down by a monster. So Tommy had put the task in the hands of Jack and Callum, assisted in some part by the Fitzpatrick brothers. Closely watched in the shadows by Ronnie.

The grapevine had delivered, just has Tommy had known it would. Yeah, he knew all about his old ally, John Senior, and the man's dissent. According to one of the landlords, John had gotten pissed one evening and begun shooting his mouth off about Tommy's old-school ways and how he'd bought a house in a gated development to hide away from any potential enemies. How Tommy wasn't the man John had known back in the sixties and seventies. John had gobbed off to anyone who'd listen and let his mouth run away with him.

And while Tommy liked John – because they did indeed go back quite away back together – dissent was dissent and needed to be nipped in the bud.

And quickly.

If John wanted out then Tommy wouldn't stand in his way.

And, anyway, Tommy was planning a different route for him and his growing family – one that no one else needed to know about … couldn't know about. It would make him look weak if it came out now, and he would lose respect, something he could never let happen.

Back in the sixties and seventies, armed robbery and violence were how he'd made his bones. Now it was cocaine and ecstasy. Had been for the last twenty or so years. And he wasn't stupid. He could see where it was all heading. Plus, he'd had a good run, hadn't he? No need for his family to be mixed up in it anymore. Besides, he'd lost the thrill of chasing the money, and all the shit that went with it, especially these past few years during which his family had been targeted by Yardie gangsters, and his dearest friend – Jack's Uncle Albie – had been murdered by those psychos. And then on top of all that there was the ever-growing stress of having the Serious Crime Squad watching his every move.

Perhaps he was just getting old. He'd already spoken with Ronnie Fisher. After the wedding he'd bring Jack in on his plans. After all, his future son-in-law was key to them.

5

A Coven of Darling Witches

The kitchen of the new residence in Primrose Hill was huge, and it needed to be to contain the excitement, anticipation and anxiety that Tommy encountered as soon as he entered the room. The hairdresser and makeup artist were running late, and Lorraine was up in arms.

'Don't worry, love,' Peggy said. 'We have plenty of time. she'll be here soon enough.'

Sitting at the breakfast bar, and being about as useful as a chocolate fire guard, or so it seemed to Tommy, was Amanda, his eldest daughter.

'It's not like she can do a lot with you anyway, is it, sis? I mean look at the state of you. She's a makeup artist, not a magician,' Amanda chirped.

'Oh, do shut up, Amanda,' Peggy said, stifling a laugh. 'If you can't say anything positive, or at least be serious, go and get your father a drink. I mean look at him – he's wearing a hole in my bloody carpet, pacing up and down like that. 'Tommy,' – she looked over at him – 'for God's sake, sit down and relax. Everything's in order and we still have two hours before the damn thing's due. Amanda's going to get you a drink, aren't you, sweetheart?' she said, and glared at her daughter.

'Yes, Mother. Right away, Mother,' Amanda said, and saluted Peggy.

Tommy had insisted that the wedding reception take place at their new home. Not only was it palatial, with plenty of room for all the guests; it was also part of a small gated community with only two other properties, and surrounded by the latest and very best security tech that money could buy. That had been a must-have after Albie's murder, courtesy of that psycho Yardie, Chambers. Tommy wasn't taking any chances. Because you just never knew, did you? Especially in the kind of business he was in. And just because Harry Parkhurst was locked up didn't mean he couldn't arrange a little something for Tommy from prison. He was, after all, a very wealthy man. And money bought serious criminal influence, not just here in London but up and down the country. And it was Harry and that rat Grover who'd primed Chambers to take out not just Albie but Eddie Harris over in Brixton, too, trying to extract information about him and his soon to be son-in-law.

Tommy sighed. Told himself to concentrate on the wedding, and forget about all that shit. Retribution would come later.

The tinkle of Peggys laugh dragged him back to the present, and Tommy felt the tension in his neck ease up a little. *Family. Focus on family.*

His daughters had their ups and downs and often bickered, as sisters often did, but his wife had always known how to smooth things over and restore the peace when things got a little emotional. And when it came to the crunch, when it really mattered, Amanda and Lorraine were always staunch allies. Today was no different. Amanda threw her little sister a wink as she climbed off the barstool, and Lorraine grinned back at her.

Then his eldest daughter sauntered out of the kitchen, heading – he hoped – for the study, where he kept what he liked to think of as his 'special' brandy.

He wasn't disappointed. A few minutes later, she was back with a bottle of the good stuff. She poured him a snifter and handed him the glass. Tommy downed it in one.

'For God's sake, Tommy,' Peggy snapped, 'you have to give your daughter away in under two hours, and God help you if you're pissed doing it.'

She was right, of course. She always was.

'Another, Daddy?' Amanda said, smirking, knowing only too well it would infuriate her mother.

Peggy shot her that look – the look every mother in the world reserved for occasions such as this – and Amanda retreated, taking the bottle with her.

'Keep your hair on, love,' Tommy said. 'I'm not going to get pissed. It's my first, and it will be my last until this thing's over.'

'This *thing*?' Lorraine said, waving a finger back and forth. 'You're talking about is my wedding, Daddy. It is not a *thing*. It's my special day and I'm marrying the man of my dreams.' She held one hand over her breast and pretended to swoon.

'I think I'm going to be sick,' Amanda muttered.

'You're just jealous, you little cow,' Lorraine said.

Amanda laughed. 'Whatever, sis.' The doorbell chimed. 'I'll get that. It'll be your magician, Lorraine. Shall I send her away and tell her you're a hopeless case?'

'Piss off and let her in, you moron,' Lorraine said, grinning. 'If you're lucky, we can get her to try her magic on you … after this princess of course.' She did a twirl and then bowed. 'But I wouldn't hold out much hope.'

Tommy just stood there, dumbfounded. He'd never understood women, certainly not his daughters. But they loved each other – that much was obvious – and that was good enough for him.

For now, he'd make himself scarce, go off and find his cufflinks.

'They're on the dresser beside the lamp,' Peggy shouted after him.

Jesus, she was a bloody witch, that one.

6

Overdressed, Overhung and Over the Handlebars

John Fitzpatrick Junior glanced up at the rearview mirror, checking for the umpteenth time that the suits and two boxes of shoes the other boys would be wearing later this afternoon were still on the back seat. He knew they were there. He'd picked the suits up from the cleaners himself. And yet the thought of turning up without the kit, and the verbal kicking he'd get, had forced him into a state of near compulsion – checking over and over that he hadn't fucked up this one job and made a dick of himself. He and Liam were already dressed for the occasion at least.

John looked down ... just to check that getting all suited and booted earlier that morning hadn't been a delusion.

All good. And they were nearly there. The hotel was just a few hundred yards down the road.

The night before had been a riot – a pub crawl that had taken them through most of Islington and had ended up with a visit to the local strip club in Camden Town.

'Jesus,' John said, looking over at his brother, 'I don't think I've ever put away that much booze and cocaine in my life. Those boys are fucking animals.'

'You're telling me, brother,' Liam said. 'I must have put away a Henry the Eighth on my own. I'm surprised I've even made it this far. How much sleep did you get? I think I got three if I'm—'

The motorbike came from nowhere.

It slammed into John's side of the car and the rider was flung at an angle over the bonnet. He landed in a heap about thirty yards down the road.

John slammed on the brakes, and the car screeched to halt. He looked over at where the poor fella lay in the middle of the road.

Time stood still for a moment.

Shit, was he was dead?

Someone started to scream. Then someone else. John looked to the side, following the high-pitched racket. Two young girls, laden with shopping bags, stood stricken, eyes wide. One started to sob.

Liam got out of the car, and John went to follow but it was like his limbs were stuck, paralysed.

His brother was ashen, and had that look on his face, like he wanted to run. Why, John couldn't fathom. The car wasn't stolen.

Irrelevant. Get your shit together.

He clambered out of the car. Thank fuck his legs had decided to work again. But the other fella's? 'He came from fucking nowhere, Liam. I never saw him. I didn't stand a chance did I, son? Of avoiding him, I mean.'

But there was no reassurance from his little brother. Liam just stood there, head in his hands, shouting 'Fuck, fuck, fuck' over and over.

Minutes later, the road was teeming with police. An ambulance arrived.

John and Liam were taken aside. The police asked questions. Liam was still in a bit of a state so John let the words tumble out of his mouth, until the coppers seemed happy that they'd got all the right facts and in all the right order.

They'd been lucky. There were a lot of people around – witnesses who'd seen what happened and been able to describe the incident. John could hear them pointing the finger at the motorbike rider. And the damage to the side of the car backed up their statements. It had been the bike that had hit the car, not the other way around, and the car had the right of way.

And then one of the officers brought out a breathalyser. Standard procedure, he said. Just routine, he said. Because John was the driver, he said.

I'm fucked, John thought.

7

Something in the Wind

Tommy's cufflinks were exactly where his wife had said they were. He allowed himself a little smile, then went back to the kitchen and asked Amanda to put them on for him. They'd be leaving soon. Not that they had far to go – the church was only a few hundred yards away.

He stared through the French windows and into the back garden. Big enough to house a full-size football pitch and more than equal to the task of hosting his youngest daughter's wedding reception. A huge marquee had been erected placed right in the middle. It was a hive of activity, with at least a dozen caterers running around like honey bees, preparing for the event. To the side was a stage where several people were setting up for the band and a DJ who'd provide the afternoon and evening entertainment. No expense had been spared.

And to top it off, it was a beautiful sunny day. Absolutely perfect.

The ceremony would be held at the Church of St Mary the Virgin. Peggy had insisted. The beautiful building was just a stone's throw from the Spillane residence on King Henrys Road, and its origins lay in Christian social activism. In 1865, two local businessmen had opened up a home for destitute boys nearby. Consequently, the local iron church had outgrown itself, and St Mary's had been constructed. Tommy wasn't a religious man by any stretch of the imagination, and couldn't give a hoot about its history, but his wife and daughter did. It was what they'd wanted, and so that's what they'd got. Not cheap. mind you, and Tommy had been required to make a not insignificant 'contribution' to church funds. It hadn't come as a surprise. Tommy had clocked the vicar's Italian leather shoes at their first meeting. Later, he'd wondered out loud who'd benefit from the donation. And had been given short shrift by Peggy. 'None of your damn business,' she'd told him. And she'd been right of course. As usual.

'Lorraine, darling,' Peggy called out. 'The car's here.'

Tommy shuffled towards the front door.

Peggy was already waiting there. 'Come on, Tommy. It's ten to one.'

'Don't worry, love. It's literally two hundred yards from here. I could walk it in five minutes.'

'That's not the point, and you know it. Our daughter needs to make an entrance, as is the bride's prerogative.'

Tommy sighed. His phone trilled in his pocket. He answered.

It was Jack. With news. They'd had a little bit of drama but he'd be there in ten minutes.

'What kind of drama?' Tommy hissed.

Peggy shot him a what-the-fuck's-going-on look, but Tommy held up his hand, shushing her, and made his way back to the rear of the house, where he'd be out of earshot.

'Nothing to worry about, Tommy,' Jack said. 'Although John Junior won't be at the ceremony …' And then he explained. How there'd been a crash – not John's fault but he'd been over the limit. The police had arrested him. The car was trashed, so Liam had called Jack, and Jack had called a taxi. They would be at the church, Jack said, but they'd be late.

Tommy hung up and returned to Peggy.

'What the hell's happened? Come on, for fuck's sake – tell me,' she said.

Tommy gave her a broad smile that he hoped would relax her. 'It really is nothing, sweetheart. But there'll be a short delay,' Tommy said gently, and filled her in on what had happened. 'Jack's in a cab. Now get yourself and Amanda down to the church and let the vicar know. I'll be along shortly with the bride.'

Peggy's face said it all. She'd never really taken to the Fitzpatrick boys, not even his old mate John Senior, who they'd known since they were both teenagers. Peggy was the kind of woman who was usually warm and accommodating to everyone – always willing to hold back judgement, giving people a chance. But not when it came to the Fitzpatricks. And his old Rottweiler very rarely got people wrong.

The thought made him feel uneasy. Like something was in the wind. He'd never pressed her on the matter. Maybe it was time to.

8

Shit Sticks

Detective Chief Inspector Sandra Bates, formally of the Serious Crime Squad, now heading up the Cold Case Review team for London and the home counties, was contemplating her next move. Ever since the brutal killings of her rogue colleague Paul Summers and the grass Mickey Grover, both of whom had been taken down by the notorious Parkhurst twins, she'd been fighting for her career. Some senior officers in the Met had questioned her methods. Said she'd mishandled the operation. Wanted rid of her. And while the inquiry had cleared her of any misconduct, the old adage was true. Shit sticks. She'd confided as much to her mentor, Detective Chief superintendent Ernie Richards. Who'd just shrugged and said it was the best she could hope for; that she should be grateful for the exoneration and the chance to keep her career and seniority.

She wasn't daft. She knew what that meant – keep your head down for a while. And so she'd done just that and gone back to her regular duties.

Not that she hadn't had support. Detective Chief Superintendent Douglas Smithers and Sandra's commanding officer on that operation, had helped enormously in the subsequent enquiry. But that didn't change the fact that she was on borrowed time. Which seemed unfair because while she accepted that she'd made a few mistakes during that operation, no one in their right mind could have predicted the awful outcome that had befallen Summers and Grover.

Later, she'd privately admitted to her ever-loyal sergeant, Mellissa Stone, that she'd seriously underestimated the Parkhursts. And not anticipated the magnitude of the mayhem they'd bring into play.

That they'd captured one alive was something at least. Perhaps now he'd play ball. After all, he was looking at spending the rest of his life in prison. Maybe he'd decide to take a few with him. And there was no getting away from it – Harry Parkhurst had been an integral part of her original enquiry into several missing persons and murders, all of which were still unresolved.

Sandra picked up the phone. 'Mellissa, can we get access to Harry Parkhurst before his sentencing?'

'You have the authority, ma'am,' Stone said. 'He's locked up tight as hell. But why would he want to talk to us? He was caught bang to rights by the armed-response units back in Hythe and has already pleaded guilty to the charges at his recent pleas and directions hearing. It's only a matter of sentencing now, and we all know the penalty for murder, especially that of a police officer. It's life without parole. He will die in prison – of that there's no question.'

'Sergeant Stone, I'm haven't just graduated from Hendon, you know. I'm quite aware of all of that, thank you.'

'Sorry, ma'am. I ran away with myself.'

'No, I'm sorry. I'm just frustrated. I was just hoping you might be able to pull a little something extra out of the box. There must be something we can offer him in return for information.'

There was a pause on the other end of the line. Was Stone miffed at her? 'He's killed a serving police officer, ma'am. And, yes, I know Summers was bent but he was still a human being, as was Grover. Besides, I don't think you'd get any support from above, no matter what he could offer you.'

'I suppose I'm just clutching at straws,' Sandra said. She slumped over her desk, deflated. 'It's just that I desperately want to solve this backlog on our desks, especially these cold cases – the Davies, Saunders and Green murders. We know Mason carried out the Saunders and Green murders acting on the brothers orders but I know Parkhurst has information as to who ordered those hits.'

Stone was silent for a moment. Then she said, 'This is all about him, isn't it? Tommy Spillane. He's got under your skin and you're willing to do almost anything to get him, aren't you?'

Stone's comment had taken her aback, and for a moment she didn't really know what to say.

'I don't mean to be disrespectful or flippant, ma'am, but unless we have hard evidence, we can't go anywhere near him. Not since his acquittal in the Anderson case. Don't get me wrong, I agree with you. We both know he had something to do with that. He probably paid the Parkhursts to use their maniac Danny Mason for the jobs. And, ma'am, I want to see him behind bars as well as you do. But we've been working on this for far too long now, and I'm not sure if the commissioner will sanction any more investment in trying to prove Spillane's involvement. We need more than just a hunch, as you well know.'

Stone had a point, Sandra acknowledged begrudgingly. Her sergeant was obviously thinking a lot harder and more clearly than she was. Was she taking all this a little too personally? Had she'd lost perspective? Her meteoric rise through the ranks had brought her to the brink of another huge leap forward in her career, but this awful Hythe business had brought her down a peg or two. Had damaged her reputation. And she wanted – no – she needed Tommy Spillane.

'You're very observant, Sergeant Stone,' Sandra said. 'But there are cases on our desk and we need closure. And there's the disappearance of Darren Davies, too. He was one of that firm's leading men, and he vanished shortly after the murders of Saunders and Green. That's not a coincidence, and I aim to prove it. Here's where we'll start.'

The report provided by the Drug Squad had speculated on a connection between Davies and the Saunders mob. Nothing concrete, but it had been assigned to Sandra and her team, and it needed dealing with. 'And that's exactly what we're going to do,' she said to Stone. 'We'll get the funding and authorisation we need, don't you worry about that. But we need to come up with something a little more solid to present to the board. And that's where you come in.'

Stone would work with Detective Constable Dave Myers, Sandra told her. He'd just been assigned to the Cold Case Review Squad, on loan from the Vice Squad, and knew a hell of a lot about the kind of business that Spillane and his cohorts were involved in.

All clear, Sergeant?'

'Yes, ma'am,' Stone said, though Sandra could hear the resignation in her voice.

'Good. Now, Tommy Spillane has quite a substantial thing going on over there, and I want as much dirt as you can possibly find on him and his firm. There has to be a weak link somewhere within his organisation, something that will give us a lead or two. It's up to us to find it.'

Yeah, shit stuck, Sandra thought. But it could be washed off. And wash it off she would.

9

Supply Chain

'He's a grown man,' Maureen O'Brian muttered to herself, 'and if that's what he wants, then that's what I'll give him.' She knew the risks. Had been in the game for years. Didn't know how to do anything else if she was honest.

The stream of young runaways from the north of England never seemed to let up. They landed at Kings Cross station, looking scared, lonely, desperate. Maureen picked them up, promising food, shelter and refuge from whatever they'd been running from. All of which meant she had very little difficulty in supplying what the likes of John Fitzpatrick needed, although she was growing concerned about that particular client's tastes. No, not concerned. Sickened.

Supplying Fitzpatrick with drugs didn't faze her in the slightest. But her girls, that was a different matter. And Fitzpatrick liked them young – as young as possible. And while he paid well, she drew the line when it came to under-sixteens. The last thing she wanted was a prison sentence for soliciting a minor. She always asked their age once she had them in her grasp. Did any of them lie? Maureen didn't like to think about that. The truth wasn't always the first thing to come out of the mouths of desperate kids. And life was always a balancing act, wasn't it? The supply chain worked both ways. Desperate old men and desperate young girls.

Maureen shuddered.

Her own career as a full-time sex worker had come to an end around ten years earlier when she'd been in her early forties. Aside from those with special requirements, there wasn't much call for women of her age, so she'd pivoted – that's what they called it these days, didn't they? Let the younger and more desirable girls fulfil the demand side of the business while she concentrated on supply. And by the age of fifty-two she'd carved out a little niche for herself. Didn't earn as much as she'd once dreamed of, but it was a living and it kept the wolf from the door.

She'd been born in Clapham but had moved over the water to Islington six years earlier, shortly after the Parkhursts had taken over the brothel she managed. They'd replaced her with a much younger model, some fancy Eastern European girl who had more tits than class. They hadn't been nice about it either. Told her she was too old and past it, and that her criminal record could cause them trouble. At the time she'd thought it a bloody cheek, that crock of crap coming out of the mouths of crooks like them. But she'd never said anything. Had known better. Instead, she'd moved on, finally settling for Kings Cross, a well-established haunt for the so-called ladies of the night.

Still, she couldn't deny it – the news about the Parkhursts had brought a smile to her face. Especially Jimmy. Him being killed while trying to escape had been no bad thing. The man had been a sadist, and she'd never really liked him. Harry was okay in small doses, and could be kind on the rare occasions he was alone. Although only then. Together, the twins were a different prospect. Very serious. Very scary. But back in the day, Harry had 'indulged' in her services often. Jimmy never had, not with her or any of the girls. Maureen had wondered if he might be gay, which had been fine by her because even the thought of being intimate with that psycho had turned her stomach.

Once north of the river, she'd settled in a small but cosy flat in Islington, which is how she'd got to know John Fitzpatrick. He owned the flat, and sometimes when he came around for the rent, they'd share a bottle of wine or two. Not once had he tried it on, even thought she'd have been flattered if he had. He'd always been the perfect gentleman.

Until about two years ago, when she'd made a stupid mistake.

One evening, just because he was curious, she'd shared a crack pipe with him. 'I want to know what all the fuss is about,' he'd told her. Maureen had managed to keep her habit under control, but John had been a different kettle of fish. He'd become hooked and craved it almost every night. His enslavement to the pipe had unleashed an altogether darker palate ... a taste for young girls that had grown to the point of depravity. He'd become insatiable, and it was increasingly difficult to keep up with his demands and ensure that the girls were of age and willing.

She often wondered what Tommy Spillane would think if he got wind of it. Everyone knew Tommy. His name was legendary around North London. Tommy was the owner of the hotel she ran her business from, and John was connected to him. One evening, John had grabbed her wrist and hissed, 'This is strictly between us, darling. Do you understand?' She'd tried to pull her arm away because he was hurting her but he'd held fast. 'You better not tell anyone. And if you do, well, you know the rest.'

Maureen hadn't told a soul. She knew all too well what 'the rest' meant.

And that's how it went with people like John Fitzpatrick. His addiction didn't stop him knowing the difference between wrong and right. What it did stop him from doing was giving a shit. Men like him felt powerful, untouchable. Never gave a thought to the poor girl who they'd just left in their room or the other poor girl who they were going to abuse later that night just to satisfy their own sick lust.

Again, Maureen shuddered.

10

Special Offer

John Fitzpatrick Senior was running late. It had been foolish to visit the brothel the night before the wedding of Tommy's daughter, but the craving for sex and drugs had been too strong to ignore. The fix had to come first. Which is why he'd cried off the previous night's stag do, citing his age. Weddings were bad enough, but he especially disliked stag parties. And stags with someone he didn't even like? No thanks. The big event was something he couldn't get out of though. It would be bad form if he failed to show up for that, and Tommy would neither forgive nor forget it.

From the bathroom in the dingy hotel room, a young girl sobbed. The madam who'd provided her – along with a rather large amount of crack cocaine – had told him that the girl, a runaway with no family, was just sixteen and would do anything for drugs and money. John had liked that, although now, in the cold light of day, he doubted her age. She'd seemed a little too experienced for his liking. He preferred them more servile, scared even, particularly when they asked him to stop.

She hadn't. And he wouldn't have anyway.

A few minutes later, she came out of the bathroom. She'd redone her makeup – rather badly in his opinion – but at least the silly bitch had stopped crying.

'What's all that about, girl?' John said. In the cold light of day and now sober, he wasn't impressed. 'It wasn't that bad now, was it? Here's your money.' He flung a small wad of cash her way. 'You know the way out, I assume?'

The girl stared at him, her expression so blank it made him feel slightly uneasy.

'What is it, girl?' he snapped. 'Is it the money? Count it. I assume Maureen told you the fee I was willing to pay so you're not getting any more.'

'No, it's not the money, sir,' she replied. 'It's just that Maureen told me that you preferred girls a little younger than me, and that I should tell you that I'm sixteen and inexperienced.'

John sighed. 'I knew you were older all the time, girl. What are you getting at?'

'Well, I'm actually nineteen, and I have a child. He's nearly three, you know. He lives with my mum in Manchester.' She smiled as she spoke about her kid but then began to cry again.

'What the fuck has that got to do with me and why the fuck should I care?'

'Well, it's just that I want to go home and get him back,' she said, looking down at the floor through intermittent sobs. 'My stepfather's in prison now. He raped me and the kid's his. I just want to go back and face my mum. She didn't believe me at first, and that's why I ran away and left the kid with her. I just need money, that's all. I can't go back empty-handed. I need to find a place to stay where I can fight to get my boy back.'

'Like I just said, sweetheart, what's this got to do with me? I'm not going to pay you extra. In fact, this is the last time you'll ever see me. You're clearly not what I'm looking for – a little too old for my taste.'

'That's the reason I'm telling you,' she said, her words more measured now. 'I know a girl who's just got in from Leeds. She stays with me at the hostel. She's only been there a few days, and she's broke. Wants to earn some money. I've told her what I do and she's okay with that. I think she's only fifteen or something. The thing is, she's quite petite and looks even younger than that, and I thought she might be what you're looking for. I want paying though … for arranging it.'

Cheeky little cow, he thought, but he liked her style. Blunt. And the goods on offer sounded interesting.

'What's her name?'

'Carly, sir. I can bring her here to you if you want. Show you I'm not lying.'

John nodded. Yeah, he'd definitely need to see her first. 'And how much do you want?'

'Five hundred upfront for me, and you pay her direct. I'll talk to her later if you want and arrange the meet.'

'Fine. Bring her here tonight at 8.00 pm, and don't be late. If I like her, I'll pay you then. Then you can leave her with me and fuck off. Deal?'

The girl nodded. 'Deal. See you later.'

She walked out of the room smiling. The tears had vanished.

John smiled too. Fifteen and petite. Something to look forward to. All he had to do was get that fucking Spillane wedding done and dusted.

11

Wedding Bells and Golden Balls

Peggy Spillane had never smoked in her life, but right now she could have murdered a cigarette. It always seemed to calm Tommy when he was on edge, and Peggy was stressed. Lorraine's face had been etched with anguish, and Peggy had pulled Tommy to one side and said, 'If he stands her up, I'll bloody kill him myself.' Her daughter had heard the remark and burst into tears. Tommy had done his best to reassure them all, but Peggy wouldn't settle until she could mark today off as having gone without a hitch.

Peggy, now standing nervously outside the church when the vicar sidled up beside her and said rather snootily, 'It's a quarter past one, Mrs Spillane. We have another wedding at 3.30 and we simply can't wait much longer I'm afraid. If we haven't started before 1.30 —'

Peggy shot him the daggers. As far as she was concerned, he could go fuck himself.

He must have got the message because he looked rather ashen, then turned and strode over to the waiting crowd without another word.

The roar of an engine came out of nowhere, and a car pulled up at the kerb. The doors were flung open, and out climbed Jack, Callum and Liam, all three of them tucking their shirts into their trousers and straitening their ties.

Thank fuck, Peggy thought. She glared at the three sheepish-looking boys as they walked into the church, shaking hands with all and sundry as they went.

She fumbled for her phone and called Tommy.

***

'Hey, golden balls.' John Fitzpatrick Senior held out his hand. 'Congratulations, my son.'

'Hey, John, how's it going?' Jack said, shaking the offered hand and hoping his broad smile would mask his annoyance over the obvious slight. 'Thanks for coming. I hope you're enjoying yourself mate.'

Fuck John Fitzpatrick. It was just past three o'clock, the ceremony had gone to plan, and Jack was a married man. No way was this prick going to spoil his day.

'Fucking top notch, Jackie lad,' John Senior said. 'Good old Tommy does know how to throw a great party, doesn't he? Where is the old fucker anyway? I haven't seen him since I got here.' He turned to Lorraine, pulled her towards him, kissed her on the cheek and leered at her cleavage. 'Hey, sweetheart, don't you look a picture.'

'My father's busy looking after our guests, Mr Fitzpatrick,' she said, wrestling herself out of his grasp. 'Besides, you're a big boy. You don't need my dad holding your hand, do you? After all, it's just a wedding.'

Jack had only known John Senior a short while and yet the old man always seemed to be digging him out, always had something to say. Jack didn't know why, only that he didn't like it one little bit. His wife – his wife! – had known the Fitzpatricks her entire life, and even though she'd told Jack that she was always happy to make time for John Junior and Liam, she definitely didn't like their father. And it showed.

Jack decided that diplomacy might be in order. 'You're almost family, Johnny,' Jack said, then gripped the man's elbow and led him away. Well, just a little diplomacy. John Senior hated being called Johnny. But the old git knew just as well that Jack hated being called Jackie. Fair game, Jack had decided. 'Tommy's just a little busy right now, looking after all the people who don't really know the family. You know how it is. Was there something particular you needed to talk to him about? I can speak to him for you if you want?'

'No, there's nothing in particular, Jackie boy,' he snapped, and freed himself from Jack's grasp. 'It'll keep until another time. But do yourself a favour, son ...' He looked Jack straight in the eye.

'And what's that, *Johnny*?' Jack said.

'Keep your fucking hands off me, and don't embarrass me like that again, you little cunt. I've known that little girl and her sister ever since they were born. She doesn't need you to protect her. Me and Tommy go back over forty years, long before you were around, son. She can trust me with her life. As can Tommy. As could your dear departed Uncle Albie. I don't appreciate being treated second best, and I definitely don't need you to arrange a meeting with one of my oldest friends.'

What the fuck? Where had all that come from? Jack felt an itch in his fingers and had to quell the urge to fold them into fists and smash them into John Senior's fucking head or wrap them round his neck and rip his fucking head off. *Easy. Breathe. Think. This is your wedding day. This is Tommy's House. And so* instead of hurling John Fitzpatrick through the nearest available window Jack replied quietly and calmly. 'I think you've had a little bit too much to drink, John. I don't know who you think I am, but I'll tell you this much. You talk to me like that any other day, me and you are going to have a serious problem. Now do yourself a favour – fuck off back to your table and give your head a wobble.'

With that Jack turned walked back to his bride, wearing his best smile. But Lorraine wasn't stupid. She'd have seen the anger in Fitzpatrick's eyes and his body language. She'd know he was seething. And the place was rammed. Others would have seen it too. Jack didn't give a fuck in that moment.

12

In the Name of the Father

John Junior knew when his old dad was upset. Just as he walked into the room, he saw the old man slump down into a chair next to Liam, his face like thunder. Great. This was all he needed after being released from custody and charged with drink driving.

'Who the fuck does that little cunt think he is, talking to me like that?' His father grabbed his nearby drink.

John Junior sat down and put his hand on his dad's arm. 'What's happened, Dad?'

'I'll tell you what's fucking happened, son. That piece of shit, Clay, just put his hands on me and led me away from his blushing bride, saying I'm pissed and that he'll iron me out if I ever talk to him like that again. I—'

'What made him say that?' Liam asked. 'Did you say something to him?'

'I only told him to keep his fucking hands off me, and not to embarrass me in front of everybody, that's all. I mean he led me away by my elbow. I was only having a laugh.'

So his dad's pride was hurt. John Junior could imagine how the conversation had gone. He and Liam knew their father well. He could be cantankerous, rude even, and it had got worse these past two years or so. Both of them were worried, but their dad wasn't the kind of man you could question about his lifestyle. And God help you if you did.

Still, he was their father, and no matter what he got up to they would always defend him. Even if he was in the wrong.

Today was no exception.

***

There'd been only a few late arrivals to the church. One had stood out for Tommy. His old friend and associate John Fitzpatrick, who'd looked a little dishevelled. Tommy suspected why but had thought it best to address the matter after the wedding. He'd looked over at Ronnie Fisher, sitting quietly in a pew on his own. Ronnie had just nodded and gone back to singing the hymn.

Tommy had hoped that everyone would behave themselves at the reception but he rarely missed a trick, and it was evident that tensions were mounting. All the boys, including Jack and Callum, were pissed. Charlied up too from the look of it. Tommy had kept an eye on proceedings and seen the Fitzpatrick situation unfold. Things weren't going to end well at this rate, and his daughter's wedding would be ruined.

John Junior marched across the room with a face like thunder, closely followed by his younger brother. They were heading straight for Jack, who was deep in conversation with Callum.

Tommy needed to intervene, and quickly.

He just made it.

'John, Liam, how are you, boys?' he said, barring the way and stretching out his hand while smiling broadly. 'I haven't seen or spoken with you both for quite a while now. Can you ever forgive me?'

Both men stopped in their tracks and shook Tommy warmly by the hand, just as Tommy had known they would. They liked him – he'd made sure of that. He'd always been the perfect gentleman and had supported them and their father when things had been tough. After the handshakes, they both embraced him like they would a favourite uncle.

Over by the Fitzpatricks' table, Ronnie Fisher had intercepted John Senior and led him away towards the bar. John seemed to be going willingly.

Stepping out of the embrace, John Junior said, 'We're good, Tommy. We were just going over to see Jack and have a little chat about something.'

Tommy didn't like the way John had said that and leant in a little closer to both men. 'Not today boys,' he hissed. 'Whatever issues you or your father have with Jack is now my problem, and it won't be settled here in my house and definitely not on my daughter's wedding day. Now go and get your old man' – he nodded towards the bar – 'and leave this house quietly and without any fuss. And don't forget to say your goodbyes to my wife and daughters on your way out. After all, you're their guests.'

Both men stood back, eyes wide, jaws slack. Tommy hoped they were scared. That it felt like he'd turned into another person. That they'd heard the menace and the intent in his voice. They'd have heard the stories from their father and others of course, but sometimes a person had to experience it for themselves to really understand how the game was played and what their role was.

'Listen, Tommy,' Liam said, glancing towards his father and the now smiling Ronnie Fisher, 'we didn't mean anything. We were just going to talk with Jack about a bit of business, that's all. We weren't going to cause any trouble, honest.'

'Even so,' Tommy replied, 'do as I say. Go and get your dad and go home – all of you. The party's over.' Then he left them, calling out over his shoulder, 'And don't forget to thank my girls.'

***

'Jack, a word please.' Not a request; a direct order. 'Let's pop into my den for a minute.' Tommy steered Jack by the arm towards his office at the front of the house and locked the door.

'What's up, Tommy?' Jack asked.

'You're going on honeymoon tomorrow, so most of what we need to talk about can wait until you return. However, there's a few things I need to clear up with you before you—'

'Like what?'

'Don't interrupt me. Ever. Just sit down, son, and listen. I'm only going to say this once, and I don't give a fuck how you take it.'

Jack did as he was told and slumped in one of the antique wingback chairs in the sumptuously furnished office. This was serious. His now father-in-law's demeanour had switched in just a few seconds. This must be about the Fitzpatrick boys and the fact that he'd manhandled John Senior just now.

'John Senior's been digging me out for some time now, Tommy, and he was quite rude to me and Lorraine earlier on. In fact, he was asking why you hadn't shown him any respect and why you hadn't spoken to him all day. Plus, he's well pissed. I just wanted to get him away from us and back to his table. That's why—'

"Which part of "Sit down and listen" didn't you fucking understand?" Tommy boomed, now looming over Jack. 'Show some fucking respect. When I ask you to listen, I expect you to listen. That's not why you're here, Jack, you fucking idiot. Fuck John Fitzpatrick and his boys. They're finished. Have been for some time. Do you think I don't know what they're saying about me? Do you think I'm fucking stupid, son?

'Of course I don't, Tommy,' Jack said, a little taken aback. 'But I thought that's what you wanted to talk about.'

Tommy sighed and slumped down into his own chair, facing Jack. 'Listen, son – I mean that. Listen. People like the Fitzpatricks are a liability. They get ideas in their stupid heads about their status in this life. Those three have been making poor decision. All three of 'em have a drug problem, especially John Senior. Indulging in that kind of stuff changes people's perceptions, just like its changing yours, son.'

'What do you mean? I don't have a drug problem.'

Tommy leapt up. 'Don't. Don't you dare fucking lie to me, Jack. Look at the state of you and that silly bollocks Callum. You look like you haven't slept in days. It's only the cocaine you've been doing in my fucking house that's keeping you on your feet.'

Jack started to protest but Tommy waved his hands.

'No no no. Don't take me for a fool, Jack. I know what's been going on. You forget – I've been involved with this kind of thing for years and I can see the signs. Now, I'm not here to pass judgement on what a grown man chooses to do in his private life but I'll tell you this. If you continue down this road, it will only lead to disaster. Poor decisions are made when people drink heavily or take drugs, and people like us, who live and work in this business, cannot afford to make bad choices. It destroys people. Jack. Is that what you want for yourself, for Lorraine, for your baby – my grandson?'

'Of course not, Tommy,' Jack said a little sheepishly. No point in denying it. Better to come clean. 'But I've got it under control. I've only had a few cheeky lines today, just to level me out, that's all. But you're right – I shouldn't have done that in your house. It won't happen again, I promise.'

Tommy sighed, sat back down and stared at Jack until he felt like squirming. 'Like I said, son, drugs are for losers, and I can't afford to have any of my men using them. The last time one of my guys got that heavily into them, it cost me six years of my life.'

He was talking about Darren Davies surely. Jack had heard the rumours but he and Tommy had never spoken about the matter directly.

'That's not going to happen again,' Tommy said. 'I'm too old for prison, son, and I won't put my family through all that again.'

'I'd never put you in that position, Tommy. What the fuck do you take me for?'

'It's not about intention, son. It's about when you make a mistake, which you inevitably will. And when your mind isn't right, it'll be out of your hands. The police are cunning, Jack. They have resources and technology at their beck and call, not to mention the grasses, which there seem to be an abundance of. No, son, times are changing. They have the upper hand now, and people like us are in a precarious position. It's only a matter of time before the balloon goes up and we all end up either dead or in jail. To stay one step ahead of them we need to change our tactics. That means drugs have got to go – not just the taking, but their distribution as well.'

Jack shook his head. 'Bloody hell, Tommy, what's brought all this on? I mean that's how we make our money. Fuck the Old Bill. We can outsmart them. We just need to distance ourselves from the front line and play it safe for a while.'

'I've made my decision, Jack,' Tommy said, and rose out of his chair as if to say that the meeting was over. 'I have ideas … other plans for how we're going to take this family forward. And it definitely doesn't involve drugs. We also need to clear up a few, shall we say, issues before that happen. But don't worry. When you get back from your honeymoon, I'll explain it all then. In the meantime, we need to get back to the reception and your wife. People will start to wonder where we are.'

They weren't the only ones. Jack was starting to wonder where he was.

13

An Ace Up the Sleeve

John Senior listened to his sons as they reported Tommy's instructions, then finished his drink and set his glass down on the table. 'This is not good, boys. Now, here's what—'

'Best do what Tommy says, boys,' Ronnie said. 'Go and see Peggy and the girls, and make your excuses. I'll talk to Tommy in a few days and smooth this all out.'

John Senior nodded. What did they say? Caution was the better part of valour. Plus, he certainly didn't want to get into anything with Ronnie. 'It's probably best,' he muttered. 'Come on, let's get out of here. Thanks, Ronnie. I'll talk to Tommy when that little prick isn't around – get it all sorted.'

Which he would. Because John Fitzpatrick Senior had an ace up his sleeve, and at the next given opportunity, he intended to play it. They said their goodbyes, Peggy was glad and a little relieved as was Lorraine. Jack smiled from the corner.

He got in the car and slammed the door. His two sons climbed into the back and sat quietly as he ranted, unable to contain his fury. 'Who the hell do they think they are? I've known Tommy and his family for years. I worked with him, Ronnie Fisher and Albie Spires before that little cunt

Jack Clay was even born.' His boys remained silent. Good job too. If they'd interrupted him, he'd have torn a strip off them. 'I mean, who the hell is Jack Clay anyway? Yes, he's Albie's nephew, but where's he been all this time? He came from nowhere and suddenly he's Tommy's little favourite just because that arsehole screwed his daughter and got her in the club. And oh, yes, she's pregnant alright. It's bloody obvious. Tommy probably put a shotgun to his head, knowing him, and made it clear he'd use it if he didn't. You—'

'We know about the baby, Dad,' Liam said. 'Jack told us the other day.'

'Shut the fuck up, you little cunt,' John Senior snapped, and glanced up into the rearview mirror just as John Junior threw his little brother a look that told him to keep his mouth shut, for fuck's sake. 'I don't need you to tell me anything. Do you think I'm stupid or something? Clay's got himself right in there, hasn't he? I'll tell you something, boys, and mark my words, he's a wrong'un. I don't trust him as far as I could kick him. Steer fucking clear of him from now on ... and that other cunt Callum McCormack. He's tight with Jack and not to be trusted either.'

His sons said nothing – just kept looking at each other. Like they were worried. Idiots. They should be worried about Jack fucking Clay, not their old dad.

He dropped them off in Islington, outside their local pub, then continued on to Kings Cross. He didn't need a drink, not with his sons anyway. He needed a fix, which meant there was only one place to go. And, hey, it was only 5.00 pm. The night was young.

And he had plans for later. Big plans.

Or petite ones, depending on how you looked at it.

14

Not On My Watch

Maureen had lined up a couple of high-paying customers for the hotel over in Kings Cross, and was almost out of the door when the bell rang.

Who the fuck could that be? Very few people knew where she lived, and those who did rarely came calling on a Saturday night, given what she did for living.

'Who is it?' she called into the intercom.

'It's me. Open the fucking door.'

Shit. What the hell was John Fitzpatrick doing here? She'd thought he'd be at the Spillane wedding all evening. Reluctantly she pressed the entry button and unlocked the front door.

A few seconds later he was standing in her lounge. Pissed and angry. Which scared her. She'd need to handle him with kid gloves, the state he was in.

'John, what can I do for you?'

'I need some of that shit, Maureen. And I need the name and number of that girl I saw last night.'

'She said you didn't like her, John. What do you want her number for?'

He moved like lightning, and the next thing she knew his hands were around her flew throat, throttling her.

'Listen to me, you old hag. She told me how old she is, and how you told her to lie about her age. You tried to trick me.' Spit flew from his mouth as he hissed at her. 'She's fucking nineteen and has a kid. You fucking owe me. Just give me her number and call your man about the other thing. And hurry up about it.'

He let go of her neck, and Maureen dragged lungfuls of air into her burning throat. 'Bloody hell, take it easy John. There's no need for violence. You know I can't supply you with underage girls. I can't get involved with that kind of thing – you must know that. The police would be all over me. Besides, it's wrong.'

The second those final three words came out of her mouth, she knew she shouldn't have said them. But it was too late. John was back on her, both hands around her neck, strangling her.

'Who the fuck are you to tell me what's right or wrong, you fucking whore? Just do as I tell you or I'll put an end to your miserable fucking life right here and now.'

He threw her down onto the floor. For a moment, she couldn't move. She took deep breaths and tried to get to her feet but her arms were shaking so much that they couldn't take her weight. A sob escaped her. She breathed hard again, trying to calm herself. Christ, if she didn't comply with his request, he'd probably kill her. 'Okay okay. Look, just calm down, John. Please. I'll give you her number and get you what you want. There's no need for this. I meant no disrespect.'

'That's better,' he said, and now he looked a little more relaxed, like the psycho had taken a step back and let the better man step forward. 'She's not a bad kid, you know. There's something about her that intrigues me. In fact, I reckon she'd make a much better fixer than you've ever been, Maureen.'

'I don't understand. What do you mean by that? She's just a kid fresh off the train from Manchester.'

'Well, my dear, it's like this.' Then John sneered at her, like she was nothing. Like she was some piece of dogshit. The better man had been nothing more than a mask. The psycho was still in the building after all. 'It seems she already has what it takes. She wants to make some decent money. And she's found me a girl that suits my requirements. I reckon she'll make a great replacement for you, sweetheart. She doesn't have any of that bleeding-heart nonsense that you seem so fond of. Now give me that number. Oh, and while you're at it, call the hotel. I need a room for the night.'

Maureen nodded. 'Alright, John. No problem. I'll fix it all up now. Meet me at the hotel in an hour or so, and I'll get you what you want. Do you want me to call the girl or do you want to do it?'

'I'll do it, love,' he replied. 'She knows what I'm after – we agreed it all this morning. Oh, what's her name?'

Maureen wrote the number on a piece of paper and handed it to him, wishing more than anything she hadn't, then said, 'Her name's Kerry.'

'Just make sure my gear's there in an hour. I'm going to the pub for a few liveners before I get to the hotel and I don't want to be kept waiting for it. Don't talk to the girl, do you understand? And call me when my parcel's landed. I want a little taste before the girl arrives.'

Maureen nodded and closed the door behind him.

Then did exactly what he'd told her not to: she called Kerry and arranged to meet her in Travis Street, just behind the hotel, twenty minutes from now. It was really important, she said.

She made two more calls, then left the house. The move was a risk. If John Fitzpatrick found out she'd spoken with Kerry, Maureen wouldn't last five minutes. But if the other girl was as young as John had intimated, she just couldn't stand by and let it happen. He'd gone too far. It was against all her principles. And Maureen knew better than most what it was to be abused as a child. As a youngster herself she'd been raped by one of her uncles, and right under her own mother's nose too. She'd run away the first chance she got, and had never gone back. And no one, not even her alcoholic mother, had come looking for her. Instead, the young and distraught Maureen had been left to fend for herself. She caught up with an old school friend, who'd told her about the Parkhurst brothers over in south London, and their many bedsits over in Southwark, and their extraordinary generosity. It wasn't long before she'd found refuge in one in one of those studios. And not too long after that she'd learned about how generosity came at a cost. Soon enough she'd been working in one of their many establishments. It was there that she'd learned her trade. 1961 it had happened. She'd been fifteen. A child. Used by disgusting older men for their own sick gratification. The trauma was something she liked to keep buried.

And now John Fitzpatrick had opened those old wounds. Just thinking about that time made her want to puke. But that didn't mean it had to happen to another girl. She couldn't let it. Not on her watch.

To hell with the consequences.

15

Just Another Punter

Kerry was already there when Maureen arrived. The girl lit a cigarette and gave Maureen the once-over. She had that look about her. Dismissive. Like she already knew what was coming. Like she'd decided that Maureen was just some old bag who was going to tell her that she was out of her league and to back off. And the nineteen-year-old wasn't far wrong.

'Listen, love, what you're planning isn't only wrong, it's bloody dangerous. You do know who John Fitzpatrick is, don't you? Do you have any idea—'

Kerry rolled her eyes. 'He's just another punter. Just another old letch who's got a thing for young girls, that's all. I mean, I lost my virginity at fourteen. I reckon it was probably the same for you, wasn't it?' She looked Maureen straight in the eyes, defiant. 'Better to be paid for it rather than someone just taking it, isn't it? Besides, the girl he wants to see is willing. She's a runaway and just wants to make a bit of money, that's all. I've spoken to her and she's up for it.'

'She might be up for it, young lady,' Maureen said, 'but she doesn't know what she's getting into. These men – these monsters – they abuse girls like that, then discard them when they can no longer do it for them. Then they move on to their next perverted dreamland and harm another frightened young girl.'

'Oh, don't be so dramatic, Maureen,' Kerry said, and placed her hands on her hips, like she was the dog's bollocks. 'You're just jealous. Your time's over, you old bitch, and you don't like the fact that I have more to offer people like him than you do. I'm doing this, and I don't need your permission.'

John Fitzpatrick hadn't been wrong about one thing. Kerry was young, but she a did have a certain something about her, a steely resolve to get what she wanted. Perfect for this business. But she was naïve too. They all were at her age. Which was perfect for being manipulated by the likes of John.

'You stupid little girl, you have no idea what you're getting into. You're foolish if you think men like him will give anything to help you. Fitzpatrick and others like him will chew you up and spit you out. But go ahead, do what you have to do. But' – she leant into the woman and pointed a finger in front of her face – 'pay attention, young lady. You'll come to regret it, just like I did. It's far too late for me, but for God's sake think about what you're planning to do. Think of the young girl you're about to place into his slimy hands. Please.'

Kerry's phone began to trill, and the girl put her hand up, shushing Maureen, and then walked a little further up the road. A few moments later she came back.

'That was him. I'm meeting him in an hour at the hotel with the girl. Don't try and interfere, Maureen. I need the money. This is happening.'

And then she sauntered off, like she didn't have a care in the world. Exasperated, Maureen walked off in the other direction, towards the hotel. She was meeting her dealer there – for Johns drugs – and she couldn't be late. He wasn't a patient fellow. They never were.

***

The Prince of Wales served a good pint, and John nursed his fourth in a seat by the window. It gave him a perfect view of the hotel across the road, and although he was a drunk, he wasn't so off his face that he couldn't recognise Maureen as she scuttled towards the hotel entrance. 'Good girl,' he said under his breath. She'd be meeting with her dealer. And, yeah, there was risks with the drugs and the underage girls, but it was his life, wasn't it? What he did in his own time was his business, and the girls were willing, for fuck's sake, so fuck Tommy Spillane.

Still, that little voice plagued him, nagged at him about how if the truth emerged, and Tommy found out, well ... The drug thing was bad enough but the girls ... he needed to do something about that. And he would, he really would ...

Just not now because there was that kid from Leeds and time to fit in just one or two more pints and his fix was coming, wasn't it. Yeah, all in good time.

All. In. Good. Time.

He ambled over to bar, got himself a refill, and ordered a chaser on the side. Just a little something to take off the edge until the parcel arrived.

16

You Scratch My Back

Detective Constable Dave Myers was just about to clock off when his mobile rang. He listened for a few moments, then said, 'Do as he asks, sweetheart, then make yourself scarce. You don't want to be around when the shit hits the fan. And thank you.'

Maureen O'Brian was an old acquaintance of sorts. More specifically, he'd arrested her for soliciting and drug offences. Courtesy of his time That was when he'd been over in South London, working for the Vice Squad. She'd received a six-week sentence for that little episode, but been out in three. Dave had felt a little sorry for her when he'd taken her into custody. Maureen was harmless, old school. Pretty straight-laced for a prostitute. And she'd offered him valuable information about a well-known paedophile and sex offender in exchange for lesser charges. And Dave, of course, had obliged. Because that was the way to get things done when it came to Vice – you scratch my back and I'll scratch yours. Dave had ended up with another informant in his pocket – a necessary evil in his profession – and in return he turned a blind eye to her drug-taking and casual supply, never pressing her for information on that particular matter. They'd been working together for several years now, and the deal came with caveats, or friendly advice as he like to think of it, one part of which was that she should keep it in house, as if the Drug Squad came calling, he wouldn't be able to help her.

Maureen had always proved good on her word, and today was no exception.

Because what she'd just told him was dynamite.

And the timing had been perfect. He'd only just come away from a briefing with Sergeant Mellissa Stone regarding the North London firm who had a controlling interest in the very hotel Maureen had mentioned. One they often used for their line of work. Tommy Spillane had bought out the previous owners when they'd fallen out with the experienced gangster. Well, bought out might be stretching it a little. They'd doubtless been given little choice in the matter. Of course, the transfer in ownership was all above board, all legit. The authorities hadn't been able to do a thing.

It wasn't just Spillane though. The call from Maureen had been of additional interest because of what she'd said about John Fitzpatrick Senior. The elder Fitzpatrick was a Spillane enforcer. And Dave's superior officer, Detective Chief Inspector Sandra Bates of the Cold Case Review Squad, would be more than a little piqued by what was about to go down. Would welcome the opportunity to talk with the old man.

Which meant there wasn't a minute to lose. Dave set the wheels in motion and headed off to Kings Cross.

17

Time to Rock and Roll

Where the fuck was she? Kerry had arrived at the hostel at the agreed time and checked the girl's room, but she wasn't there. Jesus, the kid had only jumped off the train from Leeds a heartbeat ago and already she'd proved herself unreliable. Carly Stubbs probably wasn't even her real name. But that was par for the course. Kerry had stopped using hers pretty sharpish too. Katie Finch was someone else. Another girl from another place from another fucked-up time.

Kerry knocked on doors until at last she found her. Carly was in another girl's room. The two of them were smoking drugs. Twats. Furious, Kerry stomped across the sparsely furnished room and slapped her young protégé with such force that Carly fell off the chair and onto the floor.

'You stupid fucking bitch,' she screamed. 'I told you to get ready. You're supposed to be preparing for tonight, not getting out of your face with this whore.' She threw daggers at the other girl on the sofa, who looked up at Kerry, her shocked eyes wide as dinner plates. 'Now get yourself up and come with me.'

She grabbed hold of one of Carly's arms and dragged up onto her feet. The girl on the sofa said nothing, just looked away.

'I was just getting high, Kerry,' Carly said through light sobs. 'I'm not trying to back out. I'm still going to do it.'

'Damn right you are, you stupid little cow. I'm not losing out on this because you couldn't control yourself. Now get back to your room, throw some water on your face and get ready. We have to be there in under an hour.'

Carly did as she was told, though she looked petrified. Reluctant too. Like she seriously regretted agreeing to meet this man. Kerry could imagine how the conversation with sofa-girl had gone while they were smoking who the fuck knew just now. She'd have told Carly what men like that did to young girls. So, yeah, she'd be scared. Out of her fucking wits.

Kerry couldn't care less. In fact, it could just work in her favour having someone like that to sell to him. A man like him might pay more for a scared child. Yeah, definitely.

Soon as she got there, she'd ask for more money.

***

John Fitzpatrick Senior placed his pint glass down on the table and smiled. As usual, Maureen had come through. She'd called him. Told him that all was good and ready.

Time to rock and roll.

***

On the instructions of DC Myers, Constable Chalmers had entered the pub – in plain clothes of course – and planted himself at the bar ten minutes earlier. From his stool, he watched John Fitzpatrick's every move. The man supped the last of his pint, downed his short then exited the pub and made his way across the road to the hotel.

Chalmers gave him a minute head start, then followed him into the hotel lobby and proceeded straight into the disabled toilets. There, he locked the door and called Myers with an update.

'Just let him get to the room,' Myers said. 'We need to make sure that what O'Brian says is true before we make our move. And right now, he's done nothing wrong. I don't want this messed up so give him some space.'

'Ten four, sir.'

Chalmers came out of the cubicle just as Fitzpatrick entered the lift. Maureen O'Brian had told them the room that their target had booked, so there was no need to follow him. Instead, Chalmers took a seat and relaxed. Now it was just a waiting game.

***

Maureen closed the hotel door behind her and headed towards the lift. She passed a man sitting in a cosy arm chair, reading a newspaper. Or pretending to. Maureen didn't give him a second glance. The plain-clothes officer was exactly what Myers had promised. And he'd delivered.

Relief washed over her. Not for herself. For the young girl who had no real idea of what was in store for her.

John took the drugs she'd thrust into his grubby hands, then walked over to a bedside table where he greedily opened the bag just handed to him. Within seconds he got down to business. Maybe he caught the disapproval on her face because he sneered at her, said 'Fuck you,' and then laughed. 'Who the fuck are to judge me, you fucking skank? You're the bloody whore. You've been selling this sort of thing yer whole life, and now you've decided to get all high and mighty? Really? You're a fucking joke. Well, fuck you and fuck off.'

Maureen did just that. She fucked off.

Heard the slam of the door behind her as she made her way down the hallway and back to the lift.

Moments later she was back in the lobby and into the cold night. The plain-clothes copper hadn't said a word. But he'd know.

She crossed the road and went into the pub. Allowed herself a little smile as she ordered a drink, and then another for when that was finished. Took a seat at the table near the window. The same one John had likely sat at while waiting for her to deliver his package. There was a good view of the hotel from there. The perfect spot from which to watch the show.

18

Rappity Tap

A knock came at the door. A rappity tap. One that indicated familiarity. The kind of knock John Fitzpatrick used all the time when he knew the person on the other side.

He opened the door, and there stood Kerry. And in front of her a girl.

A very young girl.

With pigtails.

Kerry gripped gripping the girl's shoulders. The girl looked scared. Which John liked. Very much indeed. He felt himself getting hard, and wondered if his arousal was evident to the young girl. He hoped so.

Kerry pushed the girl forward and followed her in. John closed the door.

Rappity tap and rock and roll! Fuck Maureen. This was more like it.

***

As soon as the two girls entered the lobby, Chalmers called it in. Myers told him to sit tight until the backup was ready.

'But, sir, they just went up in the lift. They'll be in the room now.'

'Stay where you are, Constable,' Myers said. 'We need to wait until this Kerry girl is back in the lobby and on her own.

That way we know she left the girl with him. Then we go in. Am I clear?'

'Yes, sir,' Chalmers said. It was all perfectly clear. It always was. But that didn't mean he had to like it. Which he didn't, not one bloody bit. That girl with Kerry – she'd looked frightened, and so bloody young.

***

'I need more money, Mr Fitzpatrick,' Kerry said, before the punter had even had a chance to speak. 'I don't think five hundred pounds is enough for a girl like this. I mean look at her – she's fresh. And I can get you more.'

Carly started crying. 'I've changed my mind, Kerry. I don't want to do this.'

Fuck. Carly turned and started to walk back towards the door, but Kerry blocked her way and slapped her face. Like last time, the blow knocked her to the floor.

'You'll do as your told, you little cow. There's no going back now.'

Her client appeared momentarily gobsmacked, but then he grinned. Like he approved of her ruthlessness. No, more than that. Like he was enjoying it.

'I've got your money here, sweetheart,' he said, and thrust a wad of notes her way. 'I'll give you another hundred next time but I don't have enough on me for that right now. Only the hundred for her.'

He gawped at Carly, still sobbing on the floor. Kerry studied him for a moment. Saw the longing etched into his face. And the desire causing his trousers not to hang straight. Fucking perv.

'Fair enough, Mr Fitzpatrick,' she said while pocketing the money. 'I'll get it next time. You have my number now. Just call if you need anything. Oh, and by the way' – she looked over at the bedside cabinet – 'I also have a dealer. One who can supply whatever you need. Just make sure I get my girl back in one piece.' She leaned over and patted Carly on the cheek. 'Just be a good girl, sweetheart, and everything will be alright.'

Three minutes later, two burly men approached her in the lobby, both wearing jeans and casual shirts. She wondered if they were Fitzpatrick's boys – until they introduced themselves as police officers.

Sixty seconds later they'd arrested her and bundled her away into a waiting car. Her feet barely touched the ground.

***

Dave entered the hotel lobby and called Stone. 'The girl's in the room, ma'am. Just her and Fitzpatrick. The other girl's in custody. How long should we leave it?'

'DCI Bates is on route, Myers,' she replied. 'She'll be there in about ten minutes or so. She wants to make the arrest herself.'

'But, ma'am, a lot can happen in that time. We have a duty of care towards this vulnerable young girl. That bastard could be raping her as we speak. We have to move in now.'

'No. You have your orders. Now just sit tight and make sure no one leaves that hotel, do I make myself clear?'

Dave took a breath, calming himself before he spoke. 'Yes, ma'am. But I want to make it clear – I am not happy.'

'You're not paid to be happy, Myers.'

Jesus, Stone could be a harsh bitch when she put her mind to it. Shame the priority was all about who made the arrest rather than the welfare of a child. What the fuck was all that about?

'We have bigger fish to fry here, Constable,' Stone continued. 'Just wait it out. When this is over, if you so wish, you can record any concerns you have in your notes and then report them.'

And then, just like that, she hung up.

19

A Room with a View

Sandra had nearly wet her pants when she'd read the report on what Tommy Spillane's monkey was planning to do. This was just too good, the perfect chance to get an inside man into custody and attempt to turn him. Against the big man himself. There was no guarantee, of course, but if all the rumours about John Fitzpatrick were true, he absolutely would not want Tommy Spillane knowing about it.

As Stone drove them over to Kings Cross, Sandra was almost salivating.

Stone was on the phone, tearing a strip off Myers.

When she hung up, Sandra said, 'Well-handled, Sergeant. The less he knows at the moment the better. Although if he has anything about him, he's probably already guessed.'

'No doubt about that, ma'am. I briefed him earlier about our intentions in regard to the North London mob. That's how he added two and two together and put this thing into action. We have him to thank if we get an arrest tonight.'

Ten minutes later, they arrived at the hotel. Myers gave her a brief situation report on the events leading up to the moment. She listened, then nodded.

'Okay, lads. Let's go kick a door in and get this fucking creep down to the station.'

***

Not that the door needed kicking in. The hotel manager had been only too happy to help and given them a spare key. Not that they'd needed that either, because Fitzpatrick, in his eagerness to get proceedings underway, it seemed, had forgotten to even lock the door.

They found him kneeling by the bed, very high and completely naked.

Myers pushed him to the floor and rolled him onto his stomach. He was cuffed before he could even register what had happened.

Mellissa ran over to the bed. The girl's hands were tied to the bed posts and she was gagged. Her clothing had been disturbed but, much to Mellissa's relief, she was still wearing knickers.

'Don't worry, sweetheart. You're safe now,' she said while untying her wrist binds and removing her gag.

The girl gasped and began to sob hysterically. 'I told him I'd changed my mind and didn't want to do anything but he beat me and tied me up. He was … he was gonna r-rape me, I know it.'

Mellissa stroked her hair. 'You're okay. You're safe. Let's get you to the hospital and we can talk about it there.'

'I just want to go h-home. Why do I need to go to the hospital?'

'It's just precautionary, sweetheart. Now, tell me your name.'

'C-Carly. Carly Stubbs.'

'Well, Carly, it's better for a doctor to give you the once-over, that's all. It'll be a woman doctor, I promise.'

Carly broke down again, and Mellissa wrapped her arms around her, then pulled a blanket over her shoulders. 'I promise you, everything will be okay. You're safe.'

***

Maureen sipped her drink as she watched the drama unfold. A young girl was led by paramedics to an ambulance parked outside the hotel. Police officers, including her handler, Dave Myers, spoke into walkie talkies and mobiles.

But where was John Fitzpatrick?

She shouldn't have drunk alcohol. It was clouding her thoughts, making her paranoid. *Stupid stupid stupid.*

But, still, there would be implications after what she'd done. John Fitzpatrick wasn't a man to be messed with, and if he found out it was her who'd grassed him, the consequences would be huge.

Her sensible voice told her that surely he'd think it had been Kerry. But the paranoid voice countered – what if he blamed her anyway?

She shuddered and took another sip of her drink, mourning the loss of glee she'd felt earlier, wrapping her mind around the reality of what she'd brought about. If he found out, her life would be over. Literally.

Which meant she needed to leave, get out of the area. But where?

The sensible voice was back, telling her she had time, not much but enough. He'd be held in custody while they investigated, wouldn't he? The charges would surely be serious enough.

Then again, a man of his resources could afford the best lawyers. Maybe he'd be out in a few days, maybe a day. A normal Joe wouldn't get bail, not with those charges anyway, but Fitzpatrick? He had connections. And he owned the flat she lived in.

'Oh my God, what have I done?'

Several nearby patrons turned around and looked at her, and it was only then that she'd realised that she'd spoken out loud.

20

Unreliable Witness

Despite the itch to interview Fitzpatrick, Sandra held back. She'd wait for him to sober up. Several high-profile cases had been lost over the past few years when those in custody had later claimed that they hadn't known what they were saying because they were drunk or high or some other lousy fucking excuse for their shit behaviour. If a suspect claimed they weren't compos mentis at the time of admission of culpability, the statement could too easily by dismissed by a judge as unreliable.

No way was Sandra about to make that mistake with her prize. Not a chance. Instead, she'd would let him stew in the 'comfort' of his cell until he was bright-eyed, bushy-tailed and ready to sing for his supper.

Besides, there were other trophies to put a polish on. The informant Maureen for one. Kerry, the sex worker turned pimp in the cell adjoining Fitzpatrick's. And young Carly, of course. Stone was with her at the hospital and would get her statement when the time was right.

And in this game, it was all about good timing.

***

Maureen opened a holdall and began to throw things inside – clothes, shoes, a few personal items, all the while telling herself that travelling light meant travelling fast. Three bags max.

The intercom buzzed, and terror coursed up her down her spine and into her bladder. Was he out already? Had one of his henchmen come for her? She fought the urge to wet herself, and won. One battle down.

She pressed the button. Said: 'Hello. Who is this?'

'My name is Detective Chief Inspector Sandra Bates. Is that Maureen?'

The police. Not great, but not the worst visitors to have right now.

'Yes, what do you want, Inspector?'

'Just open the door, love. It's better if we talk in private.'

She buzzed them into the lobby – what choice did she have – and a few moments later peered through the peephole. A woman was standing there, and behind her another officer whose face she couldn't see.

'Who's that with you?' Maureen said.

'I'm with Detective Constable Myers of the Vice Squad, Maureen. I believe you two are acquainted.'

Dave Myers. Someone she could trust.

She opened the door and let them in.

21

A Royal Fuckup

John had made use of his right to a phone call. Explained to his usual lawyer that he needed some assistance, but didn't say anymore. James Lawton QC had agreed to make himself available. And now, in his cell, having had a chance to consider that decision over the past few hours while the drugs and booze wore off, his head had cleared, allowing him to think straight.

And what he was thinking was bringing zero fucking comfort. Because he'd made a mistake. A big fucking mistake.

John could have kicked himself. What the hell had he been thinking? Lawton had been the Spillanes' advocate for over twenty years. It had been Lawton and his team who'd got Tommy off on a conspiracy-to-murder charge less than a year earlier. No way could he ask Tommy for help. The man frowned upon drug use, but underage sex – that was a whole different ball game. He'd string John up faster than the filth for that. And telling Lawton would pretty much mean telling Tommy.

Christ, he was in serious trouble here. Queen's Council? More like a royal fuckup, that's what this was.

The cell door opened.

'Mr Fitzpatrick,' a grumpy-looking officer said, 'your solicitor's here. Please follow me.'

John clambered off his bunk and walked out into a narrow hallway of cells deep below the police station. He followed the copper until they reached an interview room. Inside, and shuffling papers around the desk in front of him, was James Lawton QC.

'Come in and take a seat, John,' he said a little too cheerily for John's liking. Then he turned to the copper. 'Thank you, Sergeant. Please close the door on your way out. I'll take it from here.'

The sergeant did as he was told and disappeared .

'Now, John,' Lawton said, his tone now more serious, 'you're up shit creek without a paddle, my friend. The allegations just presented to me by a rather pretty young thing called' – he fingered his notes – 'ah, yes, Sergeant Mellissa Stone, working alongside the Vice Squad, are quite damning. The facts as presented to me are that you've literally been caught with your trousers down, and were about to assault a girl who by all accounts is under the consensual age. I'll get that confirmed, of course, but if that's the case, you're in real trouble here. Notwithstanding, you were also in possession of a class-A drug, namely crack cocaine. This also needs to be confirmed by way of analysis, but in the meantime, let me have your version of events. And, please John, don't leave anything out. I may can only help you if I have all the facts. Do I make myself clear?'

'This has to remain confidential, Lawton. Tommy doesn't need to know about this. Do I have your word as my lawyer?'

'Why of course, John,' Lawton said, and frowned as if affronted that John should even ask the question. 'I have a duty of confidence in these matters. Nothing said or done here will leave this room.'

John nodded, then spilled his guts. Told the lawyer everything.

When he'd finished, Lawton sank back in his chair, sighing heavily. But there was something there. Etched on his face. Contempt. John was pretty sure he could recall hearing that the QC had daughters. And while the lawyer had no doubt seen some real nasty pieces of work in his time, and had defended some of them to acquittal, he probably wouldn't be thinking to highly about John right now. All he could hope for was that Lawton would do his job and advise him on the best course of action and present a defence, no matter what his personal feelings were.

'Thank you for being so honest with me, John. And don't worry about confidentiality. Even if I wanted to, I'm not allowed by law to disclose your arrest with anyone, let alone a known gangster like Tommy. I'd be struck off.'

John exhaled. *Thank fuck for that.*

'Now,' Lawton continued, 'getting back to the present, my advice to you at this moment is to make a "no comment" statement when interviewed. We need all the facts and evidence first. For example, proof of the girl's age and confirmation of the drug class. The drug thing is minor in the grand scheme of things, and would only amount to a fine should you even be charged with possession. However, in the case of the girl, it's one thing her being underage. Kidnap and false imprisonment, well, that's quite another. Which is what you're looking at, because from what the police have told me, the girl was tied to the bed and gagged. Add that to a charge of engaging in sexual activity with a child, and any other charges such as assault and intent to rape, well, you could be looking at a substantial prison sentence should you be convicted. Double figures.'

John lowered his head into his hands, suddenly dizzy. The enormity of what he was facing hit him like a ton of bricks. And, yeah, he was used to being interviewed by the police, course he was, but not under these circumstances. The evidence was overwhelming. It would be almost impossible to escape a lengthy prison sentence. Worse, his reputation would be destroyed. Branded a nonce. It would finish him.

He couldn't have that. He just couldn't.

Unless … unless there was a way to get to the witnesses. Without them there was no case.

Lawton waited patiently.

'Do I have any other options?' John asked.

'Like what?' Lawton appeared baffled. 'Let's not be too hasty in conceding anything, John. You never know what they might have up their sleeve. Once the witnesses realise the implications, they may decide not to proceed with their accusations. Indeed, people of this ilk generally have a lot to hide and are notoriously unreliable when it comes to actually giving evidence. No, like I said, just go with no comment statement under interview, get your bail and wait for the evidence to be collated and presented. Then we can look into the options available to you. That's my advice, but as is usual, the choice is yours.'

John nodded. The choice was his. Some fucking choice.

22

Rough Justice

Sandra kneaded her temples, trying to massage away a threatening headache before it took hold. 'Maureen O'Brian won't say a thing. She seemed seriously distressed when Myers and I paid her a visit earlier. She was actually a little drunk and we thought it best to let her stew for a while and get back to her tomorrow when she's sobered up.'

'I think the enormity of what she's done has sunk in and she's now running scared,' Myers said. 'But the evidence from her is ropey anyway. I mean, what can she actually tell us that would make a difference to what we already know? She made it very clear that she wouldn't give evidence in court under any circumstances, and I believe her.'

Sandra sighed. 'So what have we actually got? Fitzpatrick was in a hotel room with an underage girl who originally stated that he was about to rape her just before we got there. He was in possession of a class-A drug, crack cocaine. There's a possibility that he may have shared it with Carly – that's also an offence. Stone, what has Carly said in her statement?'

'I'm afraid she won't make one, ma'am. She's seriously traumatised by tonight's events but she's adamant that she won't give a statement and won't go to court. It would mean having to face him again, she said. All she wants is to go back home to Leeds and forget about the whole thing. I very much doubt we could change her mind, although it might be worth trying.' Katie Finch was saying nothing either.

'Bloody hell,' Sandra said, and rose from her chair. 'What is it with these damn people? Are they prepared to let a fucking paedophile and potential rapist escape the clutches of justice? This man is a bloody menace and needs to be taken off the streets. And where does that leave us? We can't force them to give evidence. Honestly, I despair sometimes, I really do.'

'All's not lost yet, ma'am,' Myers said. 'We can still charge him with engaging with a minor for the purposes of underage sexual activity, with or without her statement. She is actually fifteen. We caught him red-handed, don't forget. And it would be very hard for him to wriggle out of that one. Plus, we can charge him with the supply of a class-A drug to a minor. That alone would guarantee a five-year sentence. At a—'

'Yes, at a minimum, but without Carly's statement it won't stick,' Stone said. 'He'd just deny it. Say she was high when she got there. And other bullshit like she'd told him a fake age and that he was unaware of her youth. Don't forget, she was prostituting herself. I really do think that without her statement, he'll walk.'

Sandra held a hand up. 'Not necessarily. Ignorance is no defence in law. We have a case, that's for sure, but possibly not the one we were hoping for. It's something to go on at least. And who knows, Carly and Maureen might change their minds once they're both sober. Then we can revisit the attempted rape and false imprisonment charges perhaps.'

'With all due respect, ma'am, I think we're clutching at straws with that scenario,' Myers said. 'I have worked Vice for some years now. I know these women, or women like them. And I've seen first-hand how unreliable they can be as witnesses. Without Carly's testimony, Fitzpatrick will just say that it was a sex game they were playing, and that he thought she was over the age of consent. I reckon we should just take the win where we can and let it go at that.'

Sandra slammed her fist on the desk. 'So we're just going to let a fucking monster get a slap on the wrist and leave it at that? I don't bloody think so, DC Myers. I've made my decision. We'll interview him and hope he slips up, reveals something we can use against him. You never know, do you?'

But even as the words came out of her mouth, she doubted them. A man like John Fitzpatrick Senior surely wouldn't give anything away that easily. He was far too knowledgeable in such matters. She could already see the way it would go. *No comment. No comment. No comment.*

23

Terminal Leave

John Fitzpatrick was out. Not out of the woods by any means, but out of the nick at least. He'd been ordered to surrender his passport, which his lawyer had duly delivered to the desk sergeant prior to his release, and he'd have to answer his bail in two weeks' time at the police station, which could lead to further charges. But for now, all they had on him was a charge of possession of a class-A drug. The other matter was still under investigation.

Now stone-cold sober, he considered his options. He'd known the interviewing officer because of the Spillane trial. Detective Chief Inspector Sandra Bates no less. And she'd made it perfectly clear that she wasn't done. Which more than anything else was worrying him. She'd go hard. Seek any evidence she could get her hands on so she could charge him with the sex offences. Christ, drugs were one thing, but being charged with molesting an underage girl? The implications were horrifying, unthinkable. At best he'd be ostracised. At worst he'd be killed. Neither was exactly palatable. This mess needed sorting, and bloody quickly.

And John knew where exactly where to start.

***

Maureen threw the last of her things into a third holdall. Ten more minutes and she'd be gone. She swallowed down the panic. It was bad, worse than ever before. Sure, she'd dealt with some serious players in her time – that came with the territory in this profession. But none like Fitzpatrick. He scared the hell out of her. He was unpredictable and violent, not someone she wanted to see anytime soon. Moving away for a while was the only option, at least until the dust had settled. She had a few quid under the mattress, enough to see her through for a few months.

Back over the water to Clapham felt like a good option. She knew a few people, there, people who could keep her safe, for now at least. It was an up-and-coming area, especially when it came to the nightlife. Lots of new clubs and bars had sprouted up over the past few years. And the transport links were good too – the train, Tube and buses providing easy access to central London. Perfect for out-of-town young professionals looking for a place to rent and company between the sheets. Which for Maureen meant there was money to be had and opportunities to exploit. After all, hers was reportedly the oldest profession in the world, wasn't it?

As she zipped up the bag, a faint odour tickled her nostrils. Smoke, booze, the sour tang of state sweat.

She spun around. And there was John Fitzpatrick, standing in her bedroom. *Shit.*

'John, what on earth are you doing here? You startled me. You should have called. I could have been naked or something.'

The bastard had a key. Of course he did. Being the landlord, he would have, wouldn't he. And in her panic, she'd completely forgotten.

'Just thought I'd pop by and have a little chat, Maureen,' he said with a crooked grin. 'Guess where I've been all night, sweetheart?'

'I've no idea, darling. How would I know?'

He sneered and walked towards her. 'Oh, come now, Maureen, do you seriously mean to tell me you know nothing about what happened last night? Are you telling me that no one from the hotel called you to fill you in? That that little tart Kerry never said a word to you once she was released from the police station? That the police haven't visited you?' He rolled his eyes. 'I'm beginning to think you're taking me for a fool, sweetheart.'

And Maureen realised she'd made a mistake, a really stupid one. John would know she'd have been told what had happened. Of course she would. She had an ongoing relationship with the hotel people. She'd have been one of the first to find out.

'It's none of my business, John. Why would anyone tell me what's going on? Besides, I went for a few drinks last night. Didn't get in till really late.' She tried to keep her voice light and steady.

'So you're telling me that you have absolutely no idea what happened at the very same hotel you use for business? Okay, then. In that case, why don't you fill me in on why you're packing a bag, sweetheart. Going somewhere, are you?'

'Just visiting with some friends for a few days, that's all, then I'll be back.'

John began to laugh.

Not a normal laugh.

An awful manic laugh that seemed to come from the pit of his stomach and spill out of his mouth like viscous liquid.

A laugh that scared the shit out of her.

His hands were by his sides. And then they weren't. A fist flew towards her face. The blow knocked her to the floor.

'What do you take me for, you old whore?' he screamed, looming over her. 'Am I a fucking idiot? I mean look.' He pointed at her luggage. 'Who packs three bags of clothes for just a few days? You're a lying fucking bitch. You're doing a runner, aren't you? Now tell me everything or, God help you, these will be your last breaths, I promise you.'

She should have left the previous evening, she realised now. But she'd been pissed and had decided to get a few hours kip. She'd overslept.

'John, for God's sake calm down,' she said while wiping blood from her mouth. 'Okay, I admit it, I knew about your arrest. I was in the Prince of Wales when it happened. I saw it all unfold from across the road. I even saw that little bitch leading the filth into the hotel.' A lie, yes, but one that might save her. 'She must have told them what you were doing. But it was nothing to do with me, John, honest. And I did warn you about her, didn't I? I told you not to go for girls that young. I said it would bring serious trouble your way, didn't I?'

'Then why the fuck did you lie to me just now? Why didn't you just come clean to start with?'

'I'm sorry. But I was scared, John. Really scared. I thought you might blame me, that you might not hear me out. Because you've got a bit of a temper, sweetheart. Honestly, I promise you – that's all it was.' She rolled onto her back, and tried to sit up, but he was too close, right in her face. 'Please, John, don't hurt me. I've told you all I know. It must be that little cow who's done this to you. It not me, I swear.'

'Where is she?' John said, and slapped her face. 'And don't fucking lie to me. She's going to get what's coming to her, and it can't wait.'

'I don't know, John, and that's the truth. She never came back here, that's for sure. I mean why would she? You should check that hostel she stays in. She can't be far. I'll check for you if you want.'

'Never mind you checking where she might be, sweetheart. I'll catch up with her sooner or later.' He chuckled, grabbed her hair and snarled. 'What do you think I am, stupid? You'll run off to your police friends and put me right in the shit. No, Maureen, you've still got a little explaining to do, haven't you?'

'You're hurting me,' she cried out. 'I don't know what happened, honest I don't. She must have set it all up.'

'*LIAR*. It was her who brought the girl to me. She couldn't have shown the filth. She didn't have had enough time. And why would she? She was making money from that deal. She even offered to supply my ... needs for the other thing. No, sweetheart, it was you who set this whole thing up, getting on your high horse with your bleeding fucking heart. And if it wasn't you, why didn't you warn me when you knew she was leading the police to me? Not only that, how could you know it was the police when you were watching from the pub? All the filth that came into my room were in plain clothes. You couldn't possibly have known unless you were in on it.'

He was right, of course. A whimper escaped her throat. She was done for. He'd hurt her. Badly. She curled into a ball on the floor and covered her head.

***

The assault was brutal and terminal. John made sure of it.

When it was over, he went into the bathroom and cleaned up as best he could, though there was an awful lot of blood.

The first call he made was to his eldest son. His boys were to come to the flat in Kings Cross and bring the cleaning equipment. It wasn't their first rodeo so John headed off home. There he made the second call. News of his arrest would get around quickly. Getting his version of events in first, before the rumour mill went into overdrive, was essential.

And he had a plan.

24

Someone to Confide In

Tommy put down the phone. *Shit.*

'Everything alright, darling?' Peggy asked as she poked her head through the door to his office. 'You're white as a ghost.'

'Everything's fine, sweetheart. Nothing to worry about. Just a bit of business, that's all. Have you heard from the kids?'

His wife loved nothing more than talking about their kids. The question had the desired effect. Peggy was immediately distracted, and started to fill him in excitedly on about how Lorraine and Jack had settled into their honeymoon suite at the beautiful Royal Bath hotel in Bournemouth, and how when their daughter had called earlier, she'd sounded very happy.

Then she gave him one of those looks, like she could read his mind. 'Why do you ask?'

'Oh, no reason, darling. Just enquiring, that's all. When are they back?'

'Just under a week, darling. But you know that – it was you who paid for it, you silly sausage.'

Tommy grunted and headed into the kitchen. Peggy sidled up alongside him and wrapped her arms around him. 'What's wrong, Tommy? Is it something you can talk to me about?'

Tommy turned around and faced his wife. 'There may be some trouble coming our way, sweetheart, that's all. Something's come up from the past that could cause me some serious problems. That's really all I can say.'

Peggy pulled away, from him. 'All you can say? For fuck's sake, Tommy, I'm your wife. I've been by your side through thick and thin. For God's sake, just tell me. I might be able to help you.'

Tommy sighed. 'God, I wish Albie was still alive. He'd know what to do.'

'About what? Just bloody tell me.' She paused a moment, looked straight at him, then said, 'Oh my God, don't tell me it's something to do with those bloody Yardies. Tommy, tell me right now, are Lorraine or Jack in any danger?' She pummelled his chest, then grabbed the lapels of his bathrobe, shaking him, and shrieked, *'Tell me.'*

'Calm down, love,' Tommy said, and took her hands in his own, squeezing gently, massaging her fingers. 'What do you take me for? if I thought the kids were in danger I would have dealt with it by now. No, love, it's got nothing to do with those bloody Yardies. It's something from the past that I can't talk to you about. I need time to think.' He smiled and kissed her cheek. 'Now be a good girl and get the bloody kettle on. I always think better with a cup of tea.'

Peggy nodded, and began to do as he'd asked. Tommy went outside to the patio and sat down in a chair that faced the beautifully landscaped garden. What he needed right now was someone to confide in, to talk things through with. Maybe the time had come for him to bring Jack into his confidence. Although the drug-taking thing was a concern. The boy would need to deal with that first. It could scupper all Tommy's plans for moving his family out of crime, relieving them of the relentless burden of having to watching out for the filth. No way did he want his grandchild growing up with that kind of fear and uncertainty. The Yardie issue only months ago had really brought it home to him, and the thought of his beloved daughters being caught up in that kind of violence terrified him. Jack was crucial to taking his family forward. He just needed to be tamed a little. Question was, could you tame a man like Jack?

'What have you got to lose?' he muttered.

'What's that, darling?' Peggy said, and placed his tea on the table in front of him.

'Just thinking out loud, sweetheart. You know me, always chuntering away to myself. Thanks for the tea.' He lit a cigarette. Peggy hated him smoking and took it as a dismissal.

'You're welcome, love,' she said, then kissed him on the forehead and went back inside.

Tommy sipped the drink, and as the warm liquid slide down his throat, his mind cleared. He took out his mobile.

***

'What can I do for you, Tommy?' Jack said, keeping his voice cheery despite the surprise. Why the hell was his father-in-law calling him now?

'I'm sorry to call you on your honeymoon, son, but I need to talk to you urgently. Where's my daughter?'

'Being pampered in the hotel spa. I'm on my own at the moment.'

'Good. Now listen carefully.'

Then Tommy explained. No names – he wasn't comfortable mentioning those over the phone, but a good friend of theirs had got himself into a bit of trouble recently with their other friends – the ones who dressed in blue. The friend in question was the same person who'd had some difficulty at Jack's recent nuptials, Tommy said. Did Jack know who he was referring to?

Jack knew alright, and said so. John fucking Fitzpatrick Senior of course. 'But if that's the case, maybe it's better for us to talk in private, Tommy. Do you want me to drive up tonight? Lorraine will be alright for a few hours. I'll tell her it's urgent, and if I mention you, she won't bat an eyelid.'

'I don't like to put this on you, Jack, but yes. This is rather urgent. Tell Lorraine I'll make it up to her once she's had the baby – all expenses paid to anywhere in the world for as long as she likes. And then you can celebrate properly without any distractions. See you in a few hours.'

Tommy hung up on him, and Jack went to find his new bride.

She wasn't happy but didn't stand in his way. 'Do what you have to do, my darling, but make sure you're back here first thing in the morning. I've booked us on a boat cruise down in Portland. Apparently, it sails past Sandbanks, the most exclusive island in the UK. I want to live there one day.'

Jack laughed and kissed her on the forehead.

Two hours later he was back in North London.

25

Putting the Squeeze On

'I still think we have a case for charging him with false imprisonment,' Sandra said to Stone. 'We have enough evidence even without the witness statements. I mean we literally caught him with his pants down and the girl tied to the bed.'

The sergeant nodded. 'But I'm still concerned that if Carly won't corroborate it with a witness statement, Fitzpatrick will just say it was consensual. And we've got nothing from Maureen O'Brian. Even if we did, it might be considered hearsay and inadmissible in court, unless she'll take the stand, which is doubtful. And Kerry's going to be no comment all the way. She won't want to incriminate herself, will she? Ma'am, I really think that the only way forward with this is to charge him with engaging in sexual activity with a child, and hope that this prompts him to talk to us. Unless, of course, we can get Maureen, Kerry and Carly to change their minds and agree to stand up in court against him. Then we could present him with all the charges. That would definitely be enough to get him talking. Someone like that doesn't want to have those charges on him, does he?'

The briefing-room door edged open and DC Myers entered, carrying three cups of steaming coffee. 'What have I missed?' he said, placing them on the table.

Sandra filled him in. Myers listened as she spoke, then sat down, nodding and chewing his lip, seemingly deep in thought. Sandra let him have a moment to collect his thoughts.

'With all due respect, ma'am, it's a tricky one. Without witness statements, the case would be fragile to say the least, and I very much doubt that the Crown Prosecution Service would go for it. But more importantly, don't you want this man for your own purposes? Mellissa told me that you believe he's crucial for gathering evidence against Tommy Spillane and others in several murder cases. If you charge him for those offences, surely he'll just clam up. He'll have nowhere to go, especially if he gets bail. He might be killed, either by someone who wants to keep him quiet, or because he's been branded a nonce, and I'm not sure that I'm comfortable with that scenario.'

'I have no interest in your comfort, DC Myers,' Sandra snapped. 'This team is tasked with gathering evidence that will prove once and for all that Tommy Spillane and his cohorts are responsible for numerous killings over the past two decades. And with bringing down his criminal empire. We know he was involved in the Giles Anderson murder despite his acquittal, and we suspect he was involved with the torture and murders of Billy Saunders and Karl Green. Fair enough, we can't go back on the Anderson case, but as God is my witness we're going to prove his involvement in the Saunders and Green cases. And we mustn't forget that there's a missing person in the equation. Darren Davies.'

Davies, she reminded them, had been a runner for the Spillane outfit and had mysteriously disappeared around the same time. Sandra believed he'd been killed.

'Why or where we still don't know, but I aim to prove it, and this Fitzpatrick fella could hold the key. He's worked with the Spillane mob for years. As a senior man, he must know something.'

'Then why do you want to charge him, ma'am,' Myers said. 'It makes no sense. Like I said, he could just clam up and you'll get nothing from him.'

Sandra laughed. 'DC Myers, are you that naïve? We'll make him *think* that's what we're going to do. We let him sweat for a while until he has to answer his bail. In the meantime, you and Sergeant Stone revisit the witnesses. I want statements from all the staff who were on duty at the hotel last night. I want Maureen O'Brian paid a visit and it made clear that if she doesn't comply, we'll make life very difficult for her. Myers, you know her better than anyone. Get yourself over there and put her under pressure. Stone and I will go back to Katie Finch and Carly Stubbs and try to get under their skin.'

Myers looked perplexed. 'But I don't understand, ma'am. I thought you wanted him for your own purposes. Gathering evidence against him will mean a trial. I was under the impression that that's the last thing you wanted.'

Stone shook her head. 'I think what the guvnor's getting is quite simple really. Forgive me if I'm wrong, ma'am, but I think you want Fitzpatrick running scared. He'll know that we're building a case against him, and that'll nudge him to approach us with a deal. Am I right?'

'Very good,' Sandra said, trying to hide the smugness in her tone. 'Do you understand our strategy now, DC Myers?'

Myers nodded. 'Understood, ma'am. I'll get over to Maureen's later this afternoon and put the squeeze on.'

They agreed to meet at six that evening.

26

Trouble Ahead

The door opened and Peggy gawped at Jack. 'What on earth are you doing here? You're supposed to be on honeymoon. And where's my daughter? Where's Lorraine?' She peered over his shoulder towards the car.

'Don't worry, Peggy love,' he said, and kissed her on the cheek. 'She's getting pampered by the hotel staff. She's in her glory. I won't be here for long – I just forgot something, that's all.'

His mother-in-law raised her eyes towards the sky. 'Oh, is that right? If you say so. Well, in you come then. Tommy's in his den. Which is really why you're here, son. I'm not stupid, you know.'

Jack glanced down at the floor, hating lying to Peggy, talking to her like she was some naïve fool. She was a lovely person, and anything but stupid.

'Don't fret, Jack. I know my husband and what his line of work entails. This isn't my first rodeo, you know. Now stop looking like some awkward schoolboy and get yourself in there. Shall I make you some tea?'

'That would be lovely,' Jack said. What a woman. Not only wise, but kind too. Always ready to bring relief to others. 'See you in a bit.'

Tommy was already poking his head out from the den at the far end of the hallway. He beckoned Jack towards him. 'Sit down, Jack,' he said, and closed the door behind them. 'I need to talk to you.'

Jack took a seat opposite Tommy's sumptuous desk. 'What's this all about, Tommy, and why the urgency? Lorraine isn't happy.' A lie but they were on their honeymoon all.

'I know, son, but this is very important and could have serious implications for the whole family if we don't get it sorted urgently.'

Tommy looked worried, more worried than Jack had ever seen him. What the hell had happened?

His father-in-law sighed. 'Where do I start?'

'How about at the beginning?' Jack said.

Tommy nodded. 'Sounds about right to me. Now, bear in mind that what I'm about to tell you would leave me seriously exposed if it ever got out. Son, I'm putting my life, and that of my family, in your hands, do you understand?'

Jack didn't, but nodded anyway.

'I used to discuss things like this with your Uncle Albie, but that's no longer a possibility. You're the nearest thing to him that I have now, Jack, and I need to know that I can trust you completely.'

'Of course you can trust me. For fuck's sake, I'm married to your daughter. I'm part of this family now, no matter what happens, and to the death if needs be.'

'Alright, son, calm down,' Tommy said, extending his arms towards Jack. 'It's just that I'm not used to talking like this to anyone. My life's on the line here, and I need to know that you're with me and the fam—'

'Tommy, your daughter is the love of my life, and is about to drop my son into this world – your grandson. What do you think I'm going to do? I'm sorry but if you need reassurances about loyalty, you're talking to the wrong man.' He stood up and marched over to the door, only to find his way blocked by Peggy. He'd not even heard her come in.

'I've got your tea, Jack. Come on sit down and hear what Tommy has to say.'

Tommy looked at her with incredulity, and Jack realised that she'd probably never before entered the den uninvited, never mind interfered in her husband's business.

'Oh, come on, Tommy,' she said. 'Don't look at me like that. The mere fact that Jack's here during his honeymoon tells me all I need to know. There's trouble ahead and I have a right to know what's going on. I'm not bloody stupid, sunshine. And don't forget, it's usually me that has to pick up the pieces when the shit hits the fan.'

Tommy's mouth hung open. Jack wanted to laugh. This was surely a rare treat, witnessing Tommy's darling wife giving him a piece of her mind. For Jack at least. Tommy didn't seem so happy about things.

'Peggy, be a darling and put the bloody tea down. Then remove yourself from my office. Jack and I have business to discuss, and if you need to know about it, I'll tell you – later, not before. Am I clear?'

'Crystal bloody clear, Tommy. Sir, yes, sir. I'll make myself scarce. But let me make something clear.' She held her finger in Tommy's face. 'If this family is in danger like last time, and anything happens to my daughters, I'll do for you myself. Am *I* clear.'

Jack sat back down. Jesus fuck, this had gone from amusing to just embarrassing. And right now he'd have preferred to be anywhere else. Was this what married life was like? A chuckle slipped out of his mouth.

'Something funny, son?' Tommy said, glaring at him.

Jack stopped laughing. 'No, Tommy, but I don't appreciate being in the middle of a domestic. If this is what married life's all about, then you can stick it.'

Peggy snorted. 'Jack, my darling, get used to it. Lorraine is cut from the same cloth as me and her father. You'll have your fair share of this kind of thing, mark my words. It doesn't mean anything most of the time; we're just blowing off steam, that's all. And I'm sorry you had to be in the middle of it.'

So was Jack. It had reminded him of his mother and stepfather, that animal was Ritchie Powers, who'd beaten young Jack and his mother whenever the mood had suited him. At the tender age of only fifteen, Jack had killed Ritchie. Uncle Albie had known of course. Whether he'd shared that information with Tommy, Jack couldn't know. If Tommy did know, he wasn't giving it up now and said, 'It's like Peggy says, son. Just blowing off steam. Me and Peggy are as strong as ever. She don't mean nothing by what she says, do you, love?'

'Don't bank on it, Spillane,' Peggy said, and then winked at Jack. 'I'll make myself scarce and go get some cyanide from Sainsbury's … just in case.'

Then she closed the door and was gone.

Tommy shook his head and chuckled. 'Now, let's get down to business. First, I apologise for questioning your loyalty. Old habits die hard, son, and I meant nothing by it. I hope you see it that way.'

Jack nodded. 'We're good.'

'Alright then. So let's start afresh. John Fitzpatrick Senior was arrested last night for engaging in underage sex with a minor, and there's a charge of false imprisonment that might be in the pipeline.'

'Might? So it it's not already? I don't get that. How can—'

'Because he'll claim she told him she was older and that she agreed to be there,' Tommy said. 'Regardless, he was released from Islington police station earlier this morning. Charged with drug possession. Just to be clear, I've known about his drug habit for some time and was going to speak with him about that after your wedding. The fact that he's not been charged with the other offences has me worried, hence my calling you here today.'

'What have you got to be worried about? That fucking wrong'un's indiscretions are surely nothing to do with you, are they?'

'Leave it out, Jack. What do you take me for? I have daughters. That kind of shit is despicable. I can't believe you would—'

'Tommy, stop. I didn't mean it like that. I just meant, how does this affect you?'

Tommy sighed. 'Well, that's the thing. It doesn't affect me, not directly, but he has something on me that I wish he didn't.'

Okay, now things were getting interesting. What could a piece-of-shit nonce like Fitzpatrick have on the great Tommy Spillane that would cause him this much anguish? And why was his boss struggling to get to the point?

Jack leant forward. 'Listen, Tommy, whatever that fucked-up prick has on you, I need to know so that I can help you. That's why I'm here, right? That's why you called me and dragged me away from my honeymoon. Because you need my help. But unless I know what I'm dealing with, I can't do anything about it, now can I?'

'I killed Darren Davies,' Tommy said.

So there it was.

'John and Albie disposed of the body for me. I never asked where. Just trusted them to clean up the mess. Clearly, your uncle's no longer around to tell me, but John knows, and I'm worried he'll do a deal with the filth … if he hasn't already. And if he has, Jack, it's all over. If he's told them about my involvement and where the body is, I'm finished. And he knows about other things too, stuff I had to settle when I came out of prison. I'm not sure exactly what he knows, but it would be enough to get the filth's taste buds tingling, I can tell you.'

'Bloody hell. Okay, we need to get on this quickly. If they've released him, it means they probably don't have all the information they need. Not yet anyway. But from what you've told me, it's only a matter of time before he spills his guts to save himself from a long prison sentence. We need to get to him now. So where can I find him?'

'Oh, that's easy, son. He called me earlier from his house when you were on your way down here. He wants a meet about the wedding night. I think he wants to smooth things out with me about almost kicking off in my house. Interesting that he never mentioned getting arrested. Interesting and extremely worrying. Surely he knows that I'd find out sooner rather than later. He can't be that stupid, can he?'

'Drugs make people do stupid things, Tommy.'

Tommy looked at him knowingly. 'You're not wrong there, smartarse.'

'I haven't forgotten what you said to me on my wedding night, and believe it or not, I did take it all in.'

'I'm glad to hear it, son,' Tommy said. 'Drugs are a bad business, and before you ask, yes, I've used them to my advantage and made a lot of money out of them, but things have changed. I truly believe that they'll be our downfall if we continue along that path. Like I told you a few days ago, I want out of this filthy business. I want to go legit so that neither we nor the rest of the family end up spending the rest of our lives looking over our shoulders twenty-four hours a day, seven days a week. The police have the upper hand now, Jack, and we just can't compete. Full stop. However, that's a conversation for another day. We have to deal with this issue first. I told John I'd get back to him in an hour or so; I was waiting to see you first. Now that I have, I'll call him and arrange the—'

'Hang on a minute, Tommy,' Jack said. 'If Fitzpatrick didn't mention his arrest when he was on the phone earlier, how did you know what happened?'

'Because his lawyer told me.'

What the fuck? A lawyer breaking his oath? What the hell was the world coming to? 'Blimey, Tommy. Don't tell me – Fitzpatrick used the family lawyer. What a stupid prick.'

'Indeed. Prickery of the highest order,' Tommy said, and shook his head. 'But let's get back to the matter in hand.'

'Fair enough,' Jack said. 'Where are you going to meet him? It can't be here for obvious reasons, or anywhere public for that matter. And we don't want him coming with anyone else either, do we?'

'No, I'll guarantee that. I'll tell him it's just me and him. He's a proud man, is our John. He's old school and would see it as a weakness if he needed support just to talk to me. Wouldn't even want his sons seeing that. As for where, the irony of all this is that we've just taken possession of a large parcel from our friends over the water, and its sitting nice and snugly in my lockup unit just by Kings Cross station. Which, incidentally, is where I done Darren Davies. John's been there many times – takes possession of the goods and moves it to wherever it's supposed to go. So it's the ideal opportunity for me to "talk" to him about the current situation.'

'Only one problem with that plan, Tommy,' Jack said. 'He'd usually arrive by car, and with someone else to transport the goods. He's paranoid about that sort of thing, you know.'

'And he has every right to be,' Tommy said. 'That's how I got caught all those years ago, don't forget. That's why you're going to call Callum. I want him to watch John's house and follow him when he leaves. Do you think Callum can manage that?'

'Definitely. Don't you worry about him – he's solid. I would trust him with my life.'

'Fair enough, Jack, and you're probably right. He'll use a driver. Make sure Callum keeps an eye out for who it is. If it's one of his sons, then too bad. There's not much I can do about that. If I insist on another driver, he'll get suspicious. But I will insist that it's just me and him in the lockup. Just make sure Callum reports back to us about the driver. Once we know who it is, I can make a decision on what we do with him. I don't want this to get messy. I need to keep it calm, at least to start with. I want you there when I question him, and I want you armed. Like you said, John's paranoid, and will be even more so now this has happened. We don't know what his state of mind is so we need to be careful. Now, you go and call Callum, and I'll call John and set up the meet for seven tonight. And Jack, just make sure you're both prepared for anything, do you understand?'

Jack nodded again. 'We will be. You don't need to worry about a thing. I have a key to the lockup, and I'll be waiting. Callum and I will be in constant contact prior to the meet so we'll soon know if anyone else is involved. I'll call you as soon as Callum has eyes on the driver.'

'Good lad. I'll see you at the lockup at 6.30.'

27

All Wrapped Up

Liam and his brother didn't move a muscle. Someone had knocked on the door and called out a name. A fucking copper. Dave somebody. He glanced at John, who'd closed his eyes and was mouthing *Shit shit shit*. The policeman rattled the door. Pushed open the letterbox. Thank fuck the bedroom wasn't in direct sight.

It seemed like an age before he finally left.

'Bloody hell,' Liam said, letting out a breath. 'That was close. I wonder what he was doing here.'

'What the fuck do you think he was doing here?' John snapped, and pointed at the corpse on the floor. 'He wanted to talk to this bitch, mate. She's obviously a grass and that's why dad's done for her.'

'I don't like it one little bit,' Liam said, feeling the panic rise again. 'Let's just get this over with quickly. Our pal Dave could come back at any time, and we don't want to be here when he does.'

'Agreed,' John said. 'Let's just get it done. Wait for it to get dark and get the fuck out of here. Grab that rug. Let's wrap her in it, then we'll have a quick clean-up and go.'

By eight that evening they were done and gone.

28

Duty of Care

Stone had already delivered her report to Sandra on Carly Stubbs. No change. Still not prepared to give a statement about the assault on her. And Katie Finch had done a runner back to Manchester. No surprise there.

Myers returned just after six. More bad news. Nothing on Maureen O'Brian.

'There's only three other flats in the block,' he said.' Of those, only one person was in, and they hadn't seen or heard anything from Maureen. I'll go back tomorrow and try again. But I have a feeling she was there – just not answering.'

'Why's that?' Sandra said.

'When I first turned up, I'm sure the upper window was open, and I'm pretty sure I saw movement, but in the blink of an eye it was gone.'

Sandra sighed. 'Not having much luck here, are we people? Maureen's being uncooperative and hiding in her flat, and Katie Finch has headed north.' She looked at Stone. 'You're sure she went to Manchester?'

Stone nodded. 'I questioned the hostel manager and two of the residents, two young girls who confirmed they'd seen her leaving in a hurry with a large holdall and heading towards the station. The duty manager checked her room shortly after. She confirmed that most of her meagre possessions were missing. It seems reasonable to assume she's headed back home.

'Not as stupid as she looks, then, is she, Sergeant,' Sandra said resigned. 'She's gone to ground while this plays out, and has taken herself out of the firing line. Quite smart considering who we're dealing with here.'

'So where does this leave us, ma'am? Without any substantial witnesses, Fitzpatrick will walk away from the main charges.'

'Perhaps, but he doesn't know that, does he? Let's stick to the plan and keep digging. I think Fitzpatrick will reach out to his paymaster, Tommy Spillane, and try to get his version of events over to him as quickly as possible.'

'Won't he want to keep this on the low, ma'am?' Myers said. 'I mean why would he tell someone like Spillane that he was arrested for engaging in sexual activity with a child? Spillane's old school. If he finds out about that he'll surely disassociate himself from Fitzpatrick without a second thought and cover his tracks, if there are any.'

Sandra nodded. 'Maybe. But Fitzpatrick isn't stupid. He knows Spillane will find out what's happened sooner or later and will probably tell him that it's all bollocks and that he was set up or something of that nature. Either way, he needs support, and I think that's what where he'll try to get it. Our best hope is that you're right, Myers, and that Spillane wants nothing to do with it. And that could lead to Fitzpatrick seeing us as his only option.'

'There's another possibility, ma'am,' Stone said quietly. 'Spillane could kill him rather than take a chance he'd turn on him. Have you considered that, ma'am?'

'I have, but it's a risk I'm willing to take. If that does happen, then that's on Fitzpatrick and Spillane. They both know the risks of operating in the world they inhabit. And there's not a lot we can do about it, is there? Unless Fitzpatrick comes to us for protection.'

The room went silent. Myers chewed his lip again, like he always did when he was ruminating on something. And Sandra could guess what it was. He probably thought her a cold fish. Myers was a softie, a copper with a conscience. She'd been one of those not so long ago. It got you fucking nowhere when you were dealing with gangsters and drugs.

'With all due respect, ma'am,' he said at last, 'if Spillane does take that path, then we've effectively sent a man to his death—'

Yup, there he went. All righteous. Because they had to keep the paedos safe, eh?

'—whatever way you try to spin it and I'm not sure I'm comfortable with that.'

'Oh grow up, Myers,' Sandra said. 'And stop with all this fake indignation. Like I said to you before, no one cares about your bloody comfort. These are serious gangsters and murderers we're dealing with here. They kill and maim people for fun and money. And I don't give a flying fuck about Fitzpatrick. He's a bloody child molester who would have raped a young girl if we hadn't intervened and he's probably done it before. No, if something happens to him then that's on his own head. He could have easily made a decision while he was here in custody and done the right thing, but, no, he's reverted to type. Thinks he's above the law. And besides, we have no responsibility to look out for him once he's off our premises. Do I make myself clear?'

Myers looked taken aback. He said nothing, just got up, shot Stone a look and left the room. Stone looked nonplussed by the rant. No surprise there. The sergeant had already been on the thick end of it during their previous case. Two men had been murdered by the Parkhurst brothers. Sandra had known that would be a possibility, but she'd ignored it. And she suspected that Stone knew it too. Her decision had nearly cost

Stone her life and Sandra her career. A reminder she didn't need that policing was fucking hard.

'Ma'am, may I interject?' Stone said, and stood up.

Sandra sighed, knowing what was coming. 'If you must.'

'Do we really want a repeat of the Parkhurst fiasco? I mean, that didn't end well, did it? Three fatalities. And, yes, two of them were involved in high-level crime and had probably killed people in their line of work but—'

'Not probably, Sergeant. We had proof of that, even if we never managed to get it to court.'

Stone shook her head. 'I know that, ma'am, but Paul Summers wasn't a killer, not that we know of. Yes, he was a bent copper but that doesn't warrant turning a blind eye to his possible murder, which is exactly what happened, isn't it?'

Sandra got to her feed. Seething. 'How bloody dare you? I didn't know that those bloody psychopaths would turn up in the middle of the day and blast two men to death. If I could have stopped it, I would have stopped it. I had an armed-response team nearby for just that eventuality, you know that. You were there for goodness' sake. And you, better than anyone, should know that all I was trying to do was gather intel on the Parkhursts and that other piece of shit, Tommy Spillane.'

'Yes, ma'am. We all recall what you said at the enquiry, but that wasn't the whole truth, was it? You knew that the Parkhursts would try get to Mickey Grover. I'll grant this – you couldn't have known about their intention to kill Summers at the safe house. But you still took the risk while trying to tempt them out into the open. You're doing the same thing here with Fitzpatrick. Yes, he's a bloody wrong'un but surely we have some responsibility, some sort of duty to protect him. We're police officers.'

So there it was. Out in the open. Stone looked contrite, like she'd gone too far. She sat back down as if expecting Sandra to round on her. It took courage to stand up to a governor.

And Stone and Myers both had. Yes, policing was hard, but that was the job. And having the guts to question your governor meant stressed-out coppers like Sandra didn't fuck up to often. Maybe she'd gone too far with Myers. Maybe he deserved better than the sting of her tongue. Maybe Stone did too.

Sandra sighed and sat back down herself. 'You're right, of course. Go and get Myers back in here. We need to step this up.'

A few minutes later, Myers – his face like thunder – slammed his backside onto chair and folded his arms.

'DC Myers, I apologise. I didn't show an appropriate regard for your professional concerns, and that was unacceptable. All my officers should be heard, no matter their rank or the situation. I also want to acknowledge that saying I have no concern for your comfort was wrong and unprofessional. I apologise for that too. It won't happen again. Now, clearly you're both concerned about the welfare of Mr Fitzpatrick, and you're both right to be. We have a duty of care towards all civilians, no matter what their alleged involvement is in any particular criminal activity. And on that basis, I want you, DC Myers, to go and pick up Maureen in the morning. Arrest her for soliciting or … whatever. I don't care what it is. I want her here. She needs to understand that she can't start all this and then bury her head in the sand. DS Stone, I want you to contact the Manchester Constabulary and get Katie Finch in custody. She's a suspect in the coercion of a minor, and as far as I'm concerned, she's broken her bail arrangement by leaving London. I want serious pressure put on her to reveal all she knows about this incident. Once she's in custody, you'll go and pick her up. In the meantime, let's all go home. It's been a long day. We can reconvene tomorrow morning at nine sharp. And let's not forget why we're all here – we still need the scoop on Spillane. If Fitzpatrick won't give it, and we can't rely on the notion that he will, then we'll need another avenue.'

'What about Carly, ma'am, the victim?' Myers said.

'Leave her alone for now. I think she's suffered enough. Who knows? If we can get Maureen to make a statement, Carly might find some courage and tell her story as well. Let's see.'

Both officers look pleased as they left the room. And Sandra would take that as a win. Because sometimes that was about as good as it got.

29

A Man Not to be Trifled With

Callum called Jack. He answered immediately and told Callum he was already in the lockup at Kings Cross. Just as Callum had expected, because Jack liked to be early and prepared. Would want to make sure everything was in place.

And they both knew that this wasn't going to end well. Because although Jack had said just to watch Fitzpatrick at his home and see who picked him up, Callum wasn't stupid. There was bad blood between his friend and John Fitzpatrick Senior, and something serious was going down.

His friend's voice has a buzz to it, like it always did when he was looking forward to something. Not an agitated buzz – more measured, calm, like he was in control. Callum had always appreciated that. It made him feel relaxed, no matter what the circumstances were.

And then Callum's heart sunk a little when the driver pulled up outside Fitzpatrick's house. Now *that* he hadn't been expecting.

'It's Ronnie Fisher, Jack.'

'Just follow them. I need to make sure they don't pick up anyone else. Call me if they do. It's important.'

'What if Fisher gets out of the car when they arrive?'

'Just call me, son. Other than that, just sit tight and wait for me to call you, understood?'

'Fair enough, mate, but if there's going to be trouble, I want to be there with you, Ronnie Fisher or not.'

Jack laughed – not a condescending laugh, but one of respect. 'Callum, you're a geezer and I love you, mate, but don't worry. If Fisher decides to make himself busy then I'll deal with him. The most important thing is that I know about it. Just call. If I need you, I'll give you further instructions.'

The line went dead and Callum double checked his weapon. Jack had said to come armed, so he had. And was now glad of it. Ronnie Fisher was notorious. If ever there was a man not to be trifled with. Fisher was that man.

***

'Don't worry about Fisher, Jack,' Tommy said when Jack called it in.

Which was easier said than done, Jack reckoned, because Ronnie Fisher was the kind of guy who probably took a gun just to visit his grandmother. He was always armed.

'Fitzpatrick will think he's safe with him,' Tommy continued, 'but Ronnie's my man. He won't interfere, I can guarantee you that.'

'Then why is he driving him?' Jack said. 'You don't bring along a psychopath like him unless you're expecting trouble.'

'Like I said, let me worry about him. Just get yourself ready. I'll be along in a few minutes. I'm only around the corner.'

'Tommy, don't get me wrong, I can handle him, but I'd rather not. Fisher's—'

'Jack. Stop. Listen. It won't come to that. Are we clear? Just be ready for Fitzpatrick. He's not to be trifled with either.'

Tommy hung up. Jack took three deep breaths, and with each one wondered what the fuck was going on.

30

To the Ends of the Earth and Back

Ronnie Fisher was smart enough to know his strengths and weaknesses. What he lacked in brains he made up for in brawn and brutality. So people said, anyway. His six-three frame and shoulders wide enough to remind people of a brick shithouse had done him no harm. Fearless. A man to be relied upon. His reputation around the streets of Islington had become legendary, as had his allegiance to Tommy Spillane.

And that loyalty had been well earned. Ronnie owed his life and his freedom to that man.

He and Tommy had first met in early 1964, when Tommy was just sixteen and still an up-and-coming young buck. Ronnie was ten years older, but he'd liked the young whipper-snapper straightaway. Despite Tommy's diminutive size – well, in comparison to Ronnie anyway – he was just as fearless. The major difference between the two of them was quite simple really. Tommy was a thinker and a planner. Clever, too. Really fucking clever. The smartest man Ronnie had ever known. Ronnie had looked up to him from day one. There'd been something about him that had commanded respect. And for Ronnie, who'd been raised in poverty and violence, that was everything. He'd needed Tommy. He still did.

Along with Albie, Tommy's right-hand man, a formidable trio had formed. One not to be messed with. They'd set about taking control of the North London pub and club scenes. And when the mood and opportunity arose, they'd grace the odd jewellery store with their attention. Tommy had always planned the robberies well, down to the armoured getaway cars. On two occasions, and mostly as a result of heavy drinking and too much talking, Ronnie had been lifted. Convicted both times. The first one had got him six years in prison, the second, eight years.

And he never opened his mouth. Not once. Just done his time like a man.

On both occasions, Tommy and Albie had looked after him, made sure he had a nice pension waiting for him on his release.

Friends like that were hard to come by, and Ronnie had never forgotten it.

Back in the late sixties, with the demise of the Kray twins in the east and the equally rapid fall of the Richardsons in the south, the whole of London had become wide open, primed for the taking. And the Legal and General gang, as they came to be known, had gone about their business ruthlessly and efficiently, even when Ronnie was doing time.

By the mid-seventies, Tommy had established himself as London's main man. His only serious rivals had been the Parkhurst twins from South London, but they'd generally kept themselves to that side of the water and hadn't bothered the boys.

What Ronnie hadn't known back then was that Tommy and Albie had stumbled upon the twins one afternoon at a spieler in the West End. That had led to the formation of a sort of friendship. It had only come out when Tommy had been in court on a charge of murder. He'd been acquitted, but Ronnie had struggled to understand the Parkhursts' betrayal and had vowed to take revenge. Tommy had ordered him to hold back.

'Bide your time, Ronnie, lad,' he'd said. 'They'll get what's coming to them in due course. Let's just celebrate my freedom. There's always a time for retribution, but it's not now.'

Ronnie had accepted Tommys decision, though reluctantly. If it had been down to him, the Parkhursts would have been propping up the nearest flyover by breakfast.

He thought back to the time he'd been released from his second stint at Her Majesty's pleasure. He'd been met at the gates of HM Prison Wandsworth by John Fitzpatrick, on Tommy's instructions. Ronnie had already known John of course –he'd joined the firm in the late sixties, but only as a bit-part player. Ronnie hadn't quite been able to put his finger on why, but he'd never really taken to Fitzpatrick. There was something off about him, but he'd figured that if Tommy was vouching for him, that was good enough. Still, he'd only mixed with him when he had no choice or at Tommy's request. Never for pleasure.

Two months after his release from prison, he'd found out that his wife of nearly ten years had been having an affair with a local villain called Reggie Taylor. Ronnie had known him quite well, as had Tommy and all their friends. Reggie had even done some work with them on several occasions. Shagging Mary had felt like the ultimate betrayal. And in the world they lived in, such a thing was seriously frowned upon. You didn't knock off friends' or associates' wives while they were banged up. Of course, everyone knew it went on, but it was usually with an outsider and discreet. After all, women had their needs too. It's just that when it came to your fella's mates, that was a complete no-no.

As far as Ronnie had been concerned, both would need to pay – and heavily.

Ronnie hadn't messed about. For once in his life, he'd formulated a plan and discussed it with Tommy. Ronnie could still recall his mentor's advice word for word.

'Don't kill them, son,' he'd said. 'She needs a good hiding, maybe even a Glasgow smile. And then you're done with her.'

Such a retribution was vicious. You took a razor-sharp knife and cut from one eye all the way to the mouth. The scarring was devastating. Always.

'He on the other hand,' Tommy had continued, as if unable to even utter Reggie's name, 'needs hospitalising. I suggest a knee-capping.'

Equally unpleasant, but perhaps even more brutal, this involved the recipient being tied to a chair, after which an electric drill or a hammer would be used to destroy the kneecaps. According to those who'd undergone the 'treatment', it was excruciating. Most ended up confined to a wheelchair for the rest of their lives.

'He absolutely cannot be allowed to walk again in my opinion,' Tommy had said, shaking his head. 'And, yes, send a message. But for fuck's sake, don't kill him, Ronnie. You don't want to spend the rest of your life in jail for that piece of shit.'

Ronnie had understood perfectly. It had been agreed that he'd use Tommy's place at the arches in Kings Cross. It had been empty for a few years, and Tommy hadn't decided what to do with it. It would give Ronnie all the privacy he needed, as long as he carried out his business after 6.00 pm. That would ensure the nearby working scaffold yard and café were closed.

Tommy had also wanted assurances that he told no one of his plans or about the affair. A bit late for that, thought Ronnie but replied.

'No chance."

Only the previous night, Reggie had been seen drinking in the Horse and Groom on Priory Road. Drinking and laughing. And it taken everything Ronnie had not to go down there and smash Reggie's fucking head in when his snout had told him.

'You done the right thing,' Tommy had said. 'Too many witnesses in pubs. You'd be back inside before your feet could touch the ground, my son. Don't forget, you're still on licence for another year or two. You'd end up serving the remainder of the original sentence, plus whatever they gave you for caving his head in. You could end up with another ten years. No, you handled it just right.'

Ronnie had agreed. This was why he'd come to Tommy in the first place. Left to his own devices, he'd have just dealt with it and to hell with the consequences.

'How are you going to get him to the lockup?' Tommy had wanted to know.

A valid question, and one that Ronnie hadn't given that any thought to. Which had probably been exactly what Tommy was expecting, and why he'd asked it. Again, keeping his eye out for Ronnie. Making sure everything was in order.

And then Tommy had stepped right up. 'I can call him if you want. He knows me and will trust anything I say. I'll tell him I have a proposition for him, and to meet me at the lockup to discuss it.'

'You don't have to do that, Tommy,' Ronnie had said. 'Besides, once I've finished with him, he'll hate you. Might even want to take out some form of retribution on you.'

His friend had burst out laughing. 'Do you think I give a fuck about him not liking me anymore, son? He's a fucking wrong'un, and I wouldn't work with him again anyway. And as for retribution, leave it out – he wouldn't dare come at me. You give him too much credit, mate.'

And then he'd laughed again, and Ronnie hadn't been able to help himself. He'd creased up too.

They'd arranged it for the next night at 6.30. Ronnie would do Reggie first and then take care of Mary. Do them both on the same day.

There must have been a look on his face, because Ronnie would still swear that Tommy had shuddered. And not much made Tommy Spillane react like that.

'Just remember, son, don't kill him. It's not worth the hassle. Promise me you won't.'

Ronnie had promised, and promised again. A pity, he'd thought, but Tommy was right, like always. That jumped-up little prick, Reggie Taylor, wasn't worth a life sentence.

Tommy had seemed to relax then. Said he'd make the call and set things up. Ronnie would be at his mum's, so he'd checked that Tommy had the number.

'Of course I do, son. I have it written down in my little book right here,' he'd said, patting his overcoat. 'Now, come on. Let's go get a beer or two. I'll call Reggie from there. The landlord has a telephone right behind the bar. If he's in, there won't be any need to disturb your mum. But either way, I'll get it sorted.'

'I know you will,' Ronnie had said. 'You've never let me down.'

'And I'm not going to now son,' Tommy had replied.

And he hadn't.

***

Tommy recalled Jack's confusion. *You don't bring along a psychopath like him unless you're expecting trouble.* True, but Tommy knew things about Ronnie Fisher. They had history together. A history of doing the right thing.

Like that time years ago. Tommy had received a call from a payphone across the road from his lockup. Ronnie had started talking nine to the dozen. So fast, he'd barely been able get the words out.

'It's all gone wrong, Tommy. I got carried away and he's died on me.'

Tommy had known this could happen. Course he had. Ronnie was borderline psychotic now, and had been borderline psychotic then, so no real surprise there. But it was a mess that he'd needed to clean up.

'Stay there,' he'd said to Ronnie. 'And don't call anyone else. I'll get hold of Albie and we'll make our way over to you.'

Ronnie hadn't answered, just hung up.

A half-hour later, he and Albie had arrived at the lockup. The place had been in total darkness, the padlock snapped back into place.

'Strange. I told him to wait here. Got your key on you, son?'

Albie had nodded and got them both inside the building. Tommy had made sure to lock the door behind them. Then he'd turned the lights on.

The sight had been horrific. A gagged Reggie Taylor tied to a chair. Both his knees done for. The power tool used to drill them sitting right in front of him, caked in blood, sinew and bone.

But that hadn't been the cause of death.

Tommy and Albie had walked a little closer. And Tommy had forced himself not to gag. Because in one of Reggie's temples there'd been a half inch-wide hole. Blood weeping from the wound, over his eye, down his cheek, pooling at over his neck and shoulders.

Ronnie had drilled into the man's head.

Really gone at it too. There'd been brain tissue on display. Tommy had tried not to look. And failed.

Then his guts had got the better of him and he'd thrown up. Albie had retched.

Tommy had seen men had killed before; so had Albie. And often brutally. But that? That had been something else.

Tommy had wiped his mouth over his sleeve. 'Jesus … I told the fucking psycho not to kill him. What a fucking mess.'

Albie had nodded. 'He tortured him, didn't he? It's the only thing that makes any sense. I mean you wouldn't drill the knees after the head, now would you?'

'No, you wouldn't, mate. That would be totally pointless.'

Tommy had instructed Albie to arrange for a clean-up crew while he went to find Ronnie, and quickly, before he did something even more stupid.

Tommy could still remember the look Albie had given him. One of incredulity.

'More stupid that what, mate? He's done the fucker, and that's that. It doesn't get more stupid than this.'

'Not quite, Albie,' Tommy had replied. And then reminded his right-hand man about Mary – Ronnie's old woman. He'd want to make her pay as well. Tommy had prayed to God that the stupid fucker hadn't already killed her as well.

Albie had shaken his head. 'Bloody hell. I mean I know she's done him wrong and all that, and a part of me empathises with him, but kill a woman? He wouldn't do that would he?'

But Tommy hadn't been at all sure of the answer to that. Because a man in Ronnie's mental state couldn't be right in the head, could he? A man like that would be capable of anything.

Albie had urged him to stay out of it. Said the Reggie thing was bad enough. That he liked Ronnie and all that, but if he'd gone fucking mental, did they really want to get mixed up in it?

But Tommy had felt he had little choice. Ronnie had come to him for help, and in confidence. And Tommy had pretty much okayed his plan and given him the opportunity. Not that he'd thought for a minute that Ronnie would ever go this far. But he had, and so Tommy had decided that he'd see it through, no matter what. That much he owed him.

'Fair enough,' Albie had said. 'But you better get going then and hope he's stopped off for a drink or something before he pays her a visit. He's got at least an hour's head start on us.'

Tommy had doubted that Ronnie had stopped off anywhere. He'd be covered in blood and fuck knew what else. And the chances that Ronnie had thought to bring a change of clothes? Zero. He hadn't said so though. Just focused on the clean-up. 'Use someone we trust for this mess. John perhaps.'

'Fitzpatrick, you mean?'

'Yes, who else do you think I mean?' He'd snapped at Albie, and felt bad about it. Albie had deserved better that night. Albie had always deserved the best, God rest his soul.

'Alright, mate, keep your fucking hair on. It's just that I don't like him very much, that's all. He's only been on the firm a few years, and from what we know he isn't the most reliable, is he?'

But Tommy hadn't backed down. 'Just do it, Albie. Get him over here and get it sorted. Those are my instructions. Call me later when it's done. No arguments.'

Albie had said no more, just nodded. Which was just how Tommy liked it. Even now, all these years later. He spoke. The other person listened. Full stop.

Then he'd walked out into the dark night.

***

Ronnie's front door had been slightly ajar. And Tommys heart had sunk.

Something bad had happened – he'd felt it in his bones.

He'd pushed it open. There'd been no lights on so he'd barely been able to see down the hallway, but he'd been there a few times. The sobbing he'd heard had been coming from the kitchen. A man. Ronnie.

He'd turned around and locked the door, then made his way through the gloom.

There at the kitchen table, with his head in his hands, Ronnie had sat. He'd looked up when Tommy entered, his eyes red from crying.

And that hadn't been the only part of him that was red. He'd been covered in blood, the stuff dripping down his face and neck, like he'd been in a war zone.

Tommy had sat down opposite him and said, 'Where's the old woman, Ronnie? Where's Mary. What have you done to her?'

Ronnie had looked up, and stared at Tommy, his expression maniacal. And in that moment, it had been clear to Tommy that the man had succumbed to complete madness.

Tommy had been determined not to move a muscle, to stay firm and resolute. Sure, any normal person would have bolted in that moment, got as far away from that lunatic as humanly possible. But not Tommy. He was made of sterner stuff – then and now. When you said you were going to help, you didn't buckle. Ever. You delivered on your promise, made good on your word.

And so he'd leaned in towards Ronnie and said, 'For fuck's sake, son, pull yourself together. And stop that pathetic crying. You look and sound like a fucking idiot.'

He'd been taking a chance, responding so aggressively like that, putting that dangerous beast in a corner, maybe making him feel a little denigrated. And it could very well have gone sideways. Tommy had been armed, as usual and just in case, though he'd hoped it wouldn't come to actually killing the man.

And then the mania had left Ronnie's expression, to be replaced by a look of incredulity.

Tommy had stared back without blinking.

Ronnie's features had seemed to soften, and then he'd thrust his hands over his face and broken down again.

It had worked.

'I'm sorry, Tommy. I really am. But they both laughed at me. Not so much Taylor, not out loud, but I could see it in his eyes. It was almost like he was saying, "I fucked your wife. What are you going to do about it?" Even when I started drilling his knees and he was screaming, all I could hear was him laughing at me. You had to be there, mate.'

Tommy had been glad he wasn't.

Imagine. Reggie having a giggle while Ronnie laid into his joints with a power tool. Yeah, right, no delusional thinking there, son.

But Tommy had kept the notion to himself. Just nodded and said, 'Go on, son.'

Ronnie had wiped his eyes with the back of his hand and taken the handkerchief Tommy'd handed him. 'Thanks, Tommy. As for her up there' – he'd nodded towards the ceiling – 'she did laugh at me when I confronted her. Out loud. She told me I was useless in bed anyway, and that Reggie was more of a man than I'll ever be. She even said that if I hurt her, Reggie would kill me. Can you believe that?'

So Mary's dead. The thought had come to him like a punch.

Would Tommy have acted the same in that situation? The truth was, he probably would have. No man liked to hear stuff like that, especially when it was his woman who'd done the cheating and then thrown it in his face.

Don't be stupid. The follow-up had taken milliseconds to materialise.

Because who had he been kidding? Ronnie had planned to kill them both all along. A man like him would never be able to let go of a betrayal like that. His reputation wouldn't allow it. Those in the circles they moved in back then would have wondered if he'd gone soft and tried to take advantage of the situation. No, it had always been going to end that way.

And what's done is done, he'd told himself. The only outstanding matter had been to clean up the bloody mess Ronnie had left in his wake.

'Ronnie, look at me,' Tommy had said. 'You need to go upstairs and clean up. Not her – leave her where she is. I'll get a team over here tonight. Whatever weapon you used, make sure it's left at the scene for the disposal team. And all your clothes, too. And I mean everything you're wearing, including the shoes. Do you understand?'

'Yes, Tommy, I understand,' Ronnie has said, as if it were the most normal situation in the world. The psychosis had been only temporary, it seemed.

Tommy had been mightily relieved. 'Good lad. Now get on with it. I'll be back in a few minutes. I need to make some calls. Don't open the door unless you know it's me, understood?'

'Understood, Tommy. And thank you.'

'You can thank me when all this is over, son. You're not out of the woods yet.'

And then Ronnie had walked out of the kitchen and headed for the stairs.

Tommy had followed closely behind, issuing instructions – how Ronnie needed to disappear for a while, that he could use Tommy's place over the water in South London. There was a phone there, too, so they could stay connected. 'The police will come looking you now, and the further away you are from all this, the better.'

And then he'd let himself out and walked into the night towards the nearest phone box. It had started to rain. 'Bloody weather,' he'd muttered while pulling his overcoat lapels up to his chin. 'Perfect, just perfect.'

No one else knew for certain what had happened that night, although Tommy was pretty sure there'd been plenty of speculation over the years. Those who lived that life had suspected foul play, no doubt, but the police had soon lost interest. Maybe they'd put it down to the two lovers running off and starting afresh somewhere else. And it wasn't as if Reggie – a well-known villain – would have been missed by the local police force.

And that had been that. Since 1975, Ronnie had been forever tied to Tommy. He'd walk barefoot to the moon and back if Tommy asked him to.

Not that Tommy had ever asked him to go to the moon.

Only to the ends of the earth.

31

Another Bit of Work

John Fitzpatrick had asked Ronnie to drive him to Tommy's lockup. The call had come at short notice, which had worried Ronnie. It was off, a glitch in the usual pattern. The elder Fitzpatrick usually used one or both his sons. As soon as the call had come in, Ronnie had fed it straight to Tommy, who'd said, 'Do as he asks, Ronnie. I'll fill you in on all the details later. Just sit in the car outside the lockup and keep your eyes peeled until I call you. I may need you at some point.'

Ronnie had accepted that. He'd known Tommy for decades and had earned well from their ventures together. He wanted for nothing and Tommy had always been there for him and his family, no matter what the circumstances. He'd follow Tommy Spillane to hell if need be. And, besides, Ronnie didn't particularly like Fitzpatrick anyway. Had always found him a little arrogant and obnoxious. There was something about him that gave Ronnie the heebie jeebies, and for the most part Ronnie had steered clear of him even though he was part of the firm, albeit a different branch.

Ronnie was an enforcer, whereas Fitzpatrick was a pimp and drug dealer who mostly used the firm as backup. Only rarely was Ronnie required to go and straighten out people who were getting out of hand. The orders usually came at the behest of Tommy, though sometimes Fitzpatrick. Both paid well, even when violence wasn't necessary. Just a simple word or two in the protagonist's ear usually did the trick. Usually. Not always.

There'd been an incident over in Camden Town a few years back when Fitzpatrick had called him, complaining about a few drunken lads causing havoc in one of the clubs he had an interest in. Ronnie had gone straight over and dealt with it. Fitzpatrick had pretty much stayed in the background while all hell had broken loose. The boys clearly hadn't known who they were dealing with and were quickly dispatched, but not before one of them had come at Ronnie from behind and smashed a beer bottle over his head. Fitzpatrick had just stood there. Hadn't lifted a finger. If Tommy had been there, he'd have been in amongst it without a second thought, even if he'd thought Ronnie was handling it.

Ronnie hadn't forgotten, and he hadn't looked at Fitzpatrick the same way since.

***

John got in the car and greeted Ronnie. Thanked him for his help. Explained that his usual people were on another bit of work at the moment. Decided to omit mention of the fact that the bit of work involved disposing of a woman he'd just killed.

'And sorry for the short notice.'

'Don't worry about it, John,' Ronnie said. 'But why me, son? I mean it's only a pick up, isn't it? You could have done this on your own.'

John looked over at Ronnie. There was something in his tone that was off. It made him jittery. Not that he'd call Ronnie out on it; he knew better than that.

'You know how it is. I've got a meeting with Tommy to discuss a few things, but after that I need to drop a parcel off to some serious players south of the river. I don't trust them, son. Hence your presence. Besides, you and Tommy are tight. He might appreciate seeing you.'

'I doubt that, John. If you and him have business to discuss, then that's between the two of you. If Tommy had wanted me there, he'd have asked. No, I'll sit in the car if you have no objections. Just mind my own business.'

The response was fair, so John nodded. That Ronnie was his driver for the evening would, he hoped, ensure a smooth meeting with Tommy and a quick exit. Although he wouldn't pretend he wasn't nervous. It was unusual for Tommy to request his presence at the lockup, and after what had gone down at the wedding, he'd been unable to shake off the feeling of dread that hung over him like a dark cloud. Still, it was a way of killing two birds with one stone, and the jitters were probably just a result of coming down from the drugs. That always made him a bit nervous, didn't it? And paranoia was just a part of the job.

Chill out, son, he told himself. Nothing to worry about. Apologise for the wedding. Pick up the parcel. Job done. Just another day in the office.

32

Underneath the Arches

The lockup was at the end of a dead-end street lined with railway arches. Only two other businesses was still operating there – a scaffold yard sitting under the mainline railway bridge into Kings Cross, which at this time of night was deserted. The arch directly to the right housed a café also owned by Tommy. He'd considered closing it down after the previous tenants had been unable make it work and moved out, but someone else had taken it on, and most days it managed to scratch enough punters to keep it on its feet. Most of the arches were in desperate need of repair, but regenerating the area wasn't easy considering the road went nowhere. And now, with all the bigger businesses moving out, there was little passing trade.

A large steel shutter provided access for vehicles. Within that was a regular door that allowed visitors to come and go on foot, provided they had the keys to the multiple padlocks. The previous tenant had constructed a ramshackle hut that served as an office in theory but looked like it had been cobbled together by children. Corrugated iron and rotting timber held the thing up. A single large window looked out into the gloomy workshop, illuminated by nothing more than an overhead strip light that flickered constantly. Several steps led down to a five-foot-deep car pit still bore evidence of the mechanic's work – a few old rags and patches of oil that had sunk deep into the concrete base.

Tommy hadn't touched the place since he'd taken it on back in 1979. It had been the dead-end location, not the interior, that had caught his eye. You could see all the way down the road to the high street beyond and being so quiet it was the perfect place from which to operate an illicit business. The only thing that ever worried him was when one of his boys drove out onto the main road. That's where they were vulnerable. Security was paramount and so Tommy never did the same thing twice or arrived and left at any defined time. Only his trusted lieutenants knew about any deliveries or drop-offs, and he aimed to keep it that way. Question was, how much longer could he keep things under wraps? The police were always sniffing around. They knew what he did for a living and were determined to catch up with him. Which meant he was on borrowed time where this sordid business was concerned. They had too many resources, including all the grasses coming out of the woodwork. It was like snitch central these days, what with all those fucking canaries singing. Tommy hated them more than the filth, and would have eliminated each and every one of them if he'd had his way. What the fuck was wrong with them? He couldn't understand why they did it. Most of them had done prison time, knew what that was like for them and their families. At least the police were just doing their job – you had to give them some respect for that. But this game of cat and mouse was sucking the life out of him. It was only a matter of time before they got something on him. Yeah, it was definitely time to hang up his gloves. There was money to be made elsewhere.

He closed the door behind him and went into the dingy office. Jack was waiting for him.

'I really need to get that fixed,' Tommy said, looking up at the strip light as he shook Jack's hand. 'But that's for another time. Let me fill you in on what I want here tonight, son.'

Jack nodded, and Tommy gestured for him to take a seat.

'So. The Darren issue. I need to know where the body is. He can never be found, Jack. Not with the way the filth are working these days – DNA and all that." he never mentioned Reggie Taylor. "They could find something that links me to his killing. John Senior's the only one left who knows. The only other person was your dear uncle, who clearly can't help us now, God rest his soul.' He paused for a moment, then said, 'The other bit of business is that pervert's arrest for sexual activity with a child. He hasn't been charged with that yet. Which doesn't make sense. Why would they release him? The charges are too serious.'

'I think—'

Tommy held up his hand. 'It's because he wants to make a deal, son, that's why. Lawton told me that John was talking stupid at the station, asking how he could get out of this situation. High as a kite, too, and still hungover from the booze. Now that, son, is a dangerous combination. He's a loose cannon, and I reckon he's either ready to make a deal, or he already has. We need to know what he's told them. And by any means. Do you understand?'

'Oh, I understand, Tommy,' Jack said. The menace in his son-in-law's tone was so palpable that Tommy could almost taste it. 'Don't worry about a thing. Whatever information he has, I'll get it out of him. And it will be a pleasure. It's obvious he's done or said something. Why else would they release him like that? Besides, we don't want a fucking nonce in the firm, do we? I mean, having sex with an underage girl while high on crack? It's just disgusting. He's got to go.'

Tommy smiled. The kid continued to impress him. He reminded Tommy of himself back in the day. Which was good. It meant he was evolving into the man Tommy wanted for his firm. It meant his family would be safe. 'Good lad. Now call Callum and find out where they are. And don't worry about Ronnie. I've spoken to him. He'll stay in the car until I call him.'

Jack looked surprised. 'Does he know what's going down, Tommy? I haven't told him. Callum neither. Don't get me wrong, I trust him with my life, but the less he knows the better, right?'

'No, he doesn't know, son, but he's not stupid. When Fitzpatrick doesn't come out from the lockup, he'll know what's happened. But that's no bad thing. Sometimes you have to do these things without totally giving the game away – let people know you're serious, not to be pissed on. Besides, I may well call him in. Who else will dispose of the body? Unless you want to do it.'

Jack laughed. 'Not really. But why him?'

'Call it … opportunity. I didn't want him involved. He wasn't supposed to know anything about this. But John Senior's brought him in, and it's too late to change that now. So the way I see it, it's better that we use that to our advantage, control the narrative so to speak. Ronnie and I have done this a few times, Jack. It's not his first rodeo, and his loyalty is with the firm. Plus, the money I give him for his help will be welcomed. John Fitzpatrick is just another piece of shit who's fallen by the wayside. He won't be the last.'

Jack's phone hummed. He glanced at the screen. 'It's Callum.' He answered, listened, then hung up. 'They're here. Ronnie's parked just up the road. Fitzpatrick's walking up on his own now.'

'Excellent,' Tommy said. 'Now get yourself out of sight. I'll let him in and get the ball rolling. Just make sure you're ready when the time comes.'

'How will I know when the time comes?'

'Oh, you'll know. Or you're not the man I thought you were. Jack.' Tommy nodded to the rear of the workshop. 'Gone on. Get yourself over there by the toilet. It's in shadow. You'll be out of sight but close enough to hear everything.'

Jack did as instructed, and Tommy walked over to the rusty door, which creaked as he opened it.

'Could do with a bit of oil that door, Tommy.' Fitzpatrick smiled and stepped into the gloom.

'Bloody thing hasn't had a drop of oil since I bought the place, John,' Tommy replied, and gestured for him to enter. 'Come and take a seat, son, and tell me what's on your mind.'

Tommy led the way, and they headed into the cabin. He left the door slightly ajar, so Jack would be able to hear.

'Well, Tommy, I don't know what you know or what you've heard about that little incident over at the hotel last night, but I thought it would be better for you to hear it from me.'

'Good man,' Tommy said. 'Always best to clear the air. Honestly, I thought you'd come to talk about the wedding. But if there's something else you want to say, I've always got time to listen to an old friend.'

Yeah, nice and relaxed. Just so the nonce wouldn't smell a rat.

Rats could be dangerous when cornered. But stroke 'em and they'd do anything for you.

33

Clean as a Whistle

Just as Dave as was about to press the buzzer for Maureen's flat, the entry door to the apartment block slid open, revealing a woman he recognised from his previous visit.

He blocked her way and held the door open. 'Hello, Susan.'

'Good morning, Officer,' she said, then put her hands on her hips and stuck her nose up in the air. 'I haven't done anything wrong, you know.'

Dave laughed. 'I'm not here for you, sweetheart. You seen Maureen today?'

'Who?'

He laughed again. Fair play. 'Never mind, sweetheart. Get on your way and on with your business. You and I can catch up another time.'

She didn't need telling twice. Just ambled off, up towards Kings Cross where Dave knew she'd ply her trade for the early customers.

He headed up to Maureen's first-floor apartment. The first thing that caught his attention was the smell from outside the door. Cleaning products. The place stunk like a bloody surgical theatre.

The second was the door itself. It was open, just slightly.

He pushed it wide and peered inside. There were no windows in the small hallway, rendering the view rather dark and gloomy, but beyond the door to the front room daylight spilled in. He stepped in.

'Maureen, it's me – Detective Myers. I need to speak with you.'

No response.

The smell of cleaning fluids was almost overpowering. *Fuck.*

He switched on the hallway light, illuminating the carpet beneath his feet.

Drag marks. *Double fuck.*

'Maureen? Are you okay?'

He pulled a cosh out from his belt and proceeded into the front room. The laminate floor had been recently scrubbed and hadn't yet fully dried. The smear of chemical residue was still visible on the faux planks. Same with most of the furniture – damp and smelling of too-clean.

No sign of Maureen, so Dave went into the only bedroom. The smell was even more pungent in there. He scanned the walls, the furniture, the carpeted floor. Everything was shipshape. Too much so. Not lived in. Which wasn't like Maureen at all.

No, she wasn't okay. She wasn't fucking okay at all.

And something was missing. A circle, like there'd once been a rug underfoot. He inspected the furniture. Clean as a whistle. Moved over to the window frame. And there it was – blood spatter, just a touch. Something the cleaners had missed.

He got on the radio and called it in. Less than twenty minutes later, a crime-scene manager had secured the area, and an incident response team began crawling over the flat. Police officers arrived and began knocking on neighbours' doors.

Shit. One of their key witnesses was probably dead. That's something DCI Bates would want to know about. He rang her private number.

34

Just Like the Old Days

'I won't pretend I haven't heard a thing or two, John,' Tommy said. 'Of course I have. You know how the rumour mill works. But my view is this – your private life is just that. Private. What you get up to outside of firm hours has nothing to do with me. Like I said, I thought you wanted to speak about that little incident with my son-in-law.'

Thank fuck for that. Tommy seemed calm, like he didn't give a shit about that little tramp. John relaxed, and berated himself of getting in such a state about things. Tommy was old school, yeah, but John was his old friend. They went back aways, didn't they? And that counted for something. And to think he'd been shitting himself about coming here and got so worked up about. What a silly cunt he was!

John nodded. 'Well, that's good to hear, Tommy. And that incident was part of why I wanted to speak to you but then something else happened and … look, it's all nonsense, you know. That bitch Maureen set me up with the Old Bill by getting an underage girl to prostitute herself to me. I didn't know she was underage, I swear.'

Tommy raised a hand, cutting him off. 'Like I said, John, that's none of my concern. What I'm more worried about is you falling out with Jack. I can't have bad blood in the firm, son. It's not good for business or morale.'

'Oh, don't worry about that, Tommy. I was a little pissed, that's all. A storm in a tea cup. I'll make it up to him when I see him, I swear.'

Tommy stared at him, and there was a strange look on his face. The room seemed suddenly colder, as if a window had been opened, and John shuddered.

Tommy stood up and walked towards the far corner of the cabin. There was a little cabinet there. He opened it and pulled out a bottle of whisky and two glasses.

'Tell me more about what the police have charged you with, John. I may be able to help. Fancy one?' He nodded at the bottle.

'Yeah, why not?' John said, and laughed. 'I've got a mouth like an Arab's sandal.'

Tommy didn't laugh back. There was had a crook in the corner of his mouth, almost like he was stifling a growl, but who cared? The man was offering to drink with him, and it had been a while since that had happened. Felt just like the old days, like he was part of the family again. And the whisky would take the edge of things until he got his hands on another fix.

John took the whisky and gulped it down in one go.

'Steady on, John,' Tommy said. For a moment, he looked annoyed, but then he he the crooked mouth turned into a smile. 'There's plenty more where that came from. No need to slam it like that. Now, son, tell me what the filth had to say about your predicament. Like I said, maybe the firm can help.'

'Oh, it's nothing, Tommy. I just gave a no-comment statement and they released me pending further enquiries. If you ask me, they've got nothing. I mean it's not likely that Maureen will make a statement, is it?' Because he'd done for that snivelling bitch, hadn't he? Not that Tommy needed to know that. 'Besides, I never laid a hand on the girl. Didn't have a chance to. The filth burst into the room before we'd got down to it, so there's no forensics. It's her word against mine really. Don't worry, I'll beat it.'

Tommy dismissed him with a wave of his hand. 'Oh, I'm not worried, John. Though one thing is puzzling me.'

Tommy's words hung in the air, like he was waiting for John to say something.

'And what's that, Tommy?'

And in a flash Tommy was out of his seat and looming over John. 'Do you expect me to believe that nonsense? The charges levelled against you are far too serious for you to be released pending further enquiries. No, son. No no no. I've spoken with James Lawton, and he tells me that those charges relate to false imprisonment and kidnapping among other things. Those allegations alone would ensure a visit to the local magistrate before bail would be given, if indeed it was given at all. He also tells me you were looking for a way out. A deal maybe. And that a certain fucking cold-case inspector is involved. Sandra Bates no less.'

The door swung open and Jack fucking Clay was in the room, appearing like a fucking genie magicked out of a bottle. He held a gun. Aimed it at John's midriff.

'Jack. What … what the fuck are you doing here?' He looked at Jack. Then down at the gun. Then up at Tommy. 'I thought this was just between you and me. Why the gun? I'm not armed.'

'Just a precaution, John,' Tommy said. 'Your behaviour over the past few days has given me some cause for concern, so I asked Jack to accompany me here. Now get up, turn around and face the wall.'

'Bloody hell, mate. What the fuck? We go back years. I'd never do anything to harm you. Or Jack for that matter,' John said, fighting his rising panic and wishing he'd asked for a double whisky.

'That's as may be, John, but I still need to make sure you're clean,' Tommy said. 'We need to discuss a few things and I don't want to be worrying that you have something up your sleeve. You forget – I know you very well. Now just do as you're told.'

John complied. There was no point in doing otherwise. Tommy was always good on his word. A second later, he felt a thump on the back of his head and the world went dark.

35

Red Carpet Treatment

'My God,' Sandra said. In the bedroom, a team of investigators in white coveralls were taking samples. 'So what have we got?'

A man held out his hand. 'Detective Inspector Ryan Jones, crime-scene manager. I know who you are: DCI Bates. This one of your cases then?'

Sandra nodded.

'See the window frame? There's blood there. Is there anything you can tell me about the woman who used to live here?'

'Used to live here?'

'Yes, ma'am. If this is her blood, then I suspect she's shuffled off this mortal coil. It's not just the window. There's blood spatter everywhere in this room. And other indications that all's not well. Whatever happened here was brutal. And, I suggest, fatal.' He looked over at another officer gathering evidence. 'Sergeant Thomas, if you could show the chief inspector, please.'

Thomas talked her through the evidence – a missing rug, the cleaning-chemical residue on the furniture and floors in both this room and the lounge. 'If this is evidence of an attempt to clear up blood, then it was a big job ... because there was a lot of it.'

Sandra felt sick. She'd been at crime scenes before, of course, but never one where she'd just spoken with the victim only a few days before. A situation like that brought an additional degree of empathy into play, one that made the reality all the more difficult to stomach.

'Not only that, ma'am,' Jones said. 'We also have a witness who says she saw a rug being loaded into a van sometime around eight yesterday evening.'

'Don't suppose she got the registration plate. Or names for that matter.'

'Unfortunately not, ma'am. However, there are cameras further up the street that may shed some light on what happened here. I've dispatched several members of the team to go knocking on doors. Hopefully they'll turn something up, but it's early days. The witness lives in this building – flat one on the ground floor. Her name's Susan Morrison. She was arriving back home when we turned up. I told her to stay put and expect a visit for a statement later.'

Myers stepped forward. 'I know her, ma'am. She was here earlier this morning when I tried to gain access. She's a local prostitute. I nicked her once when I was with Vice.'

'Then let's go knock on her door.'

36

Pour Yourself a Large One

'Tie him up son,' Tommy said. 'John's a dangerous fella when cornered, and we can't risk there being any problems when it comes to talking to him. When you've done that, get on the blower to Callum and tell him to get Ronnie in here. After he's done that, Callum can himself off home. Tell him we won't be needing him anymore tonight.'

Tommy and Jack stared down into the car pit. John Fitzpatrick lay on the floor, blinking. Good, he was coming around. It would take him a wee while to work out where the fuck he was, and that was alright with Tommy.

Fitzpatrick shuffled, tried to sit up but failed. He fell onto his back and strained his neck backward. Gawped into the space above him.

Well, it sounded to Tommy more like a muffled high-pitched roar, but that was because of the gag. Tommy smiled.

'I suppose you want to know what's going on, sunshine,' Tommy said.

Fitzpatrick stilled, and glared at him. Tommy reckoned he could almost smell the man's fury.

'See, Jack, that's what I'm talking about.' Tommy chuckled. 'John's staunch. Can you imagine what he'd do if he wasn't tied up? He'd try to rip our throats out, wouldn't you, John boy?'

Fitzpatrick narrowed his eyes. Dipped his head once. *That's right.*

Tommy looked over his shoulder and nodded. Ronnie Fisher stepped forward and peered into the pit.

'Hello again, John,' Ronnie said.

It took a moment for that to sink in. Tommy could almost see the cogs turning. And surely John would realise now that he wouldn't get out of the lockup alive.

Ronnie pursed his lips, then shook his head. 'Tommy and Jack have been telling me all about your recent escapades, you dirty little fucker. How could you, mate? She was only a child.'

Fitzpatrick didn't move, just looked up at them with the same contempt as before.

'And a fucking grass, John,' Ronnie continued. 'I never thought you'd do that.'

Fitzpatrick started struggling with his binds while roaring through the gag.

'What the fuck is he on about?' Tommy said. 'I can't hear a word he's saying.'

'I can translate for you, son,' Ronnie said. 'Well, I can try. I imagine he's trying to tell you that grassing isn't in his blood, that you and he go way back, that he'd never do any such thing. That he hasn't spoken to the police and done a deal. It's all bollocks. Have I got you right, Johnny boy,' Ronnie said.

Jack chuckled. 'I think you've hit a nerve, Ronnie.' He leant over the edge of the pit and aimed his gun at Fitzpatrick's head. 'I mean look at him, squirming around like the wrong'un he is. He knows what he's done and now he's shitting his pants. Pathetic. Let's just put one in his nut and get the fuck out of here, Tommy.'

'No,' Tommy said, and placed his hand on Jack's arm, lowering it. 'I need to hear what he has to say. Jump down there and remove the gaffer tape from his mouth. Let him talk.'

'But—'

'Do it,' Tommy snapped.

Jack complied, and the words spewed out of Fitzpatrick's mouth like a burst dam. 'What the fuck, Tommy? You think I'm a grass? What on earth could I say about you that the filth don't already know? We go back decades, mate. And even if I had something on you, I'd never tell them bastards about it, I swear to you on my—'

'Like I said earlier, John, why did the filth release you without any charges? It doesn't make any sense.' Tommy paused. 'Unless you told them something, or were going to. You were the one who set this meeting up. Why would you do that? And don't tell me it was to apologise for the wedding or to inform me about what happened over at the hotel. You'd have known I'd get wind of that sooner or later. No, you wanted to talk about something else, didn't you? Darren Davies, perhaps?'

Fitzpatrick said nothing. But he lowered his head, and Tommy knew he'd hit on something. His old pal was in deep shit with this police thing, and it would've been only a matter of time before they'd had had him singing like a canary. What better than to disclose Tommy's involvement in the disposal and the whereabouts of Darren's body.

'Leave it out, Tommy,' Fitzpatrick said, his voice a pleading whine. 'I'd never tell them that. And you're forgetting – we were supposed to be arranging a drop later today. Yes, I was going to talk to you about Darren, but Albie, God rest his soul, told me on that fateful evening to leave you completely out of it and to never speak of it again. And I haven't, I swear.'

'That's as may be, John,' Tommy replied, 'but there's only you left that knows where Darren is, now isn't there? If you tell me where he is, we can put this to bed and you'll be free to go. But can never work with us again. I don't work with child molesters, John, you know that. Am I clear?'

'I can't remember exactly where, Tommy, I promise, but I can take you to the area. That might jog my memory. We can dig him up and then you can move him somewhere else. I'll go my separate way and we can forget all about it. That way the police can never question me on it. Not that I'd tell them anything anyway.'

***

Because he couldn't. Because he'd been high on drugs that night and hadn't been in a fit state to dispose of the body. Albie had used his two boys. And then John had begged Albie not to tell Tommy, which Albie obviously hadn't, because otherwise it would have been his sons in this fucking pit.

'Just tell me where he is, John,' Tommy said. 'I'm losing my fucking patience here. I can't believe you don't remember. It wasn't that long ago, for goodness' sake. Have the drugs scrambled your fucking brains, son? No, I'm not buying it. So just tell me and you're free to leave.'

And then John began to laugh. Because it was a fucking joke, wasn't it? Everybody in the room knew exactly what would happen if he told them.

'Do you think I'm that stupid, Tommy? You forget – I know how these things play out, and goodness knows we've both been here before. The minute I tell you where Darren is, golden balls over there will put a bullet in my head.'

He shot a glare at that prick, Jack, who simply smiled knowingly.

'So, you're not going to tell me then?' Tommy said. 'Fair enough, son. You leave me no option. Jack, go get the can by the office.'

Jack disappeared from the edge of the pit, and John began to sweat. The fucking stuff was running in rivers down his back, under his pits, in the creases of his groin. It was like he was swimming in his own cold perspiration, like his skin was pissing itself.

'Tommy, for Christ's sake, there's no need for this. I really don't remember where he is. Just take me down to Sussex and I'll show you, I promise.'

'Now we're getting somewhere,' Tommy said, and clapped his hands. 'Whereabouts in Sussex?'

Jack appeared back at the edge of the pit. Holding the can. A bloody petrol can. He started to undo the cap, and the sweet tang of fuel wafted down into the pit.

Shit. 'I told you, I really don't know. It was dark, but I do know it was the in New Forest, just off the A22. I'll recognise the spot when we get there.'

Jack began to pour the petrol can into the pit. It's splashed over John's legs, arms, face. John couldn't help it – he began to scream. And then plead.

'No, Tommy, not this, please. I'm being honest with you. I really don't know the exact place where we buried him. On my kids' lives, I don't know.'

And Tommy, his old friend from way back, just stood there stone-faced, staring into the pit.

***

Tommy believed him now. In his time, he'd buried a few people in the dead of night, and for the most part wouldn't be able to give an exact location either. He looked over at Ronnie, who nodded. Jack did the same. They all believed him. Because the thought of being burned alive would make even the most hardened people talk.

'You know what, John?' Tommy said, 'I believe you. I think you're telling the truth.'

Fitzpatrick looked relieved.

'But the thing is, son, I can't take that chance, can I? There's only one person alive who knows where Darren's body is. And that's you. And it's one too many. Besides you're a child molester, a nonce. And a heavy class-A drug user. Not the kind of man we want in this firm. You can't be trusted, son.'

He nodded at Jack, who lit a match.

Fitzpatrick started screaming.

But not for long.

Tommy went back into the cabin and poured himself a large one. 'Anyone else want one?' he said, waving the bottle through the doorway. Ronnie and Jack joined him in the cramped office.

'Ronnie, get rid of that filth once we've gone, and make sure it's found in a few days. I want to send a message.' Tommy looked through the doorway and beyond to the smouldering pit, where flames were dancing and spitting over John's now lifeless body and the smell of burnt flesh and hair filled the lockup.

Jack wrinkled his nose and said he was going out the back to get some fresh air. 'He got what he deserved, Tommy. The filthy animal got what was coming.'

Tommy ignored him. 'Do it yourself, Ronnie. I don't want anyone else involved, am I clear?'

'No worries. I understand.' And then Ronnie laughed. 'I'll need to let him cool down first. Then I'll take him to one of my special places. Make sure his body isn't hidden too carefully. They'll find him in a couple of days.'

Tommy shuddered. He liked Ronnie, always had, but he was dark beyond comprehension, and even the most die-hard gangsters who moved in similar circles steered clear of him. The man was brutal. Had no qualms about exacting extreme violence on those who opposed him. Most people were fearful of him.

But not Tommy. Tommy had always known how to manage him, manipulate him. And he knew Ronnie's darkest secrets, didn't he? Like that serious trouble back in the mid-seventies. Tommy had helped him out, and ever since Ronnie had pledged his undying loyalty to Tommy.

He'd need to let Jack know all about that. It was important. Ronnie needed to be on Jack's side, have his son-in-law's back, particularly as there were some serious problems coming up that need putting to bed. Ronnie would be the perfect ally in those matters.

'Is that wise, Tommy?' Jack was back, crinkling his nose again. 'Surely it would be better if John's body's never found. People would still get the message after he fails to materialise in the future, and—.'

'No. I want that bitch copper Bates to know what happens to her little grasses. Besides, she won't be able to prove it was me that done for John, will she? She'll suspect, of course, and it'll probably make her very angry, but that's what I want. The angrier she becomes, the more mistakes she'll make. Don't forget, she tried to get me life only last year. And she also told us both while you were in hospital that she's investigating Darren and is determined to find the evidence. With that rat gone' – he nodded towards the pit – 'she's got nothing. And I want her to know it.'

Jack sighed. 'Fair enough, but you should know that I don't like it. I mean, it could make her even more determined to come after you. I'm telling you, if she had a cock, it would be hard. Such is her lust for you.'

Tommy grinned. 'Noted, but that's a chance I'm willing to take. Now, let's get out of here. Jack, you need to get back to my daughter. I have a dinner reservation with my darling wife at my favourite restaurant. And Ronnie, clear this up and meet me at my house in a couple of days. I'll settle up with you then. And by the way, his two sons need to go away for a while, perhaps permanently. I know they're your friends, Jack, but if they get wind of this, they could become dangerous. See what you can find on them, Ronnie, and let me know. Jack, you need to distance yourself from them, and let Callum know the situation. Once John's body's found, they'll be looking for suspects. We need to keep an eye on them.'

Tommy led Jack outside, and Ronnie locked the door behind them.

'Do they have anything on you?' Jack said. 'John Junior and Liam, I mean.'

Tommy laughed. 'Those two? Leave it out, Jack. They would only know what you've told them about me. I always dealt strictly with their father, as did your uncle. They don't know shit about me. And they won't know that we done their father, now will they? And that means we have to act just as outraged as they will once his body's found. Even so, I don't like them very much. They're not like you or me. They don't have what it takes, believe me, and I want them phased out, am I clear?'

'Crystal, Tommy.'

All in all, a good day's work. Tonight he'd have the fish. For some reason, cooked meat wasn't tickling his tastebuds.

37

See No Evil, Hear No Evil

The coppers had arrived. No surprise there. Not after what she'd seen, and what with that Vice bloke Myers sniffing around. She knew what they said about her – Susan Morrison, hardened criminal, prostitute, druggie whose use had gotten out of control. Not far wrong, but it's not like she'd woken up one morning and chosen this life. Sometimes life chose you.

She'd lived in the apartment block for nearly three years now, and knew Maureen well. John Fitzpatrick, too, what with him being her landlord. The man terrified her. So when she'd seen him arrive at the block yesterday, and with a face like thunder too, she'd shrunk away from the window and locked the door. She'd had dealings with him before, usually over problems paying the rent. *Dealings* … a nice way of describing the penalty he'd doled out while out of his mind on crack and booze. She called it rape. She'd she never reported it. Who would have believed her?

The knock came on the door, and she let them into the hallway.

'Susan, I'm Detective Chief Inspector Sandra Bates and this is Detective Constable Dave Myers. I think you know each other.'

'Yes, I know him. He's nicked me a few times haven't you, DC Myers?'

Myers smiled. 'Yes, I have, but we're not here for you, Susan. We're here regarding Maureen. I believe you two are acquainted?'

'I know of her of course. I mean she's my neighbour, isn't she? But I don't know anything about her.' A lie but she needed to see where this was going before she spilled her guts. 'What's happened?'

'I was hoping that you'd tell us,' the chief inspector said. 'Where were you late yesterday afternoon?'

'I was here, sleeping, Chief Inspector.' She folded her arms and stared the woman in the face. 'I went out about four in the afternoon and came back about nine. Your DC can confirm that, can't you?' she said, and glared at Myers.

'Relax, Susan,' he said. 'We're not here to interrogate you so stop being so bloody defensive and aggressive. You must have noticed the vehicles outside and the constant footfall up and down the stairs. That should tell you that something more serious is being investigated than a bloody Vice raid, no?'

'I suppose so. But I don't know why you're here. I don't know anything.'

'Oh come on, love,' Bates said, and rolled her eyes. 'You told one of our sergeants that you saw a rug being loaded into a van. Are you trying to tell me that you heard or saw nothing else? Listen, we believe Maureen's been killed – in the flat directly above you. And if the blood stains are anything to by, her end wasn't easy. It was brutal.'

Myers winced, but his boss seemed nonplussed.

Bates continued. 'Do you honestly expect us to believe that you heard absolutely fuck all? Do me a favour – the assault must have gone on for a good few minutes and would have been noisy. Really noisy. I can hear our officers up there right now, tromping through her apartment. Can you hear them, DC Myers?'

'Why, yes, indeed I can, ma'am,' Myers said, looking skywards. 'Can't you, Susan?'

'Yes, I can hear them, but like I just told you, I was sleeping. I heard and saw nothing. If I had I would've done something, right? Maureen's been pretty decent to me if I'm honest, and I'm upset that she might have been killed. And thanks for breaking it to me so gentle, Chief Inspector.' She glared at the officer. 'But I'm sorry, I can't help you. Now please leave me alone and get out of my apartment.'

'What about the carpet you saw being moved out of the building?'

'Yes, I told your fella I'd seen that, but I didn't see who was carrying it, and I certainly didn't know it was connected to what's happened to Maureen.'

Bates shook her head. 'You must have known something wasn't right.'

'I swear I didn't,' Susan said. Her eyes stung as tears welled up. 'If I'd known Maureen was in that carpet, I would have told you, wouldn't I? I'm not a monster.'

'Listen, Susan love,' Myers said, 'we need to know who was carrying that carpet. I accept that you didn't know what was in it, but if you have any knowledge about them – and I'm assuming there were two of them – you need to let us know now.'

And the truth hit her like a hammer. A sob escaped her throat. 'Oh my God, he killed her, didn't he? That dirty rotten bastard.'

Myers stepped forward and touched her arm. 'Who's that, love?'

'John.'

'Are you referring to John Fitzpatrick?' He glanced over at his boss.

'Yes. Yes, I damn well am. I saw him here yesterday afternoon, and I heard them arguing. But I had ... I had, you know, an appointment. So I left and I didn't return until last night.'

'Was that when you saw the men carrying the carpet,' Myers said gently.

Susan nodded. 'Yes. It was about 8.00 pm. I was walking up the street when I saw them coming out of the block. They didn't see me because I stopped when I saw who it was and hid behind the dustbins just up the road.'

'Who was it, love?' Bates's tone was kinder now. 'Was it John? And who was helping him?'

'Yes, I mean no. It was John Senior who was arguing with Maureen in the afternoon, but the carpet thing later? No, that was his sons, Liam and John Junior. I saw them clear as day even though it was dark. I'd recognise them anywhere.'

'What did they do with the carpet?' Bates said, and Susan could hear the excitement in her voice. 'Was it placed in a vehicle?'

'Well, duh. How else do you think they'd take it away?'

If the chief inspector was pissed off by the sarcasm, she didn't show it. Just pressed on. Good job too, Susan thought, because the question had been on the stupid side and had deserved the response she'd given it.

'What kind of vehicle was it, and did you get the regis-tration number by any chance?'

'Registration number? Are you joking? Of course I didn't. And I don't know anything about motors, only that it was a white van. It drove off down the road towards Kings Cross.'

Bates pulled Myers to one side and whispered a little too loudly in his ear. 'Go and get a uniformed officer from upstairs and get Susan to the nick. We need this in writing.'

'No way. No fucking way, you bitch. I've told everything I know. I am not going to the police station, not on any account. I have an appointment in an hour with a very good customer who pays extremely well, and you can't make me.'

'Detective Constable Myers,' Bates said, 'arrest this woman on suspicion of soliciting and withholding evidence. Get her to the station immediately, please.'

'Oh, come on, please,' Susan said. 'There's no need for that. I'll make a statement here and sign it. Surely that's enough. I have to live, you know.'

Bates turned to Myers. 'What do you think, DC Myers? Can you write it up in your notes and get it signed?'

'Yes, ma'am, I can.'

'Good,' Bates said, then poked her finger towards Susan. 'But a word of warning to you, missy. Do not talk to anyone about this, do you understand?'

Susan folded her arms again. 'What do you take me for, Chief Inspector? I'm not stupid. Do you know who the Fitzpatricks work for? One word of this in the wrong ear and you'll have another body on your books. Believe me when I tell you I won't be discussing this with anyone. Oh, and by the way, a word of warning to you too. I won't stand up in court and identify those boys or point the finger at their father. You'll have to find another way to convict them. I'm only going to say it looked like them, but I can't be certain. It was dark after all.'

'Fair enough,' Bates said, and sighed. 'I have no wish to put your life at risk either. And you've been more than helpful. To be honest, the way the flat upstairs has been left we should probably have enough evidence to place them there. Even so, don't stray far. We may need to talk to you again, okay?'

'Does that mean I'm free to go?'

'It does.' Bates nodded towards Myers. 'Just get her statement in writing and then we can get back to the nick and let the team get on with their work.' Then she faced Susan again. 'For fuck's sake, love, keep your head down until all this is over. If I were you, I'd disappear for a few weeks, just in case.'

Susan said nothing, just opened the door and let them out.

Disappear? What a luxury that would be. That was the problem with the filth. They lived in a fucking bubble where people had choices. Disappear, my arse. She had an appointment to keep.

***

'Charming, that one, isn't she,' Sandra said as she walked with Myers towards their waiting car. 'She knew something alright – I could see it in her eyes. Call it woman's intuition if you want, but I knew.'

'Yes, I felt that too, ma'am,' Myers said, 'but I call it copper's intuition.'

Sandra laughed. 'You're right, of course, Detective Constable. Being a woman doesn't necessarily give me any special powers, though most people would accept that it does have its own advantages.'

Myers grinned, then said, 'I suppose we'll just have to wait and see what the surveillance cameras and interviews with the locals turn up then, wont we?'

'Indeed. Now let's get back to the station. I want to get a warrant for the Fitzpatrick arrests, and quickly – before he and his sons do any more damage. In the meantime, let Stone know what's going on. We need to bring the other witnesses into custody just in case Fitzpatrick attempts to strike again.'

'Sorry to interject ma'am, but we don't know for sure that Fitzpatrick carried out this assault? I mean, I reckon he's capable, and it's reasonable to assume that he had something to do with it, but he could have paid someone else to do his dirty work, couldn't he?'

Sandra shook her head. 'No, it was him alright. The timing's just too perfect. And don't forget, he owns that apartment block. He'll have keys.'

'Woman's intuition again, ma'am?' Myers said.

'No, Detective Constable. Experience. There was no sign of forced entry on either door, was there? And I don't think

Maureen would've willingly let him in, do you? Especially not after what happened the previous night. Besides, Susan's placed him at the scene around the probable time of the alleged murder. Just cause, I'd say. Not only that – Fitzpatrick thinks he's invincible, that he can behave however he likes. We need to remind him that he can't. He killed her alright, but it wasn't him who disposed of the body, now was it?'

Which meant they needed to find out where Fitzpatrick's boys had taken that poor woman. And quickly. Because that was the key.

38

The Smell of Oil

Jack arrived back in Bournemouth just after 10.00 pm.

Lorraine was delighted to see him. 'Darling, you're back already. That was quick! I wasn't expecting you until the morning. What did Daddy have to say? Is he okay?'

'Yes, sweetheart,' Jack said as he collapsed on the bed. 'It was nothing really. Just a bit of business, that's all. Don't worry about it. Your dad's fine, and so is your mum.'

'Anything you can talk to me about, my darling husband?'

'Like I said, woman,' Jack said, and stuck out his tongue, 'it was just a little business, and nothing for my gorgeous wife to worry about. Now get your knickers off and get over here. We have some catching up to do.'

'What makes you think I'm wearing any?' Lorraine said as she allowed her dressing gown to fall to the floor and reveal her nakedness. Her bump was noticeable, but Jack didn't care. He wanted her right there and then.

He pulled his shirt up over his head. 'My word, Mrs Clay, whatever will I do with you, you naughty girl?' And then he grabbed her and pulled her onto the bed.

Lorraine screwed up her nose. 'You smell of oil. Did you have car trouble or something?'

Shit. He'd not even considered that. At least that was all she was smelling, and not the barbeque that had gone with it. 'Just a bit. The bloody thing wouldn't start so I had to get under the bonnet and sort it out. A light tap on the starter motor did the trick, and now here I am.'

'Well, I like it,' she said, and ran her nails across his chest. 'It's almost like you work for a living.'

Jack laughed and pulled her towards him. 'Is that what you want, Mrs Clay? A bit of rough from the local garage to ravage you while your husband is away, working hard in his office?'

She giggled. 'You know me too well!'

39

Fantastico

'What's wrong, darling?' Peggy said. 'Can you tell me?' She took Tommy's hand and squeezed it.

He was about to reply, but before he could, the owner of the restaurant was by their side.

'Mr Tommy and the ever-beautiful Mrs Tommy! What a pleasure to see you both here again in my humble establishment. Can I get you some drinks?'

Tommy looked up at the restaurateur. 'Luigi, my old friend.' He stood up and extended his hand. 'How lovely to see you. We thought you'd retired.'

'Who me, Tommy? Not bloody likely, boss!'

His English was heavily accented but, Tommy reckoned, probably grammatically better than his own.

'You know my sons, right? I couldn't leave them to run this place. I'd be in the poor house by the end of the week.' He sighed, then laughed.

The friendship between the Spillanes and Luigi was well over thirty years old. Tommy and Peggy's first date had been in this very restaurant, when Luigi was a waiter, working for his own father. They'd seen each through the trials and tribulations of the restaurant and their own family's problems.

Luigi was a great host and wonderful company – always had been. And he knew when to leave, unlike some restaurant owners, who tended to hover over their guests for far too long and make things uncomfortable. Tommy and Peggy had liked him immediately.

'Kids, eh?' Tommy said, and slapped Luigi on the back. 'I know the feeling, mate. You think you have it all sussed out, and then you suddenly realise that if you want anything done you've got to do it yourself. Am I right?'

'Spot on, Mr Tommy.' Luigi beamed. 'Besides, my wife reckons I'd be climbing the walls at home if we didn't have this place to keep me busy.'

'So where have you been then, son?' Tommy said, and sat back down. 'We were here last week for dinner, finalising the arrangements for our daughter's wedding, and the server told us you'd both retired back to the old country. We thought it was odd because we were sure you'd have told us.'

'Stupid bloody idiot, telling people that.' Luigi threw his hands in the air. 'No, Tommy, I was back in Sicily for a few weeks, that's all. One of my uncles passed away in Palermo, and I was helping the family with the arrangements.'

Peggy reached out and placed a hand on his arms. 'I'm so sorry to hear that, Luigi. I hope he didn't suffer. Please accept our sincere condolences.'

'Bella donna,' Luigi replied, cupping her hand in his and kissing it tenderly. 'You're so kind and considerate for saying that. My uncle, God rest him, was like a father to me. You have made an old man very happy. *A salute* to you both.' He clicked his fingers, beckoning a nearby waiter. 'Giuseppe, bring over our finest bottle of wine for this beautiful couple and three glasses.' He turned to Tommy. 'If it's okay with you, we shall celebrate my Uncle Vittorio.'

'We would be delighted and honoured, Luigi,' Tommy said. 'Please take a seat.'

'Fantastico.' The old Sicilian pulled up a chair.

Which was indeed fine by Tommy. It wasn't even unusual. They'd been eating at Luigi's for years, thought when Luigi joined them it was more often because they were celebrating rather than sharing condolences with an old friend. And anyway, Tommy welcomed the distraction, what with everything on his mind. He was pretty sure Peggy had an inkling that something was up. At least Luigi's interruption would give him some breathing space. Not least because what was worrying him wasn't for her ears. He needed Jack back, and quickly.

'Well, anyway, that does explain why we didn't get a reply to the invitation to our daughter's wedding,' Tommy said, then regretted the clumsy comment immediately. He'd simply been trying to keep the conversation going again but Peggy shot him on of her looks, then placed her hand on Luigi's shoulder and apologised.

Luigi just laughed, so Tommy coughed and tried to change the subject. That only encouraged Luigi who started rocking back and forward in his chair, breaking his balls over Tommy's obvious discomfort.

'You're about as subtle as a car crash, Tommy Spillane!' Peggy said, though there was a small grin on her face. 'I despair, I really do.'

Tommy wished the ground could swallow him up. But even if it had tried to, it would have failed, because the next thing he knew, Luigi leant forward and embraced him. And so what? Even if he was the butt of the joke, it wasn't him who'd found himself doused in petrol while someone stood over him with a lit match, was it?

'Your health, Luigi,' he said.

And took a moment to be thankful for his.

40

I Am What I Am

Jack couldn't sleep. He looked over at Lorraine, her bump rising and falling as she snored lightly next to him. A small smile played over her lips, like she was dreaming nice things. She looked so peaceful, so beautiful ... he'd die for her in a heartbeat. For their unborn child, too.

Which was making him think. What was he becoming? Where was he going? Did he really want to bring a child into this world, given what he was capable of, the life choices he was making? Christ, only hours ago he'd killed a man in cold blood. Poured fuel over him and set him alight. And then had walked away with no remorse or regret. Just another day at the office. And then he'd come back to the hotel and made love to his wife like he didn't have a care in the world.

'I am what I am,' he muttered, but even his own words couldn't convince him.

And something was brewing, wasn't it? He could feel it in his bones. An instinct. Primeval almost. Tommy's conversation the previous day had rattled him, no doubt about it. Why Tommy had told him about Darren Davies was obvious, of course – he was worried that the police would find the body and link it to him. But there was something else – something missing. Getting rid of that piece of filth Fitzpatrick would ensure the police could never find Darren's body, but what else wasn't Tommy telling him? That was the key. He'd need to push for more information when he and Tommy met in a few days. Because how could he help his father-in-law if he didn't know what was going on?

Lorraine stirred. 'You okay, Jack,' she said, her voice thick with sleep.

'Just finding it hard to settle, darling. Go back to sleep. I'll be alright in a moment.'

Lorraine muttered something unintelligible, turned over and began snoring again, leaving Jack to his thoughts. He still couldn't help thinking that Tommy had made a huge error in wanting Fitzpatrick's body found. Message or no message, that was going to bring that chief inspector to boiling point, and she had all the resources and all time in the world. No, a different tack was required here. And Jack would need to persuade Tommy to change his mind.

Unless it was already too late.

41

An Economical Truth

'I need to say something,' Peggy blurted. 'Stop the car – just for a moment.'

Tommy pulled over. There must be something troubling her badly because this wasn't like her at all. 'Go on then, sweetheart. I'm listening.'

He turned and looked at her. She was close to tears.

'I know you don't like to share your troubles with me, and for the most part I'm grateful. I know what you do for a living and understand that certain things can't or shouldn't be discussed with me. And that's on top of your bloody pride, Tommy Spillane, which doesn't allow you to open up anyway. Bloody men.' She took a hankie from her handbag and dabbed her eyes. 'But things are different now, aren't they? The attack on our family by that psychotic Yardie Patrick Chambers and his henchman is still fresh in my mind, and it's made me think differently. Oh, yes, Tommy, I know. You told me that's all over now, that he's dead—'

'Sweetheart, don't do this to yourself.'

'—and the other one – Tommy, let me finish – got life in prison. But who else is out there, just waiting to kill us all and take over my husband's business? Answer me that. It's not like the old days any more. Women and children used to be left alone for the most part, but those days seem like a distant memory. The news is full of up-and-coming gangsters killing everyone in their path. Those people have no regard for the sanctuary of the home or the innocents living within them. No regard at all. And I'm frightened, Tommy. I mean Albie, gunned down like that in a suburban street. And it wasn't just him who was killed. Those bastards took the life of an innocent woman, too. She was just out walking her dog, for God's sake. I mean what's the world coming too?'

Shit, fuck, piss and bollocks. God, he wanted to talk to her – so desperately that it hurt. She was his rock. His everything. But honesty wasn't going to work here. It would only scare her even more. He hated lying to Peggy but sometimes you had to be economical with the truth. That's the way it worked.

The past few months had been traumatic to say the least – for the whole family – and he genuinely couldn't say with any certainty that it was over. Harry Parkhurst had survived the shootout in Hythe and was now awaiting sentence in jail. Would he give Tommy up? Would Harry tell that flat-footed bitch everything he knew about him? If he did, then the game was definitely up. But Tommy couldn't get near him. It would've been easier to take out the prime minister such was the ringfence around Harry. *Stop it*, he told himself. *You're thinking stupid, son.* Harry was a lot of things but he wasn't a grass, was he? Which was a good question because the truth was that Tommy couldn't say with any certainty that Harry wouldn't make himself busy.

'And he's got nothing to lose, has he?' The words had come out of his mouth before he could stop them.

'Who's got nothing to lose, sweetheart?' Peggy said.

'Sorry, love. I was just thinking out loud. Listen, I don't want you worrying about a thing. Your old man has everything in order. Have I ever let you down? Haven't I always looked after you and the girls? I know it's been a tough old few months, and you're right about the world changing around us. But you, my love, just need to do what you always do. Focus on our girls, and our grandchild once they're here. Family, darling. Family. That's all there is. That's all there'll ever be. Now then, dry your eyes, and let's get you home.'

Peggy nodded and gave him a weak smile, but Tommy had a funny feeling this conversation wasn't over.

He started the car and pulled out. Focused on the road in front of him and the other one ahead – the one where the business end of things got done. Getting back to Primrose Hill was easy. The other journey – not so much. He thought back to the Fitzpatrick episode. That business was still weighing heavily on his mind. Anger had got the better of him, and although he hated grasses and nonces with a passion, he'd let himself down. Let his fury and the desire for retribution lead the way. Usually he'd have considered all the options, weighed them up and then decided on a course of action based on what was best for him and his family. Not this time though. And when he thought about it, it was obvious – he'd reacted the same way when he'd found out about Darren's betrayal. Yeah, that was it – it was the betrayal that caused him to be so reckless. And that kind of knee-jerk reaction needed to be reined in. Otherwise it would be the death of him.

He'd meet Jack, talk to him. A plan was taking shape. Tommy wanted to get it moving. Fast.

And Jack and Ronnie were two of the prime players.

42

Prime Suspect

Sandra glanced down at her trilling mobile. A withheld number. And she wasn't in the mood for nonsense calls, especially not when, thanks to the intensity of the past two days, she'd had very little sleep. The manhunt for John Fitzpatrick and his sons was full on but all of them had slipped off the radar. Which made her seriously worried. Had she sent Fitzpatrick Senior and his boys to their deaths? Or had they simply gone to ground somewhere outside of their normal routine? Fitzpatrick was a resourceful and powerful man – one with a lot of friends – but to disappear without a trace was no mean feat. To make matters worse, the hugely experienced team leader of the Serious Crime Squad had leant on certain known villains and associates of Fitzpatrick's. And they'd come up with nothing. There wasn't a trace of the man, not a sniff.

A murder usually got people's tongues wagging, mainly because they didn't want to get dragged into it. And Sandra had made it very clear to her team that they should withhold nothing about the case, including informing Fitzpatrick's associates about the nature of the charges soon to be thrust upon him, her reasoning being that even the most notorious villains would find that utterly distasteful and want to distance themselves from it, even if that meant to give him up. But so far, no one had.

She picked up the call. Said, 'DCI Bates.'

'Are you the detective looking for John and Liam Fitzpatrick?' The voice was male, cagey, barely a whisper.

'Who is this?'

'Never mind that, Inspector. Just write this down if you want to know where they are.'

Sandra had heard that voice before, despite the obvious intention to disguise it, but couldn't quite put her finger on the caller's identity.

'Go ahead, sir.'

The man spilled the details then hung up.

Sandra called DCI Mike Peters from the Murder Squad. He was sceptical – of course he was. That lot always were when you couldn't tell them who'd given up the information. But she insisted anyway.

'I know it's frustrating but I need you to trust me on this,' she told Peters. 'The lead's hot. I'm sure of it.'

'Okay, okay. I hear you. I'll get a team over there immediately and let you know if we have any luck,' he said, though his voice lacked enthusiasm. 'Did your informant mention Fitzpatrick Senior?'

'No, he didn't,' Sandra said, 'but if this turns out to be factual, at least it's a start.'

'Agreed. I'll dispatch a team straight away. And who knows? The old man might be holed up at the same location.'

Sandra doubted it. It seemed more likely that the hole Fitzpatrick Senior was in was deeper and darker – the six-foot-under kind that that someone else had to dig for you. But she didn't say that, just replied, 'Let's see what you find, Inspector. And please do report your findings to me as soon as practical.'

The phone went dead. And with it, her spirits. Fuck, she had a bad feeling about this.

Her grim mood must have triggered something because the identity of voice popped into her head. She was ninety per cent sure at least.

She called Stone and updated her.

The sergeant listened, then said, 'Bloody hell, ma'am, why would he give up the Fitzpatricks just like that?'

'I agree. He's a serious player in that world, and a well-known enforcer for Tommy Spillane. It doesn't make any sense to me either. But I'm sure it was him. I interviewed him a year or so back as part of the Saunders investigation, but it led nowhere. He was staunch, that much I can tell you. So, yeah, it's just as much of a surprise to me as well. I can't work out why he'd do that, what he has to gain.'

There was silence for a beat, then Stone said, 'Could it be personal? Maybe there's some reason why he despises their father and hopes their arrest will lead to him. It's common knowledge out on the streets what Fitzpatrick Senior's done. Not just in relation to the kidnap and attempted rape of a minor, but also Maureen. He's the prime suspect in her disappearance too. And people know he's out. Free.'

'I know. Gimme a moment to think.'

None of this made any sense. Unless it was another ploy to distract her from Tommy Spillane, just like when the Parkhursts had murdered Grover and Summers. Spillane would know that the Fitzpatrick investigation was taking up her time. That was valuable for him. It would give him space to clean up any skeletons in his cupboard. *Very clever, Mr Spillane.* Well, nearly. What he didn't know was that she was handing this investigation over to the Murder Squad.

'You're not getting away from me again, sunshine,' she muttered.

'Ma'am? I didn't catch that. Did you say something?'

'Just thinking out loud, that's all. Get back to HQ as soon as you can. Hopefully we'll have the Fitzpatrick boys in custody soon, and we can hand them over. We've got other things we need to concentrate on.'

'I'll be there within the hour, ma'am.'

'Oh, and by the way, Sergeant, we have back the blood tests from the lab boys. It's human blood as we suspected. But guess what?'

'Go on,' Stone said quietly.

'We have a partial print in the blood by the living-room door. It's John Fitzpatrick's.'

'Then we've got him, ma'am,' Stone said, and Sandra could hear the excitement bubbling in her sergeant.

'Not quite. Don't forget, we don't have a body yet. And without one, we can't prove anything, especially murder.'

'You're right of course, ma'am. But when we do, he's going to find that very hard to explain. The quicker we get his sons into custody the better. I reckon we've got enough evidence to place them at or around Maureen's house at the time of the incident, so hopefully they'll lead us to her and encourage them give up their father.'

Sandra shook her head. 'But it's not going to be that simple. We mustn't lose sight of the fact that we only have the word of a convicted criminal at the moment. Susan Morrison. I wouldn't rely on her testimony, would you?'

'No, ma'am, I suppose not,' Stone said, sounding a little deflated. 'But at least it's a start. I mean those boys … they don't seem that bright, now do they?'

Sandra laughed. 'No, they do seem to have been a little clumsy on this one. But time will tell. We'll get them into custody and see what comes of it.'

And let the bastards sweat for a while. When it came to loosening tight lips, nothing beat a little time in the nick.

43

Number Withheld

The incident room was buzzing. Mellissa tapped the shoulder of the nearest officer. 'What the hell's going on?'

The officer turned and faced her. It was one of the uniforms working on gathering witness statements from the crime scene, and Mellissa knew the constable well.

'We have the Fitzpatrick boys in custody. The tipoff given to the guvnor earlier was spot on.' The constable grinned. 'They've just brought them in. Oh and Inspector Bates told me to tell you she's waiting for you down in the custody suite.'

Mellissa shook her head. 'Marvellous, just bloody marvellous.' She'd had the day from hell with very little rest, and now she'd have to sit in on a fucking interview. Just perfect.

She must have scowled because the constable said, 'But its good news, Sarge, isn't it?'

'Yes, it's good news,' she said, and a huge sigh came out. 'It's just that I'm so bloody tired, and I could do without this right now, that's all. Go and tell her I'll be down in a minute, will you? I need some coffee, and not that slop they serve to the prisoners.'

***

Sandra was elated. With the Fitzpatrick boys in custody, it would only be a matter of time before they found out where Maureen was.

She took herself off to the custody suite. The custody sergeant was sitting in his usual elevated position, designed to intimidate newly arrived prisoners.

'Good evening, Chief Inspector,' he said cheerily. 'I suppose you're here for the two Fitzpatrick boys.'

'Yes, I am indeed, Sergeant,' she replied, though with rather less cheer. When you'd been at it for the best part of two days, with virtually no quality sleep, small talk wasn't high on the agenda. The custody sergeant was known for his banter, too, and Sandra was in no mood for that either. Better to nip the conversation in the bud now. 'What's the situation?'

'Not good news, I'm afraid, ma'am,' he said, his tone more serious now. 'They've both requested a lawyer, so you shouldn't be expecting a statement from them any time soon. And I've been advised that owing to the lateness of the day, their council won't be able to make it this evening – unless you insist on speaking to them now.'

Sandra wasn't surprised. These boys were pros and knew their rights. That they'd taken this path was to be expected. And if she was honest, she was relieved. It would mean she could get some much-needed kip. That way she could go at them fresh tomorrow.

She'd need to be careful, of course. Those two wouldn't give up their father freely. The more likely scenario was that when faced with the evidence, they'd admit to the disposal of the body but would say they were never told who'd done her in. And that meant the prison time would be negligible. Five to seven years at best, though they'd be out in three if they kept their mouths shut and behaved themselves.

Sandra knew it, and so would they. Still, that wouldn't stop her trying. And Sergeant Stone was sharp as a needle. She might be able to think of a way of coming at them that would loosen their tongues. A different angle.

She'd call Stone for sure. But not now. For the time being, she'd let the boys sweat it out overnight. The interview could wait until the following morning.

'No, that's fine, Sergeant. If you could inform their council that I intend interviewing them at ten tomorrow morning, I'd appreciate it. By the way, did DCI Peters conduct any form of interview when he arrested them?'

'He did attempt to, ma'am,' the sergeant said, 'but he told me he hadn't got anywhere. They wouldn't answer a single question. It was no-comment all the way. Between you and me, ma'am, DCI Peters walked out of here a very angry man.'

'Totally understandable. There is, after all, a woman missing, presumed dead.'

'Well, if she's dead, ma'am, there's not a lot we can do about that, is there? They'll keep until the morning.'

Sandra ignored the officer's casual tone, turned on her heel and almost bumped into Stone. She told her to go home and get some rest. Stone didn't need telling twice, just thanked her guvnor profusely and speed-walked towards the exit.

It made Sandra grin. She liked her sergeant a lot. A lot a lot. Perhaps a little too much. *Get a grip, you silly girl.* That was wishful thinking. A straw-clutching exercise. Stone wasn't gay. And besides, even if she was, a relationship with any work colleague just wouldn't be right. So why the yearning?

The truth was, Sandra was lonely. Her entire professional life had been spent in the police force in one form or another, and the hours were horrendous. As a consequence, she'd never found the time for relationships – not ones that were meaningful anyway. There'd been casual liaisons, of course. Sandra had her needs like everyone else, but maintaining something serious was almost impossible.

Just another day of being a tired, grumpy, stupid old cow. She let out a sigh, then got herself home and hit the sack. Sleep enveloped her within seconds.

***

Her mobile was ringing, and her alarm hadn't gone off, so it was definitely before 6.00 am. Who the fuck was calling her at this hour?

They weren't giving themselves away – the number had been withheld again.

Still half-asleep, answered, stretching out her neck and shoulders as she listened.

'Am I talking to Sergeant Bates?' the voice said.

'It's actually Detective Chief Inspector Bates, sir. May I ask who you are and how you got this number?'

'Never mind that, Master Bates—'

That old chestnut, for fuck's sake. Shame he didn't realise it was him who sounded like the wanker.

'—I just thought you should know that the person you're looking for can be found under the Hammersmith flyover, just past the roundabout at Giggs Lane.'

The line went dead. She recognised the voice. The same person who'd given up the Fitzpatrick boys. Ronnie Fisher, she was sure of it. Though she'd never be able to prove it. But why would he want to help her? Why would he give up the Fitzpatricks?

And then the answer surfaced. How could she have been so fucking stupid? It was obvious – so obvious she couldn't believe she hadn't considered it until now. She sat bolt upright. Tommy fucking Spillane. It had to be. She recalled their previous meeting at St George's Hospital in Tooting. Jack Clay had been recovering from the injuries sustained during an attack by Yardie gangsters. Hadn't Spillane called her 'sergeant' back then, even though he knew she was a chief inspector. He'd referenced her sexual orientation back then too. And now Fisher, if that's who it was who'd called her, with his use of 'Master' had simultaneously taken the piss out of her and called her a wanker. Yes, that's who was behind this. Fisher was just Spillane's messenger boy, sent to deliver a message, more or less telling her that he could do what he wanted with impunity and there was fuck all she could do about it.

Fuuuck.

Oh sure, she'd dealt with some seriously unpleasant people in her career, but Tommy Spillane had gotten under her skin like no other. Who the hell did he think he was?

She got up and called DCI Peters, though didn't reveal her source. Not just because she couldn't prove it was Fisher, but also because she didn't want Peters to know anyway. She'd pay Fisher a visit in her own good time. Try to find out his motives. Not that she held out much hope. He was top of the tree in that world and knew how to play the game. Still, worth a try.

But right now, her priority was to get stuck into the Fitzpatrick boys, especially now that Fisher had given up their father's body. She probably wouldn't be able to prove that Spillane had killed him, or had someone do the dirty work for him, but it was a start. And the Fitzpatricks might just start talking. About Tommy Spillane? Unlikely. They wouldn't have anything on him; they were only bit-part players in his organisation.

But but but ... you never knew. And so it never hurt to ask. Life had a way of throwing out curve balls. And now and then, you caught one.

Sandra jumped in the shower, thinking over her next steps as the warm water bathed her back. Ronnie fisher had pointed his finger, and she wanted to be first at the scene. If it panned out, and the body was where he'd said it would be, she'd be on hand to confirm the identity. Spillane would have left her a message there too, surely.

She certainly hoped so.

44

Staunch

'They're here!' Peggy squealed, and pressed the entry button that would open the gates to the drive.

Jesus, she was almost dancing.

Tommy grunted. 'About bloody time.'

'Oh, leave it out, you old grumpy boots! They're entitled to take their time. They're still officially on honeymoon, you know. Besides, it was you who insisted they come back early. Why the damn rush anyway? You told me everything was good.'

'Never mind about that, my girl,' Tommy said. 'Just open the bloody door and let them in.

'They're just pulling up now.' Peggy clapped her hands and stepped around their two dogs, both of which were going bonkers. It was that weird canine instinct, like they knew Lorraine would be coming through that door any minute.

'Kayak, Pawnee, for heaven's sake, calm down!' Peggy said, laughing. 'I'm going to let them in!'

His wife had hardly got the door open when the two dogs almost knocked her off her feet and loped toward the car. His daughter held out her arms, and let them slobber all over her. Jack ignored the hounds and came into the house.

He kissed Peggy, then nodded at Tommy.

'Usual spot, Jack,' Tommy said.

They entered the den, and Jack took a seat without being invited to.

'Make yourself comfortable, son, why don't you?' Tommy said, making no effort to hide his sarcasm. Son-in-law or not, a little manners went a long way.

'Sorry, Tommy,' Jack said. 'That was out of order. Didn't mean any disrespect.'

'Never mind. Now, fancy an early-evening snifter?'

'Don't mind if I do. It's been a long few days if I'm honest, and I could murder one. Scotch and Coke if you don't mind.'

Tommy made the drinks in silence. The boy deserved a break. He was still none the wiser as to why he'd been summoned home so soon, and it was bound to be on his mind. If things had been different, he'd have been able to let the honeymooning couple stay on in Bournemouth for the remaining two days of their booking, but things were what they were. Neither Jack or his daughter had argued, and Tommy was grateful for their trust.

'We've got trouble, son.'

'I'm all ears,' Jack said, and a little too casually for Tommy's liking.

'This is bloody serious, so listen up. I've found out a few things since you've been away that you need to know about. Now, I'm not quite sure yet what impact this will have on us, but I've got a gut feeling that something's not quite right and I haven't lasted this long by ignoring it.'

'Like I said, I'm attentive. And I'm not being flippant, Tommy. I'm taking this seriously. It's just that you called me on my honeymoon with no explanation, told me to get my arse back here, but left me completely in the dark. But I did as you requested, no questions asked. And here I am. So what's troubling you?'

Tommy took a deep breath, raised his glass, and took a large gulp of his drink. Jack raised his own and leant back in his chair.

'Well, it's like this, son …'

And then he told Jack about how his snout down at Islington police station had informed him that there'd been a murder over in Kings Cross.

'Blimey! Who?'

'You don't know her – a woman called Maureen O'Brian. She was a prostitute-turned-madam who used to work for the Parkhursts back in the day. I took her on when they dumped her, and she was working her ticket at my hotel in Kings Cross.'

'Wait a minute,' Jack said. 'You own that dump? Kept that quiet, didn't you?'

'I'll tell you all about that in a minute, son, but its irrelevant right now. My snout tells me that the prime suspect is John Fitzpatrick, who's still being hunted, and that his boys Liam and John Junior are wanted for disposing of the body. Apparently, they have a witness.'

Jack shook his head. 'Crikey, he must have done her the same day he was released, just before—'

'Yes, yes, I know,' Tommy said. Christ, didn't this kid know how to just listen? 'Now, I don't think it would have changed anything, to be fair. In fact, it might be that we've done ourselves a favour. Dead men can't talk, can they? However, what does cause me some concern is his boys. How staunch are they, Jack? You know they'll get a substantial prison term for disposing of a body.'

'They might have helped him kill her, Tommy. Have you thought of that? If they did, then they'd be looking at life.'

'No, they couldn't have,' Tommy said. 'They were seen leaving the house with a rolled-up carpet around eight that night, around the same time we were "talking" to John. He's used them before for clean-ups, and I very much doubt he'd have involved them in any killing anyway, especially that of a woman. I mean why would he?'

'You have a point. But then why kill her in the first place?'

'Only he could tell you that, son. But I suspect that it's down to her in some way – perhaps his arrest was something to do with her. We'll probably never know, but I suspect it had something to do with his drinking and drug-taking. It changes people, Jack. It makes them act differently. You saw how he was, what he was becoming … a fucking liability. I swear—'

'Okay, I can accept all that, but what has any of this got to do with you? I mean you didn't kill her or dispose of the body, did you?'

'No, Jack, I didn't. You have my word on that. Maureen was a good'un. But there's something else.' He paused for a moment, making sure he picked the right words. 'Ronnie called me yesterday and told me that he'd given that bitch inspector the location of John's remains. And even more stupidly, he also gave up where the boys were hiding out.'

Jack groaned. 'Why the fuck would he do that? I know you wanted John's body found to send a message to her – against my advice, I might add – but why would he give up the boys' location as well? And more importantly, how did he even know that the police were looking for them anyway?'

'I can answer both of those questions, son,' Tommy said. 'Firstly, I told him to make sure that John's body would be found, but I never thought for a moment that he'd make a bloody phone call. Secondly, he has his own resources. In fact, probably the same as mine to a degree. I can only assume that someone told him about the boys removing the body, and that he thought he was helping in some way. He's not the brightest ticket, Jack.'

'Clearly,' Jack said, and nodded as Tommy refilled his glass. 'But how does this affect you?'

'Quite simple really, son. We weren't to know that John had killed Maureen, were we? Or that his sons had helped him in some way. Now that they have John's body, that bitch will let them think that I had something to do with it. Me and my stupid ego. We should have buried him ten feet under and forgotten about it.'

Jack thought for a moment. Then said, 'The boys have no factual information to give the police, do they? What I mean is, and don't take this the wrong way, is there any way in which you might somehow have let them in, without meaning to?'

Tommy laughed. 'Those two idiots? What do you take me for? They know diddley squat about me or this organisation. I purposely kept them at arm's length and let you and Callum deal with them.'

'Charming,' Jack said, and rolled his eyes. 'That's lovely, that is. Are you trying to tell me to expect a visit from Mr Plod sometime soon?'

'I'd say definitely, Jack. That's a given, I'm afraid. Especially when Bates tells them who her main suspects are. They'll want revenge and they'll know you probably had something to do with it.'

Jack's jaw dropped.

'Now don't go getting your knickers in a twist, son. It's all part of the game. We all get lifted once in a while, and as long as you keep your mouth shut everything will be fine.'

'For fuck's sake, Tommy.' Jack slammed his glass down on the table and stood up. 'This isn't my first rodeo, mate, and I know how to manage myself. It's not getting lifted that bothers me – I'll be out in a few hours, I guarantee it. It's having to look them two in the eyes and tell them I knew nothing about their father's death ... and knowing full well that I played a part in it. I told you on the night that it was a bad idea, didn't I? Why didn't you just bloody listen?'

'Oh, come on, Jack. What's done is done.' Tommy got up too and faced his son-in-law. 'But you're right, I should have listened. We just have to deal with situation at hand – no changing that, is there? This—'

'She'll come for you as well,' Jack snapped back, 'and you know it. She has a serious hard-on for you, and it seems you've now handed her your arse on a fucking plate.'

'You watch your fucking mouth, son,' Tommy barked, and stepped towards, Jack. This little fucking upstart needed a lesson in who was in charge around here. 'Don't take me for some two-bob cunt, son. Yes, I've made a mistake, but it's nothing we can't swerve. We just need to keep our nerve, that's all. And as for the two boys, you can't seriously think they could harm us in any way, do you? They're just a pair of fucking idiots who we were going to phase out anyway. Or did you forget that?'

'No, I didn't fucking forget, Tommy. And I don't think you're a two-bob cunt either. But for Christ's sake, we're now in a situation where not only do we have to fend off that bloody policewoman and her pals, but we've also made two enemies that that were formerly our friends, and all just to satisfy your bloody ego.'

Tommy sighed and sat down. Jack did the same. There was still tension in the air but Jack seemed to have found his measure again.

'Like I said, son, what's done is done, and we have to deal with it. The first thing we need to do is make sure that there's no evidence in the lockup. Get Callum over there immediately to make sure. Tell him to be thorough. There can be no trace of that fucking animal, do you understand?'

Jack nodded. 'I'm on it. What else?'

'Nothing else that needs doing, but there are a few that things you need to know and that will be of benefit to us both.'

Jack grinned and winked. 'I'm all ears. Again. What pearls of wisdom do you intend to bestow upon me now?'

Tommy laughed and relaxed back into his chair. 'Fix us both another drink and I'll fill you in.'

In the background, Tommy could hear the best sound in the world – that of his girls laughing and giggling. Amanda was in the mix too, and was quizzing Lorraine about her honeymoon. Stuff Tommy didn't want to hear. No father did.

He got up and put some background music on.

45

Smart Cookie

Mike Peters greeted Sandra with a grin. 'Come to see what we've found on this bright and glorious morning, have you?'

'Only if there's a body,' she said, and gave him a wry smile.

'Oh, there's a body alright. It just … how can I put it? A little distorted, shall we say. Identification may take a little longer than you might expect or want.'

'Okay, yes, from a formal position. But this is me, Mick. Is it Fitzpatrick or not?'

Peters sighed. 'You know just as well as I do that making assumptions isn't in the handbook. It's probably him, but until we have a formal identification, I'm not prepared to say anything more. The lab boys are working on the dump site now, but it's clear he wasn't killed here.'

'What makes you say that?'

'Simple. The body's burned. And I mean badly. Hence the need for proper identification. And as you'll see, there are no signs whatsoever of fire around the body. No, he was killed elsewhere and brought here.'

'Bloody hell,' Sandra said. 'Even though I know what he was, I still hope they killed him before setting him alight.'

'The autopsy will determine whether that was the case, but like I said, it'll take a day or two. May I suggest that you go back to your informant? He or she clearly knows something. Perhaps they can tell you where he was killed or indeed who killed him.'

'Oh, he knows alright, but getting anything out of him would be almost impossible.'

Peters stared straight at her. Didn't ask her to reveal her source. Just waited. And she respected him for that, for not ramming it down her throat that he was the officer in charge of this investigation.

'It's one of Tommy Spillane's henchmen, Mick. Ronnie Fisher.'

Because Peters needed to know. And this was his case now. All she could hope was that he found enough evidence to bring Spillane in and secure charges against him.

'Spillane and I go back a little way,' she continued.

Peters nodded. 'I'm aware of him and his recent acquittal. But what makes you think he participated in this murder, and why would one of his trusted lieutenants give it up like that? I mean there's nothing to gain for any of them, is there?'

'He's taunting me, that's why. He thinks he's getting to me and wants me to know that he can do this sort of thing without retribution. That man laughed in my face, Mick. Right then and there on the steps of the Old Bailey after his acquittal. He thinks he's untouchable.'

'I know of him, of course, but don't let his arrogance affect your judgement. If there's any evidence linking him to this case, I need to know about it now, do you understand?'

'If there was, I'd let you have it, believe me. I don't care who gets the arrest as long as he's taken off the streets and wipes that fucking silly grin off his face. But unfortunately, I only have my copper's instinct to go on with this one.'

Peters sighed. 'Fair enough, but look, why don't you go and interrogate his sons back at the nick? Let me and my team wrap this up. You never know – they may have something of use to us that we can use against Tommy bloody Spillane. And I suggest you go and pick up Ronnie Fisher too. Again, you just don't know what might come of it. It could be that he has a grudge against Spillane, and that's why he's helping you.'

Sandra doubted that but acknowledged him with a nod and said she'd get on it.

She got back in her car and called Stone. Filled her in on the barbequed body that was probably but not definitely Fitzpatrick. 'In the meantime, I need an arrest warrant for Ronnie Fisher. Get that done, then go and pick him up. He needs to answer a few questions back at the nick.'

'Burned. You mean someone set him alight? Was he dead beforehand?'

'The autopsy will tell us.'

'Oh my God. Who are we bloody dealing with here? What kind of monster sets people alight like that, and why?'

'People who want to send out a message, Sergeant, that's who. People like Tommy Spillane.' She almost spat out his name. 'He wants to let everyone – including us – know that he's not to be messed with. Well, I'll tell you something. He's got the wrong girl on this one. This has made me more determined than ever to put him behind bars for good. Our day will come, mark my words.'

'I'm with you, ma'am. Let's get the evidence and put this guy away once and for all, alongside all his fucking cronies. I have a feeling that Jack Clay, his new golden boy and now son-in law, has played his part in all of this, and I aim to prove it.'

'That's my girl!' Sandra said. 'Now get Ronnie. I'm heading to the station to interrogate the Fitzpatrick boys about Maureen and their possible involvement in her death and disposal. And I might just mention their father while I'm at it. Despite assuring DCI Peters that I wouldn't.'

'Is that wise, ma'am?' Stone said. 'You don't want to mess up any possible murder enquiry given that there's no formal proof yet that it's him. I think you should wait a day or two until the autopsy results are in. And you promised a colleague. If you break his trust now, that could have consequences further down the line.'

Sandra sighed. Smart cookie. 'You're right of course.' She often was. 'Besides, the boys aren't going anywhere anytime soon, are they?'

46

Too Drunk to Do It

'What are you bloody sniggering at, Jack?' Tommy said. 'Grow up, for fuck's sake! I don't want to hear about you and my daughter doing whatever. Even if you are married to her.'

Jack wanted to laugh. Tommys face was a picture. He'd played right into Amanda's hands, just as she'd known her father would. Tommy was smart when it came to business, but hopeless when it came to how women's minds worked. Jack hoped he'd fare better once he'd been around as long as his father-in-law had.

'She's playful, that one. And, come on, Tommy – it's just girls being girls. Listen to them, laughing away like hyenas. They're happy, and that's the most important thing, right?'

'I suppose so, son,' Tommy said, seeming a little more relaxed now, 'but you wait until you have girls, my son. You won't think it's funny then.'

Which was a fair point. 'I'll deal with that when the time comes,' Jack said, 'but for now, can we get down to business again, please? I'm tired out from all the you-know-what.'

Tommy threw him a glare, and for a split second, Jack thought he'd overstepped the mark. But then the old man burst out laughing. 'You little prick. I ought to put a bullet in your nut for that remark, you dirty little git!'

Jack laughed. 'Yes, but then who would raise your grandchild? You're knocking on a bit, son, and I don't fancy my child being taught the words to a Nat King Cole record!'

'Cheeky fucker,' Tommy said, still laughing. 'Okay, down to business. So, where do I start? This Fitzpatrick thing has made me nervous. Obviously I knew nothing about him killing Maureen, or that his boys disposed of the body. If I had, I may well have taken a different path. John Senior would have still needed to be killed cos he was the only person left who knew where Darren's body was, but I'd have made sure he'd never be found.'

Jack looked at him knowingly.

'Yes, I know smart arse, you told me it was a bad idea and I should have listened, but I didn't and here we are.'

'So, what's the problem, Tommy? Found or not, he can't speak up about it now, can he? The secret died with him.'

'Yes, yes, I know all that,' Tommy said, waving Jack's comment away and rolling his eyes, 'but I still don't know if Albie or John told anyone else, or used someone else for Darren's disposal. I have this niggling feeling that I wasn't told the truth about it.'

'What makes you think that? I mean if they said it was done, then it was done. Or is there something you're not telling me, mate?'

Tommy sighed, a deep deflated sigh that seemed to come from deep within him, and he slumped back in his chair.

A knot formed in the pit of Jack's belly. Something was coming. Something awful. Something that could turn everything on its head. He stared at Tommy, waiting for him to reveal what was on his mind.

Tommy stood up and began pacing the room. Then, after what seemed like an age to Jack but was probably no more than thirty seconds, Tommy spoke.

'The thing is, Jack, when all this came out the other day, I recalled a conversation I had with your dear Uncle Albie last year. We'd had a few beers and were talking about Darren, Danny Mason, and others … about that fateful evening back in the lockup when I done him. Now, of course we knew by then that Danny was dead even though a body hadn't been found. And don't forget that Danny was a witness to what happened to Darren, and with him out of the picture as it were, I was more relaxed. But anyway, what's more important is that we touched on Darren and his … his disappearance. You see, I was worried about any potential witnesses, and I remember Albie telling me not to worry about it. That was unusual for him, Jack. He normally told me everything – and I mean everything … down to the finest details. But not this time. And I didn't press him. I wish I had now.'

Jack was confused. Still didn't get why it was such an issue for his father-in-law. 'But if all the witnesses are dead, including my uncle, the police won't be able to prove a bloody thing, now will they?'

Tommy moved his head from side to side and pursed his lips. 'Perhaps not, Jack,' he said a little gloomily. 'But my gut's telling me that there's more to this. I don't think Albie told me the whole story. I think there could be someone else involved.'

'Got any names? And why would my uncle hold back something like that? You've said it yourself many times – he was staunch, and the best friend a man could ever have. And I knew him, Tommy. He'd never have betrayed you. I'm willing stake my life on that. That you could even think—'

Tommy held up his hands, palms out. 'Jack, Jack. Hold on. I'm not saying that your uncle betrayed me in any way. Not a fucking chance. I'm just saying that I don't think he told me everything about that night. And the reason I'm saying that is because when I questioned him about John Senior's involvement that evening, he said the strangest thing, and it's only now that—'

'For fucks sake, will you spit it out? What did my uncle say to make you so nervous?'

Another deep sigh from Tommy, almost a groan. Jesus, he'd never seen his father-in-law this uncomfortable, like the words he was searching for were too difficult to find, let alone say.

'Albie said – and I quote – don't worry about that drunken prick. He's sworn to secrecy. I doubt if he'll even remember it when he's sobered up. Even I don't know the exact location … so you see the issue, son.'

Jack didn't. 'So, what's the problem then? Like I said, everyone involved in that night, except you, is now dead.'

'There's two problems,' Tommy replied. 'Firstly, your uncle would never have used a drunk for that kind of work. He never did, I can tell you that much. But second and more importantly, Darren was no lightweight. Have you ever tried to lift a dead body, Jack? I know I have, and it's almost impossible on your own. There's a reason people use the term "dead weight".'

And it suddenly made sense. Jack said nothing, just thought it through. Albie must have used someone else – someone other than John Fitzpatrick Senior. But why the hell hadn't he told Tommy? It didn't make any sense.

'I can hear your thoughts, Jack. And I can see it in your eyes. You know what's happened, don't you?'

'I reckon I do,' Jack said. 'But why the secrecy? Why not tell you what arrangements were made. That still doesn't make any sense to me.'

Tommy shrugged. 'He was probably too embarrassed, son. Abie was a professional in these matters, and a proud man. He probably didn't want me to know, and thought, what's the harm? It was over and that's all that mattered. That's the only conclusion I can get to.'

'Who do you think he used then? If Fitzpatrick Senior was too drunk to do it, and Uncle Albie didn't do it, who did?'

'That's what we need to find out. And quickly. We can't afford loose ends. We can't have someone running around knowing our business, son. They must be found and taken out before the Old Bill get wind of it.'

Jack nodded. Thought a minute, chewed on his bottom lip, and used the slight discomfort to help him think. An idea came to him. 'Now, here's a thought. What about Ronnie? He'd have been the obvious replacement for Fitzpatrick Senior, wouldn't he? Perhaps has more to offer the Old Bill than we think. Perhaps he's been lifted on something else, and that's why he was so keen to give up the entire Fitzpatrick family.'

'No. Not a hope in hell, Jack. Ronnie wouldn't give me up. Wouldn't give anyone else in the firm up either, for that matter. Not without my permission anyway. And I'll tell you why. Because it's time you knew about this stuff anyway, and now's as good a time as any.' Tommy walked over to the drinks cabinet and poured himself a large one. 'Another son?' he said over his shoulder.

Jack nodded and smiled. 'I might as well. I reckon this is going to be a long night.'

You're one cheeky bugger, Jack Clay!' Tommy said. 'But I like you. Fortunately for you.' He filled Jack's glass and handed back the tumbler. 'So, back in 1975, Ronnie murdered his wife and her lover. I won't go into specifics but, essentially, it boils down to how when Ronnie was away, doing a stretch in prison, this complete fucking wrong'un was knocking off Mary. Ronnie got wind of it when he came out, and the rest is history as they say. And it was gruesome, for both of them. There's ways of disposing of people, son. Sometimes it's clean and sometimes it's dirty. We both know that. And this was dirty. The only problem was, Ronnie's wife was the sister of the boss of a rather naughty firm from across the Thames – the Saunders family. Travellers. You know who I'm talking about, don't you, son?'

Jack nodded. 'Yes, I know who the Saunders family are. Doesn't everybody? They're not to be messed with by all accounts.'

'Exactly, Jack,' Tommy said, his expression grave. 'They would have cut his bloody knackers off if they'd found out what happened. And then they'd have come after me and my firm if they'd known I had any involvement. I helped to clear up the mess, you see, and put the word out that Mary and Reggie fucking Taylor had eloped, running scared as it were. Eventually the heat died down and it was forgotten. Not by Ronnie though. He's another very proud man, Jack, and he declared his loyalty to me on that evening. Up till now he's done anything I've asked of him, and I mean anything. No, he wouldn't betray me, never in a million years. Besides, if Albie had used Ronnie, he'd have told me. He knew about our connection, and there'd have been no embarrassment on his part in that regard. Which means your uncle used someone else. But who?'

'Let's break this down,' Jack said. 'We can eliminate my uncle, John Fitzpatrick Senior, and Ronnie Fisher. Who does that leave who could have disposed of Darren's body? Who else could have taken that on? It would have to have been someone Albie knew that he thought he could trust.'

Tommy closed his eyes for a moment, seemingly deep in thought, then said, 'I can only think of a few tried and tested people that he'd have gone to, son. Firstly, there's Micky Evans. We used him on a few occasions for this kind of thing. Then there's Johnny Thoms, a big blond-haired bloke from south of the water; we used to call him the Viking. He was, and still is, loyal to this family, especially your uncle, God rest him. However, I've not seen or used Johnny or Micky for quite a while. Your uncle dealt with them almost exclusively. The only other person I can think of is Jimmy Stevens, an enforcer from Hackney who used to run with the Krays back in the day. But I doubt Albie would have used him. I mean he's in his late sixties now – probably too old for that kind of thing.'

'Not necessarily,' Jack said. 'I know who you're talking about, of course. In fact, he was at my wedding at your invitation, if you recall, and he looked as fit as a flea.'

'True, but still, I just can't see it. Jimmy's far too big a player to be involved in disposals. I very much doubt that Albie would have even asked him.'

'Okay, what about the other two then? Micky and the Viking. Can we talk to them?'

Tommy was already picking up the phone. Seconds later he was talking to someone associated with Micky. The called ended. Tommy shook his head. Micky couldn't have been involved – he was doing a five stretch in Parkhurst and had been out of the game since January 1995.

'Well, that's one eliminated then, son,' Tommy said. There was an odd expression on his face, like he was feeling guilty. Which gave Jack the jitters.

'What's up, Tommy?'

'Oh, nothing to worry too much about, son,' Tommy said. But the gloom was back. 'But I should have known that Micky had been sent down. That's the thing - your uncle kept me in the loop. He was great with that sort of thing, and now he's not here I'm finding gaps in my knowledge, and holes where I've not paid people the right attention. Like his old woman—'

'You can blame yourself for someone else's misfortune, Tommy,' Jack said.

Tommy shook his head. 'Nah, it's not that. It's about what you do afterwards. About having a process in place. So what would usually happen is that I'd be told, and then I'd go round and pay my respects. I should have been to see Micky's old girl and slipped her few quid, a pension if you like. And I haven't. She must think I'm a right cunt, ignoring her all this time.'

Jack said nothing, just gave Tommy a moment. He scribbled something on a piece of paper, and handed it to Jack. He'd printed a name and address.

'Go round to this house tomorrow, son, and give her this.' He reached into his desk drawer and pulled out a large wad of cash. 'It's the least I can do. Let her know that this is a back payment, and tell her I'm sorry but I've been tied up with my own things.'

'Bloody hell, Tommy, give yourself a break, man. Don't forget that you were banged up on remand, awaiting trial, when he got his sentence. You definitely had more important things to worry about.'

'That's as may be, but I want this done. I never forget my friends, no matter what the situation, and neither should you.'

'Fair enough. I'll deal with it as you've asked. Now back to the matter in hand. What about the Viking?'

'I don't know how to get in touch with him. Like I've said, your uncle used to deal with him. But maybe I can find out.' He was writing again. Soon, he handed Jack another piece of paper with an address written on it. 'That's the boozer he used to drink in. The landlord's a friend of mine. There's a chance he'll know where to find Thoms. Meanwhile, I'll call Jimmy Stevens myself, just to be sure.'

'I'll deal with all this first thing tomorrow, including Micky's old woman,' Jack said, and stood up. 'Are we done here? I need to get my wife and me off home. I'm bloody knackered, and I need some shut-eye.'

'Yes, we're done, son,' Tommy replied, and Jack could hear the exhaustion in the man's voice. 'Call me tomorrow with an update. I want to put this to bed quickly.'

Jack turned around and was about to open the den door when there was a thud behind him.

He spun around. Tommy had fallen into his chair. One side of his face had dropped, and his eyes stared ahead, pleading.

'Jesus fucking Christ, Tommy. Can you speak? What's going on?'

Tommy's mouth twitched, like he was trying to reply but couldn't quite get the words out. He mumbled something incoherent, and saliva pooled at the corner of his mouth where the muscles in his cheeks now drooped, flaccid.

Jack yanked open the door and called for Peggy. Seconds later, she rushed into the room.

'He's having a stroke. Call an ambulance. Now.'

Jack dialled 999, while Peggy knelt in front of Tommy, stroking his hand, assuring him that everything was going to be alright, that help was on the way. A few seconds later, Lorraine and Amanda came in. Lorraine took her father's other hand, encouraging him to speak, while Amanda cradled Tommy in her arms and stroked his hair.

Jack gave the 999 operator the address and answered her questions. Yes, Tommy was conscious. No, he couldn't speak. Yes, he was able to breathe, but his movement was severely restricted. 'It's doing him in. It looks really bad, love. Please hurry.'

Jack hung up.

Peggy glared at him, demanding answers with her eyes. 'Well?'

'They're on the way. She said to keep him comfortable until they arrive.'

Lorraine looked at him, desperation etched in every pore of her face. But what could he say? He was no medic. Had no idea what to do in a situation like this. And just like when he was a kid, when his stepfather had lifted his fist, a sense of utter impotence settled over him. He was completely out of his depth.

The room was stifling, too small for five people. So he left the women to it.

47

No Comment

By 10.00 am, the Fitzpatrick's' lawyer had turned up. Sandra asked the custody sergeant to bring in John Junior first. Fifteen minutes later, he was sitting opposite Sandra, his brief in the chair next to him. A uniformed police officer stood to attention right beside the door. Sandra wasn't expecting any trouble but standard procedure called for it. And wasn't it always better to be safe than sorry?

She kept her expression neutral as she switched on the tape recorder. It whirred, then beeped, and then went silent.

'For the benefit of the tape, I am Detective Chief Inspector Sandra Bates and I will be conducting this interview. The time is 10.15 am. To my right is ...'

'Police Constable John Egan, WD357,' the officer by the door said.

Sandra nodded at the solicitor.

'My name is Marcus Kingham from Kingham and Kingham Solicitors, and I've been appointed by my client beside me.' He gestured for John Fitzpatrick to speak.

The elder brother gave his name but nothing more.

'Good,' Sandra said. 'Now that we have the preamble out of the way, I'll begin. John Fitzpatrick, what can you tell me about a woman named Maureen O'Brian?'

'No comment,' John replied.

'Okay. What can you tell me about a white vehicle, registration L293 56Z, namely a white Ford transit van?'

'No comment.'

'That's strange, Mr Fitzpatrick, because we have your fingerprints all over it. And samples of Ms O'Brian's hair and blood from the interior. Not to mention carpet fibres that match samples taken from her flat in Kings Cross. Do you deny knowing anything about this vehicle, even though your prints are on the steering wheel, gear stick and rear door handles?'

'No comment.'

Exasperated, Sandra stood up and lent forward over the desk. 'Come on now, John. We have you bang to rights. Why did you kill her?'

'I never fucking killed her!' he shouted, and got to his feet. 'What are you talking about?'

'Oh, so you do talk then, Mr Fitzpatrick.'

Kingham looked over his client, a look of bewilderment on his face, and Sandra was pretty damn sure that this wasn't what he'd been expecting.

'When you start accusing me of murder, then, yes, I can talk, Chief Inspector, but I'll tell you this – I didn't kill anyone.'

'Then who did, John? And please and sit down.'

He did, though his reluctance was obvious.

'And let me be clear,' Sandra continued, 'Maureen O'Brian certainly didn't beat herself to death, wrap herself up in a carpet and jump into the back of your van, now did she, sunshine?'

'No comment.'

Sandra sat back down, and let the silence hang for a moment. Then she leant back in her chair and said, 'John, you're looking at life here. For murder. As is your little brother. We have his dabs all over that vehicle too. Rather clumsy of you both, wasn't it? That or rather stupid. Either way, your prints and DNA place you both in that vehicle. We also know there was a dead body in that van, John. Shall I tell you how we know?'

John said nothing, just folded his arms and rocked the chair to and fro on its back legs.

'Our cadaver dog went bloody crazy when we offered him the chance to sniff it out.'

John's eyes widened and his jaw dropped. Dumbstruck – that was how he looked. Utterly dumbstruck.

'That doesn't prove the death of the person you're referring to, Inspector,' Kingham said in the officious tone that any brief worth their salt had down to a fine art. 'The smell of death could have been lingering in that van for some time, even before my client took possession of it.'

'Sir, please,' Sandra said. 'Don't treat me like a fool. Consider the evidence. We have enough to charge both brothers for the murder of this poor unfortunate woman, and you know it.'

'I'm afraid I don't *know* any such thing, Detective Chief Inspector. Without a body, you're going to find a murder charge rather hard to stick, are you not?'

He had a point. This was getting them nowhere. And while she desperately wanted to drop the bombshell about the barbequed remains of Fitzpatrick Senior, now wasn't the time, and certainly not in front of his solicitor, that was for sure.

'That's as may be, Mr Kingham,' she continued, 'but you know as well as I do that I have enough to hold them both on suspicion of this murder …' She looked at John. 'And I intend to do so. So, again, where's the body? I'm sure we'll find even more evidence at her address – the place where you murdered her. And so unless you can give me any useful information as to why you clearly transported a dead body in your vehicle and why you dumped her where you did, I'm going to recommend that you're both charged with her murder and the unlawful disposal of a body. With your form, I reckon you'll get life with a twenty-five recommendation. And so will Liam. Now's your chance to tell your side of the story. So do you have anything else to say?'

Which he did. And charming it wasn't.

'Fuck you, Inspector Bates. I have no further comment, so there.'

Sandra caught the whine in his tone, and was reminded of a petulant child.

'Fine,' Sandra said, and terminated the interview. She turned the tape off and asked Egan to escort the brother back to his cell. 'And then bring Liam to this interview room. We'll see if he has anything to add. Is that alright with you, Mr Kingham?'

The solicitor nodded.

John Fitzpatrick stood up. 'My brother won't tell you shit, Inspector. And here's why. Because he don't know anything about it. His prints might be on that van, but he had nothing to do with any of this, I'm—'

Sandra laughed. 'It's all a bit too late for talking now, John. You had your chance to put your version of events forward on the tape, and you blew it. Besides, I'm dying to see what Liam has to say. Take him away, Constable. Mr Kingham, we'll see you back in here in, say, ten minutes.'

'Fine. I just want a few minutes with John and then I'll pop back here.'

'Fair enough, Mr Kingham, but five minutes only. I have other duties to attend too and I cannot be delayed.'

48

Bad Form

'What am I going to do, Mr Kingham?' John said once the officer had left them alone. 'That bitch knows we had something to do with it, and by all accounts she can prove it.'

Kingham sighed.

It was the sound that all educated men made when they thought they were better than everyone else around them. John wanted to fucking punch him, but held his temper and his fists in check.

'It's certainly not looking good, John, but without a body they have very little to go on. And she knows it. However they do it, it will involve the use of a not insubstantial amount of circumstantial evidence and the suspicion of foul play. Now, that *is* enough to hold you both. And so, as I previously advised, I recommend you keep your mouth shut until such time as we're presented with something more substantial than just guesswork. And be advised that you'll probably be charged at the very least for the unlawful disposal of a body, and perhaps even murder.'

'But we didn't kill her, Mr Kingham. Honest we didn't.' John looked his solicitor square in the face, imploring him to accept the truth.

Kingham seemed nonplussed. Another thing men like him were good at. 'It's not me you have to convince, John. It's the police and then a jury if it goes to court, I'm afraid. However, as I said, without a body they'll find it hard to convince a jury of your peers to accept murder. And as your council, I can only repeat: Say nothing more and wait until such time as they present us with hard evidence. I've already advised your brother of the same and I hope he'll comply.'

'Don't you worry about Liam, Mr Kingham. He knows the score and won't tell that bitch anything. Or anyone else for that matter.'

Kingham nodded and said – rather pompously, John thought – 'Delighted to hear it. Now, I best be off. Keep calm and don't worry too much. We will of course try for bail at the magistrates tomorrow, but it's unlikely that you'll get it, not with your form anyway.'

John just shrugged. 'Tell me something I don't know. Even with purely circumstantial evidence, the magistrates nearly always side with the law.'

'Indeed' Kingham replied, and rapped on the cell door.

49

Stirring Up Trouble

The interview with Liam went pretty much the same way it had with John. Sandra left with nothing. The younger Fitzpatrick had even seemed a little vacant at times. She went to find Stone. They needed to find Maureen's body, that was for sure. The blood and hair samples from the van wouldn't on their own be enough to prove murder. Nor would the cadaver dog's reaction or the Fitzpatricks' finger prints. Which meant it was entirely possible that the boys could walk away from this.

If they kept their silence.

She needed to make sure they didn't.

There was an ace up her sleeve, of course, and she was desperate to use it, but that would have to wait until John Fitzpatrick Senior was formally identified.

And Sandra hoped to Christ it was him, because if it wasn't, she didn't know where they'd go next.

Stone was already waiting in the incident room on the third floor. The look on her face was that of an eager schoolkid with their hand in the air. *Me, miss. Pick me!* Which could mean that she had some good news for Sandra and was desperate to tell her guvnor.

The notion clearly hadn't wiped the despondency from Sandra's face though, because Stone said, 'Why the gloomy face, guv?'

'So spill it, Stone. What have you got to be so bloody happy about?'

Stone's grin was so wide that nearly split her face in half. 'I'll tell you if you buy me a coffee.'

Sandra spun around and walked towards the lift, calling out over her shoulder, 'Come on then, Sergeant. You're obviously dying to cheer me up. Let's see what you've got for me.'

'I shall reveal all, ma'am. And I guarantee that you'll be happy you forked out your hard-earned cash to loosen my tongue!'

The canteen was bustling. Stone gestured to a spot by the window that overlooked the main street below, and Sandra got them a cup each of hot brown liquid that loosely resembled coffee.

'It's Fitzpatrick alright,' Stone said, beaming again.

Sandra was about to respond but the sergeant didn't give her a chance.

'Before you ask, ma'am, let me explain. DCI Peters called me while you were interviewing the boys. They have a partial print that matches John Fitzpatrick Senior. It's been checked and it's definitely him.'

'That's excellent news,' Sandra said. 'How on earth did they manage that? Pardon my coarseness, but the body looked like an overcooked spit roast.'

Stone snorted and put her hand over her mouth, catching most of the coffee she'd been about to spit over table.

Several officers on nearby tables looked over. Sandra gave them all her best superior-officer glare, and they went back to their business.

'Ma'am,' Stone said, giggling. 'That's awful!'

'Oh, reel your panties in, Sergeant. A sense of humour is much needed in our line of work. If we took it all personally, we wouldn't be able to do our job properly. Besides, this particular victim was a vicious gangster and child molester. I have no sympathy whatsoever.'

Stone stopped laughing. She looked at Sandra quizzically for a moment, and Sandra realised, not for the first time, that she didn't always do the best job of containing the stoic side of her personality. And that it came across as a lack of empathy.

'So come on then, Sergeant, tell me how the coroner managed to get a fingerprint off a hog roast.'

Stone cleared her throat, took out her notebook and started reading from it. 'Have you heard of the pugilistic stance, ma'am?'

'Isn't that something to do with fighting or boxing or something?'

'Yes, ma'am. I believe the term originates from such activities. Essentially the pugilistic stance happens when a person's experiencing extreme pain. Their hands clench into fists in an attempt to manage the impact of that pain. It's an attempt to curl up into a protective ball and assume the foetal position, which protects their vital organs.'

'My goodness … which means he must have been alive then when they set him on fire.'

Good fucking God.

'It definitely seems that way, ma'am,' Stone said. 'Why else would he be in that position?'

'What a horrible way to end someone's life. I cannot even begin to imagine the agony he suffered … the poor guy.'

'You've changed your tune,' the sergeant said. 'A minute ago he was a spit roast. Now you feel sorry for him?'

'I'm human too,' Sandra said, her voice barely above a whisper. 'There's being burnt, and there's being burnt alive. And, yes, he was a wrong'un, but I'd have much rather banged him away in prison than see him killed that way. I'm not a monster, you know.'

'I know that, ma'am,' Stone said, and rested her hand on top of Sandra's. 'I was just pulling your leg, you silly thing. I know you wouldn't wish that kind of thing on anyone.'

Sandra looked down at their hands. It was a rare moment of intimacy and kindness, and she felt a warmth, a coming together, a tingling. The sensation travelled up her arm and spread throughout her whole body, sparking thoughts and feelings that were clearly inappropriate considering where they were, and even more so given that they were colleagues.

She pulled her hand away, not quickly or forcefully, but slowly and deliberately, maintaining eye contact with her sergeant. Stone held her gaze, then lifted her hand and picked up her coffee as if nothing had just happened between them.

But it had, hadn't it? There'd definitely been something there. She hadn't imagined it. And yet, Stone was hetero-sexual. She'd split up with a boyfriend only a few months ago. Fuck, why were relationships always so confusing?

Sandra felt the heat in her cheeks. Double fuck, because that would mean her cheeks were flushed. Stone was attractive, there was no denying it, and it wasn't the first time she'd appreciated her from a physical point of view. But just now things had felt like it was more than that. The question was, was it a genuine connection or just a silly sex-starved detective inspector clutching at straws? Either way, there was a job to be done, and this shit wasn't getting her anywhere. She told herself to focus, and then nodded at Stone.

'So, where do we go from here, Stone? Do I step all over Mike Peters' investigation and get the boys to talk about their father, or do I tell Peters everything and let him take all the glory?'

'I think I know what you're going to do, ma'am,' Stone said coolly. 'Your objective all along has been to gather information on Tommy Spillane. You're hoping the Fitzpatricks have something on him, aren't you?'

Sandra laughed. 'You know me too well. I do indeed need information on that bastard, and I aim to get it. The Fitzpatricks are just a starting point. Hopefully they have something we can use. Come on. Let's go and stir up some trouble downstairs.'

50

Bullseye

'This is all rather irregular, ma'am,' the custody sergeant said from behind the reception desk. 'I mean this is, after all, another detective's case. I'm not sure if it's appropriate for me to grant you access to the prisoners again and without their lawyer.'

Stone stepped forward an put her elbows on the elevated desk. 'Come on, Sarge. Do us a favour. This is important. And we really believe that it's in the best interests of the case that the Fitzpatricks answer a few questions. If they agree to, of course. All we're asking for is us five minutes. If they don't agree, we'll walk away and let DCI Peters take over. Promise.'

The sergeant scratched his chin as he mulled over the request.

'And don't forget,' Sandra said, taking the opportunity get her tuppence worth in, 'we have a missing-presumed-dead woman to consider here. Prostitute or not, she has family. They'll want to bury her, do the right thing by her. And in light of new information we've just received, I believe those two boys will be willing to tell us about her whereabouts when they hear what we have to say.'

The chin-scratching continued. Then he looked Sandra straight in the face. 'Five minutes and that's all. And you can talk to them through the hatch. I'm not letting you into the cells, and that's that. I'm going for a cup of tea. I was never here, are we clear?'

'Crystal, Sergeant. And thank you,' Sandra said.

The sergeant lifted his hatch. Once he was out of sight, Sandra led the way towards the cells.

**

John Fitzpatrick lay on the bunk in the sparce cell, reading messages left by previous occupants. *Jonny loves Becky* had been scratched in big bold letters above the toilet. Beside the intimate love note, someone had etched *All coppers are bastards* and *It fucking stinks in here* into the wall. John didn't know Jonny or Becky so couldn't possibly comment, but the other two remarks were pretty accurate. If he'd had a marker pen or something to scratch with, he'd have added *DI Bates is a whore*, but he didn't, so he lay back on the two-inch plastic-covered mattress and contemplated his position.

And what a fucking position it was.

For one thing, where the fuck was his dad? Kingham had said he hadn't heard from him in two days, and that wasn't like the old man. Despite his obvious issues, he'd always been there to support his sons. Which worried John. Something didn't smell right.

The cell's food hatch clanged open, and behind it stood Bates. She stared at him, her expression deadly serious.

John jumped off the bunk and marched towards the door. 'What the fuck do you want, filth? I got nothing more to say to you, so piss off and bother someone else.'

'Oh, I'm not here to question you, Mr Fitzpatrick,' she said. 'I'm here to deliver some news … news you need to hear. News you're entitled to.'

John laughed. 'Don't tell me, sweetheart. My brother's confessed to it all and wants to turn to Jesus. You must think I'm fucking stupid, love. I've heard it all before. It's a little game you lot play to drive a wedge between people in the hope that one or the other spills his guts. Well, you've got the wrong man here, darling. I know that game and I'm not playing.'

'Have you quite finished, Mr Fitzpatrick?' she said, reminding him of the patronising tone his schoolteachers had taken back in the day. 'That's not why I'm here. And, John, unfortunately I have some bad news for you and your brother. But what with you being the eldest, I thought I'd give it to you first.'

John just shook his head and folded his arms. 'Go on then, sweetheart. Let me have your pearls of wisdom or whatever it is you need to tell me. But make it quick. It'll be lunchtime soon and I'm hungry.'

'Do you know Tommy Spillane?'

'I thought this wasn't a question session, Chief Inspector, but I'll answer that anyway. It's an easy one for your simple mind to get to grips with. No, I don't, but even if I did, what's he got to do with my situation?'

'Everything, John, I'm afraid. And I know you and your brother *have* worked for him, and still do to some degree … as did your father. And I'll tell you why he's important in this—'

'Hang on, must wait a minute,' John said, growing nervous. 'You just referred to my father in the past tense. What do you mean "as *did* your father"?'

'I suppose there's no good way of telling you this,' she said, and her voice was soft, sympathetic even. 'But your dad's dead, John. His body was recovered earlier this morning, and the coroner's confirmed it's him. I am genuinely sorry to have to pass on this news to you in your situation, but it's important that we catch the person responsible quickly, and I thought you might be able to help.'

Shit, was this actually happening? Was it even true or was this bitch playing with him? If it was true, was it possible that she'd actually be this callous, knowing that he could do absolutely nothing about it as long as he was trapped in this cell? Yeah, it was possible. She'd have an ulterior motive – course she would.

Which made him think – because while he knew that his father had killed Maureen O'Brian, Bates didn't. There's no way she could. Which meant this filth was trying to get him to give up his old dad by springing a shock on him, by talking a load of shit about him being dead. Silly bitch. Did she think he was fucking stupid?

He shook his head, unfolded his arms, pointed a finger at her. 'Nah, you're fucking lying, you stupid bitch. Did you think I'd crumble, fall on my hands and knees and confess just because you threw me some bullshit sob story.' He started laughing. 'My father is alive and well, and he has nothing to do with all of this, so just close the hatch, fuck off and try your tricks on some other mug, preferably one with a spanner missing in the toolbox. Oh, and don't waste your time trying this crap with my brother. He won't fall for it either. Go on – piss off.' He turned his back on her.

He heard Bates sigh heavily, and then her droning voice started up again. 'Don't you want to know how he was killed, John? Or by whom? I mean you might not believe me right now, but why would I lie to you? We know your father killed Maureen. Forensics will prove it, of that I'm certain. And you and your little brother will do some substantial prison time for disposing of the body. We have enough evidence on you two to make that stick. Obviously, we won't be able to get your father in the dock because he's dead. And for that I'm sorry. Sorry because I can't see that justice will be done, and sorry for you and Liam because regardless of this situation, he was still your dad, your family. It's your shout, but when the autopsy is carried out and we have further evidence by way of DNA or his teeth, it will be proved beyond doubt that the badly burned body lying on a slab at the mortuary in Hammersmith is your father.'

'Badly burned?' John turned around and faced the hatch again. 'And what does *further evidence* mean? You don't know its him, do you? It could be anyone.'

'We managed to pull his prints, John,' Bates said gently. 'Like I said, I'm sorry to break this news to you considering your current situation, but I thought you needed to know.'

'You fucking cunt, Bates,' John yelled and lunged towards the door. The chief inspector took a step back even though he couldn't get to her. 'Trying to pretend you're doing me a favour? Fuck off. Your kind don't do anyone any favours, you pig filth. You're a liar and a fucking whore. Now like I said, fuck off and stay fucked off. I'm done with you.'

He spat through the hatch, and a glob of phlegm landed on the bitch's face. Bullseye.

Bates looked like she was about to throw up. The copper with her handed Bates a handkerchief.

Bates wiped her face and said, 'Thank you, Sergeant Stone.'

Then Stone was at the hatch. 'It's all true, Mr Fitzpatrick. You'll find out soon enough. But just so you know, we suspect that Tommy Spillane and your dear old friend Jack Clay, and maybe others, did this. And your dad didn't have it easy. They tortured your father, and set him alight while he was still alive. We know this because his hands were clenched in a protective manner. The coroner confirmed it. Do you hear me? He was alive when they did this to him. What we don't know is why. Not yet anyway. But perhaps you can shed some light on that. Still, like my guvnor said, that's your call, sunshine.'

What she and that other bitch has said was horrible. John felt dizzy, wondered if he might piss his pants or puke. He took deep breaths, told himself think it through. The thing is, you couldn't trust the police – ever. His dealings with them over the years had proved that. You had to consider everything they said with suspicion. Those bastards would use any and all tactics to get their way. And what he needed right now was time to think. If it was true, then there was no point in protecting his father any longer. All that would do would increase the likelihood of him and Liam doing longer stretches for no reason. But if it wasn't true, he'd be condemning his father to a life in prison. And John would be labelled as a grass, the consequences of which didn't bear thinking about.

No. Trust the process, not the filth. Kingham had told him to keep his mouth shut, and that's what he'd do until he had more evidence rather than just the word of this pig.

'I don't believe a fucking word of it,' he said finally. 'Jack Clay is my mate. Tommy and my father go way back, even before I was born. Why would they kill him? And why would they torture him? I just don't believe it. And that's why I'm not saying another word to you bastards until you bring me proof. And like I said to that bitch' – he pointed at Bates, who seemed to have recovered her composure and was standing behind Stone – 'you can fuck off and leave me alone. I have nothing more to say.'

'Fair enough, Mr Fitzpatrick. That's your prerogative,' Stone said. 'But know this – Tommy Spillane and Jack Clay have no loyalty to you or your family. If they can kill your father like that, what chance do you think you and your brother have if you fall foul of them? Just think about that while you're serving the long sentence that's inevitably coming your way. They kill for fun, John. They don't think twice about low-key players like you and Liam. You're nothing to them. Think about that when the lights go out.'

There was nothing more to say. Bates's sidekick had sounded serious enough, and for a moment, John had almost been convinced, like it was all true. But why would Tommy and Jack want to kill his father? Had it been something to do with that prostitute. Had she known something about Tommy. Had his dad turned against Tommy in some way and that's why they'd killed him? It was all a headfuck. None of it made sense.

He recalled the wedding it and his father's behaviour. That hadn't gone down well, but surely it wouldn't have been just because of that. The incident had been minor, a mere blip, the kind of thing that happened from time to time among men like them.

So where did that leave him? If only he could just think this all through, rather than being pressured to give it all up now. But that was their MO, wasn't it? Wear you down, fuck with your head so you said the shit they wanted you to say. And look where it got you. Look what had happened to the Guildford Four and Maguire Seven. False confessions based on lies and pressure by relentless coppers who'd stop at nothing to make sure it was their agenda that was steering the ship.

Stone leant towards the hatch again. 'If you know something, John, now's the time to tell us. Where is Maureen O'Brian's body? That would be a good start, I reckon. You know it's only a matter of time before we get to the bottom of all this and find her. But if you help us now, we could make sure that your sentence is reduced. Like my guvnor said, we know you and your brother didn't kill her, John. Your father did it, didn't he?'

'You don't know that, Constable whatever your name is,' he said. Maybe it would piss her off, thinking he'd not caught her name. A small win. Childish perhaps. But it wasn't like he had any other fucking leverage at the moment.

'I'm Detective Sergeant Mellissa Stone, and please accept my apologies. I should have told you that before jumping in and talking to you. Nonetheless, you know and I know that a guilty plea for disposing of the body would give you credit. The judge would be duty-bound to give you a thirty per cent discount on normal sentencing guidelines if you were to cooperate.'

'I need time to think, Sergeant,' he said, shocked by how quiet the words sounded. 'I need to speak with my solicitor again. I'm not admitting anything until I have the chance to get all the facts, and that's that.'

Stone sighed. 'You do know that you and your brother will be remanded to prison tomorrow. Once that happens, the chance to come clean will be lost.'

'Oh fuck off. We both know that I have time. Tomorrow will only be a bail hearing. I won't be expected to plead. I know I won't get any bail, but what I will get is another chance before pleas and directions, and then another chance before any trial goes ahead. What do you take me for? This isn't my first rodeo, you know.'

Bates stepped in front of the sergeant. 'Leave it, Stone. We're not getting anywhere with all this toing and froing. Mr Fitzpatrick has made his mind up, and it appears he's willing to risk it all to protect his now-dead father. Come on – let's go and get some lunch. Goodbye, John.'

And the hatch closed.

Leaving him with nothing but the sound of his own fury and sense of loss the likes of which he'd never encountered. Because if it was true, his father was gone and his friends had betrayed him.

***

'I don't think he's happy, do you?' Sandra said.

Stone grinned. 'I'm just glad that those cell doors are made of iron. He's a treasure that one, isn't he?'

'Indeed. But enough of John Fitzpatrick Junior. Let's eat. After that I want you to go and arrest Ronnie Fisher. I want to know how he knew about John Senior's demise and location.'

'But you don't know for sure that it was him who made the call. You just suspect it. Fisher will just deny it, and we have no way of proving it.'

'Think of it as rattling some cages. Bring him in and let's see what he has to say.'

'Fair enough, ma'am, but on what charge?'

Sandra turned and faced her sergeant. Shook her head. 'Come now. You're an experienced senior officer. I'm sure you'll think of something.'

51

The Real Deal

'It's just as I thought, ma'am,' Stone said. 'Ronnie Fisher isn't talking. He flatly denies making that call. He basically laughed at me when I told him we suspected his involvement in Fitzpatrick's murder, then told me to fuck off and try that shit on someone else. It sent shivers down my spine, I can tell you. And I've dealt with a few like him before.'

'Yeah, Ronnie's the real deal, that's for sure,' Sandra said. 'He's old school, so it doesn't surprise me. His kind can play the game with the best of detectives. Thing is that people like him know how to get under your skin. The only way of dealing with that kind of man is to find hard evidence. And sadly, in this case we have none. Release him. And now, before he gets a solicitor involved. We could do without the bloody headache.'

Stone looked a little surprised by Sandra's sudden turnaround, but she didn't press it, just offered a perfunctory 'Yes, ma'am' and walked back out.

Of course, getting anything out of Fisher had always been a non-starter. She'd know that when she ordered his arrest. That hadn't been the objective. Instead, the goal had be to send her own message, to let him and Tommy Spillane know that she was on the case. And if she got a little bit lucky, that just might lead to one of them making a mistake. Not that she'd be holding her breath. These were serious players, experienced villains. Fisher and Spillane knew the system inside and out. To snare such big fish would mean she'd need to be clever or extremely fortunate, though probably a combination of the two. And it was that bastard Spillane she really wanted. Fisher was just his messenger boy, and if it turned out she couldn't reel him too, well, that was something she could live with.

**

The following morning the two Fitzpatrick brothers were remanded in custody at the Highbury Corner magistrates court on Holloway Road. They were charged with murder and the unlawful disposal of a body. Neither were under any obligation to make a plea, and neither did. They were carted off to Pentonville on the Caledonian Road shortly after. The whole thing had taken less than ten minutes.

Jack and Callum had watched the proceedings from the public gallery. Jack had found out about their arrests through Ronnie but only just now had it become clear what John Junior and Liam had been charged with.

As they left the building, Jack experienced a sense of disquiet. This was serious. They clearly hadn't killed Maureen O'Brian, and yet they'd been charged with her murder. Which meant that fucking copper Bates was up to something. He said as much to Callum as they navigated the London traffic back to Callum's place.

'She's just stirring the pot, mate. Casting her net out and seeing what she can haul in, that's all. She's got fuck all on Tommy or us. I wouldn't let it bother you. After all, we didn't kill Maureen, did we?'

'And neither did Tommy,' Jack said. 'But there's something in the air – I can feel it. Ronnie making that stupid call on Tommy's instructions was a mistake. All it's done is make her more determined to hunt him down and find something to harass him with. That or annoy him into making a mistake. In my opinion, we should have just dumped Fitzpatrick's body where he'd never have been found, and that would have put an end to it. But, no, Tommy wanted to send a message to her. I just don't get what he had to gain from doing that.'

Callum shrugged. 'Maybe he's not taking her seriously, being a woman and all.'

'Well he fucking should,' Jack snapped. 'She's smart, and she has the weight of Scotland Yard and the Metropolitan Police behind her. Think about it. All the means she has at her disposal compared with us. Tommy would die to have that kind of resource to call on, and if he thinks he can compete with that then he's not the man I thought he was.'

Callum looked over at Jack, frowning. 'Mate, I've never seen you like this before. Never heard you make any negative reference to Tommy's abilities.'

Jack just grunted. What else could he say? Callum wasn't stupid. He'd no doubt asked himself whether trouble was brewing.

And it was the right thing to ask. Because it was. Big time.

***

Mike Peters glanced up at the public gallery, where two men familiar to him from previous enquiries were sitting quietly at the rear. When the proceedings were over, he followed them as they left the court building, keeping a little distance between himself and them.

As he walked, he made a call to a colleague, and updated her on what had happened.

Sandra Bates was delighted. 'Let the games begin,' she said.

The smug thrill in her voice was clear as day, and it made him wonder what the hell was she was on. And whether it came in a bottle. Because some days, everyone needed a little bit of that in this job.

'Okay, Sandra, I'll play, but if you have something that I need to know, you need to spill it as soon as you get it. I hope we're clear about that because, don't forget –I've allowed you to step into *my* investigation—'

'That's—'

'—And don't insult me by assuming that I don't know out about your little extracurricular visit to the cells yesterday. What the fuck was that all about? Totally unacceptable. This is my investigation and I don't appreciate you stomping all over it. So, I'll say it again – if you have something on those boys or you're building something else that affects my enquiry, you need to tell me. And I mean now. Do I make myself clear?'

The more the words tumbled out, the angrier he felt.

'Oh, calm down, Mike,' Sandra said.

He could hear the underlying chuckle in her voice, which only pissed him off even more.

'I'm just stirring the pot,' she continued. 'Hoping to catch much bigger fish than the Chuckle Brothers you've just charged and remanded. You know as well as I do that they didn't kill that poor woman. Worse-case scenario is that they dumped her body somewhere. They'll get five years or so for that. Me? I'm after much bigger players. It's part of the Cold Case Review team work I'm doing, and I have the full backing of the boys upstairs, not to mention the home secretary, who wants these bloody gangsters off the streets, and quickly.'

That last bit shouldn't have come as a surprise, but he was disappointed in Bates, nonetheless.

'Seriously, you're rank- and name-dropping on me? I'd expected better from you,' Peters said, shaking his head. 'I know who you have backing you. But if you fuck up my investigation by playing silly games, you'll regret it.'

***

Sandra put the phone down.

'Can you believe that smug arsehole?' Sandra said. 'Who the hell does he think he is, telling me I'll regret it if I fuck up *his* investigation? We were on the trail of these bloody gangsters long before he came along. He clearly doesn't understand how these things work. The fucking cheek of him!'

Stone shrugged. 'Ma'am, he has as much right as you do to go after these men. And the murder of Maureen is *his* case, isn't it? You're equal in rank, but he was first on the scene and that means he gets precedence. I'm not surprised that he's angry about our interference, if I'm honest.'

'Leave it out. Peters knows we're not after her killers. Maureen's blood spatter's everywhere. There's a van that has clear signs of a cadaver in it. Add to that the enormous amount of DNA extracted not only from the van but from the apartment as well. He has a cut-and-dried case, and he'll get his glory moment, of that I'm certain. I think he's just jealous of our position within the force. He's just a gumshoe, if you ask me. And a lucky one too. Imagine being handed a near one-hundred per cent solvable case, with near certain convictions, especially regarding disposal. And even though Fitzpatrick Senior is almost certainly dead and therefore unable to be tried, he'll be able to wrap that up without too much trouble and close the case with no loose ends. What more does the man want?'

'I think your being a little unfair, ma'am. He's a senior officer, and a decent bloke I might add. His only motive here is to assert some authority on his case. Yes, he's been lucky on this one and probably won't have to put in the hard yards to wrap things up but that doesn't make him a gumshoe.'

Sandra sighed. 'You're right, Stone, as always, but I don't like being threatened. Peters is a decent copper, that's for sure, but he needs to understand that there are bigger fish to fry here, and I won't let him stand in my way.'

Stone's phone started ringing, and she answered. Listened. Said, 'It's the pathologist. He has the results.'

Sandra could only hear one side of the conversation, but by the look on Stone's face, it was good news.

A few minutes later, Stone hung up. 'It's John Fitzpatrick alright, just as we suspected. Dental records are conclusive.'

'We already knew that,' Sandra said, and regretted her haughty tone. 'Fingerprints generally don't lie. Still, it's good to get definitive results. Did the pathologist say anything else that could be of help?'

'Not really, ma'am, but he did confirm that Fitzpatrick was burned alive. The amount of smoke and soot in his lungs confirms it. Dreadful.'

Sandra nodded. 'It really is, but now we have something of real substance to bring to the Fitzpatrick boys. Autopsies don't lie either, so get yourself down to the mortuary and get the report. I want John Fitzpatrick to see it. Hopefully he'll realise the game is up and disclose where Maureen's body is. He has no reason to keep that a secret now. I mean he can't protect a dead man, now can he? He's better off just disclosing it all and reducing his sentence to disposal of the body rather than the actual murder.'

Stone agreed and left for the hospital. Sandra got on the phone and made arrangements to visit the prison. John Fitzpatrick Junior could refuse permission of course, as could the prison itself, but she made the circumstances surrounding her request crystal clear to her commanding officer. The guvnor agreed with her – this news would be best coming from an official source and not through the grapevine or the news. 'Hearing something like that would awful at the best of times, but with the poor chap being incarcerated … well, you never know how someone in that situation is going to react, do you? Leave it with me. I'll set it up.'

52

Better TIA than DOA

Transient Ischaemic Attack. Or TIA. That's what had knocked Tommy for six. And his distraught family for that matter. The cause – high blood pressure. They'd kept him in overnight, just as a precaution, even though he was now fully compos mentis.

He could remember everything from slumping in his chair to the paramedics arriving.

And being very, very frightened.

He still was. A mini stroke? Bloody hell, he really did need to slow down or he was going to be six feet under. This past year, these past few days especially, had taken their toll on him and his family. The list wasn't pretty. The murder of his best friend and confidante, Albie. The attack on Jack and Callum. His daughter's wedding and the stress that went with that. And now the Fitzpatricks' recent shenanigans, including the disposal of Darren Davies' corpse. To top all that, he had a nagging feeling that he was missing something, but couldn't quite put his finger on it.

And no doubt Peggy would put in her tuppence worth about his smoking and drinking the first chance she got. Not that he'd ever done either to excess but she was always nagging him to pack in the smokes. And she was probably right.

At least he'd been given the all-clear and discharged. Jack was coming to pick him up. While he waited, he ruminated. The fact was this: No one was safe. Times were changing. The old-school gangsters were almost obsolete these days. The relatively new influx – gangs from all over the world – had no respect for anyone. The whole culture was different; those bastards would take out a whole family for a debt of peanuts. Drugs played a big part in the problem, because the money that could be earned from that business was huge. The gangs thought nothing of taking out their rivals to enhance their status and increase their share of revenue. No, it was time to move on. Tommy Spillane was getting too old for this game, and he had no stomach for the way it was being played. He considered his six decades, and in that moment it was as if he could feel every single one of them. It wasn't just his own mortality at stake. It was also the impact of this lifestyle on Peggy and the kids.

Peggy had known what he was before they married, of course, but the girls? They'd been born into it, hadn't they? They never asked to be involved in this. They had no say in it. They were innocent victims in every way, and had to be protected at all costs. And there was a grandchild on the way. That littl'un had to be considered too.

Stability and safety – that's what he wanted for his growing family. Not least because he wouldn't always be there to protect them. Like if things had gone pear-shaped and the paramedics hadn't arrived fast enough. Where would that have left his beloved family? He didn't even have a will yet, and while Peggy would inherit all his known assets including the house even if he died intestate, she didn't know the half of how he earned his money. In fact, he'd deliberately excluded her from some of it, just to protect her and his daughters. But that was naïve. The vultures would be circling and be picking at his bones the minute he wasn't around to challenge them. Which meant getting his affairs in order was an absolute priority. It had to be. For far too long he'd kept his cards close to his chest. And with Albie gone, he needed a replacement – someone he could trust, confide in and educate.

It was as if that person had read his thoughts. There he was. Jack Clay. Walking through the reception area, looking around for his father- in-law.

Tommy got up and greeted him with a hug, even surprising himself with the tenderness of it. 'There you are, my boy.'

'What's brought all this on?' Jack said, patting Tommy on the back.

'Oh, nothing son. Come on. Get me home and all will be revealed.'

53

What's Cooking?

Jack drove them back to Primrose Hill. Every time he looked over at Tommy, he felt unnerved. The old man had this strange look on his face, almost like he'd changed overnight.

Amanda and Lorraine bolted out of the door the moment the car pulled up. Kayak and Pawnee bounded ahead and were the first to reach the car. Their tails were wagging like windmills in a storm, and almost knocked Tommy off his feet, but they were just a touch gentler than usual, as if they knew that something wasn't quite right. It was almost uncanny.

The aroma of home-cooked food wafted down the hallway.

'What's cooking, good looking?' Tommy said, and beamed.

'It's your favourite, darling' Peggy said.

Roast lamb and all the trimmings. One of Jack's favourites too. His stomach rumbled.

As soon as lunch was over, Tommy's demeanour seemed to change. Peggy asked if he was feeling alright. He reassured her that everything was okay, that the food had been delicious, as had the company. 'However, I have some rather important things to discuss with Jack and need some privacy.

'Can't it wait, Tommy love? You've just got out of hospital and need your rest.'

Tommy stood his ground, and led Jack to the den.

As usual, he offered Jack a stiff one.

Jack shood his head. 'Not for me, mate, and with all due respect, it's not a good idea for you to be having one either.'

'Never mind about me, son. If yesterday's taught me anything, it's fuck it. Life's too short.' He poured himself a large scotch.

'Oh, go on then you lunatic. You're right. Make it a large one.'

Tommy laughed. Said, 'That's more like it.' Motioned for Jack to sit.

And then he started talking.

Jack listened.

'No one knows how I really make my money,' Tommy said, 'and what I've put in place over the years to ensure the survival and prosperity of my family. You're now part of that family, hence my willingness to open up to you. First is this ...'

The firm's drug income was to end, and end right now, Tommy said.

And then he told Jack about the property portfolio. It was managed through a trust fund that had been set up several years ago to keep Tommy's name out of the picture. The fund was run by an old Jewish friend of the Spillanes who wasn't involved with crime. Well, sort of wasn't. He wasn't exactly straight-laced, or a shrinking violet. If anything, he skated very close to the edge of the law with what he did for Tommy, but from what Jack could gather, he was essentially a very good accountant with an overwhelming goal of making as much cash as he could for his trouble.

How did he launder that money? Jack asked. Tommy didn't know and hadn't asked. But things were going to change. The money the firm had been making from coke was a big part of that gravy train and that that to stop. 'And Ezra is the smartest man I've ever met, and will advise us on the best way forward.

I've known him for the best part of thirty years, son. We can trust him.'

Jack asked how much the portfolio was worth.

'At the last count, around twenty million … should I want to sell up now. Which I don't.'

It brought in over a hundred grand a month after expenses, but Tommy reckoned that in another ten years or so it would be worth nearly double that once the final payments had been made. Only a few properties were currently owned outright, like the house they were setting in. 'The rest are mortgaged and managed by the same guy and the family company he controls. His name is Ezra Solomon and his offices are on Brick Lane. I intend to introduce you to him shortly.'

Jack had expected that to be it. Twenty mill in bricks and mortar sounded like enough. But Tommy, it turned out, wasn't done.

'The second thing you should know about is the family interest in some pubs and clubs around London. We have an interest in fifteen or so.'

He'd 'invested' in the landlords. Not with anything formal like a paper contract. These contracts were personal, between them and Tommy. Esra knew nothing about them. A gentleman's agreement, he called it. Sealed with a handshake. In return for a small take every week. Jack had known about some of these, but fifteen?

'Ever since your uncle's death, Ronnie and I have been doing the rounds and picking up our dues. Which bring in around ten thousand a month, though that can vary depending on the situation. I'll fill you in on the arrangements later.'

'So that's where you've been disappearing to,' Jack said.

'Never mind that now, Jack. Please, just let me finish. Your chance for questions will come in due course.'

Jack apologised and relaxed back into his seat.

'You and I will need to visit all of these establishments over the next few weeks, son, and let them know that there's going to be change coming. By which I mean that I'll need to introduce you formally to them and let them know what's coming. It will be down to you to impress the fuck out of them and advise them should something happen to me, that they honour our agreement. That's why I'm going to suggest that you use Ronnie Fisher as your right-hand man. He can ... assist you in this matter, shall we say. Now, don't take that personally, it's just that Ronnie's well known to these people and they respect him. He's a very dangerous man, Jack, and loyal to a fault. A good man to have in your corner.'

Why the hell was Tommy was telling him all this now? Was he retiring? Had the doctors told him something while he was in hospital? Was he dying and hadn't told anyone?

Tommy must have seen the confusion in Jack's face, because he gestured for Jack to speak. 'Go on, son.'

'Okay, that's a lot to take in. So, first, I have my own man. Callum. He's more than capable of helping me out should that be necessary. And I trust him. Unlike Ronnie Fisher, who I don't know all that well. And, honestly, Tommy, that little thing he's just done makes me question whether his brain's working properly. I mean why would he go the whole hog and give up all the Fitzpatricks? That's not what you told him to do at the lockup. I just don't get it.'

'Oh, that's simple. Because that's actually exactly what I instructed him to do. I told him to get the whole lot of them off the streets. They're wrong'uns, Jack, and you know it. They're too heavily involved in getting high on their own supply. And I'm going to be honest here' – he leant forward – 'if you weren't my son-in-law and father of my grandchild, you probably wouldn't be sitting where you are. I've told you before, Jack, I don't like people who do drugs, but I'm trusting you to stick to your word about knocking it on the head.'

That took Jack aback, and for a moment he was lost for words.

Perhaps Tommy had realised he'd gone too far, because now he redirected the conversation back to Fisher. 'Listen, son, I know you have Callum, and I like the kid, but he's not a Ronnie Fisher. He doesn't have the same amount of experience. Besides, Ronnie's made his bones with me and your uncle over the years and is seriously respected within certain circles, whereas you and Callum are not. Circles, I might add, where you would not be taken seriously at the moment. I'm not saying that Callum can't play a part in this. I'm simply saying that, for now at least, you need a Ronnie Fisher. Please trust me on this one.'

'Fair enough,' Jack said, still digesting what Tommy had told him. 'But why are you talking like this? Is there something you need to tell me? Has something happened that's made this necessary? I mean don't get me wrong, I'm seriously flattered that you're even considering me to step into your shoes, but why, mate, and why now?'

Tommy sighed heavily and refilled their glasses. 'The bottom line is that I want to retire,' he said quietly. 'I'm sick and tired of all the bullshit that goes with this lifestyle. I'm planning to leave for Spain in a few weeks or so. Peggy doesn't know yet, so keep it under your hat for now. And for fuck's sake, don't tell Lorraine either. I need to make all the arrangements with my people over there. Peggy won't be a problem; she's always talking about it being a possibility, and loves it over there, as do the girls. The only stumbling block now is the baby, though it's not exactly a million miles away, is it, son? You could visit as much as you wanted.'

Jack got up and paced the room for a few minutes, turning everything over in his head. Then he said: 'When do we start?'

Tommy got up, and wrapped his arms around Jack. 'Welcome aboard, son.'

There was something in the way he said it that Jack hadn't heard before. More than business. There was love in there too.

'We get started immediately. First, you need to cover the items we discussed before my episode last night. Get yourself over to Micky Evans's old woman and give her that money I gave you, and be sure to tell her that there's three hundred quid a week coming her way until her old man gets out of prison. Make sure that happens without fail. Then find Johnny Thoms. We need to know whether he was involved in the Darren Davies issue. You have the address, right?'

Jack patted his shirt pocket. 'Yes, I have the details right here.'

'Good. I'm going to get in contact with Jimmy Stevens. I don't think he's involved but best to find out, I'd say. And Jack,' he looked him square in the eyes – 'don't underestimate the importance of these things. Doing your research and looking after those who need our help will always hold you in good stead. Even more importantly, it will bring about the respect that's needed in this world of ours. Word gets around quickly in this murky business, and if you're seen to be neglecting your duty or taking your eye off the ball, they'll come after you like a pack of wolves. And I don't mean the police. Always remember that, son.'

It came at Jack like a thunderbolt … a shift in his emotions. Intimacy didn't come easy for him. Never had. Keeping his distance in times of disaster and chaos was how he'd always survived. Tommy's TIA for example – that had left him feeling awkward, especially when Lorraine and her sister and mother had been all over Tommy like a rash. All he'd wanted to do was get the hell out of the room. It had been the same when they'd visited in hospital and seen Tommy for the first time, sitting up in bed while the doctor gave them a run-down of what had happened. Tommy was Jack's father-in-law, and yet all that he'd thought in that moment was that he hardly knew the man. He liked him of course, but as he'd looked at that vulnerable old man, he'd felt only a coldness as to whether he lived or died. Had that been that a defence mechanism, or had he simply not cared? He'd experienced something similar when Uncle Albie had been brutally murdered. He hadn't really known him that well either. Perhaps indifference was a way of blotting it all out.

But just now he'd looked at things from different angle. Considered a situation where something happened to his mother, Lorraine or his unborn child. That was the emotional shift, or the first part of it anyway. Indifference morphed into rage and anger, so powerful and profound that he knew in that moment he would gladly die to prevent anything bad happening to those he loved. And then those two things changed into to something else – love, trust, loyalty, all of it mixed up into one big thing that Jack couldn't find a word for. But he'd seen it in Peggy, Lorraine and Amanda as they'd tended to the father they dearly loved. And Jack now knew – knew it in every cell of his being – just what it meant to be a father and a protector, someone to be relied upon, someone to shield the family from the horrors of the world.

That's what Tommy was. That's what Jack would be. He was stepping up, ready to face his new role in life.

He looked at Tommy in a new way. In awe of him, like Jack was a boy again, and wanting to please him.

And with that came a deeper insight. Tommy's approach was artful. Because if Jack took the reins, it would be him, not Tommy, it would be him open to all kinds of scrutiny, not only from the police but also from their so-called friends. He'd have to tread very carefully, stay on his toes. Without proper support, he'd very quickly become a target, and he wouldn't last long. Ronnie Fisher having his back when times get tough, as they inevitably would, was sensible. Even so, he planned to give Callum a more advanced role in what was going down. His friend had earned it. Ronnie would understand, and so would Tommy. Jack would insist.

'I hear you about Ronnie,' Jack said. 'I'll get on to the Thoms thing this evening. And you can count on me.'

He patted Tommy on the shoulder, then asked him about Spain.

It would happen in a few weeks, Tommy said, and stood up. He needed to get away, take time to reflect and get his health back on track. 'And I don't want to burden you with this, son, but I've got an overwhelming sense of doom hanging over me. I'm hoping that a little rest and recouperation will put that right. Meet me here tomorrow morning and we'll set about putting all this into place.'

Jack took that as his dismissal, shook Tommy's hand and was about to leave the room, when Tommy grasped him by the arm and pulled him towards the wall safe just behind his desk.

'One more thing,' he said, and opened up the safe. 'Take this and keep it safe. It's a record of all of the things we just discussed – names, addresses, telephone numbers and so on. This information is invaluable and it *must* be kept secret, away from prying eyes if you know what I mean.' He handed Jack a small notebook. 'That there is mana from heaven for certain people, especially the police, who'd have a field day if they got their grubby little hands on it.'

'Understood,' Jack said, and tucked it into his pocket. 'It'll be safe with me.'

54

Pent Up in Pentonville

The notorious category-B men's prison had housed and hanged it's fair share of the famous and infamous over the past hundred and fifty years or so. The freshly painted exterior belied the grim interior lurking behind the boundary walls. Sandra shuddered. She hated these places, though God knows how many criminals she'd condemned to them. She put that out of her mind, and knocked on the fortified gate just inside the main compound. A rather grumpy and officious prison guard demanded to see her identification. She duly obliged and was led through the dismal building to the guvnor's office. He was expecting her.

Sitting behind a sumptuous desk was the rather imposing Sir Cecil Creighton OBE. He was surrounded by photos of the current monarch. Her Majesty had knighted him only a year earlier. Sandra knew this because he'd ungraciously made sure to put the images of the event front and centre. It made her want to puke.

Creighton gestured for her to sit down, then studied his notes and said, 'You say that the father of two of my prisoners is dead, Chief Inspector. John and Liam Fitzpatrick, is that correct?'

'Yes, sir,' Sandra replied, hating the almost apologetic tone that seemed to have slipped from her mouth.

'And that you want to relay this news personally to them.' He peered over his glasses. 'May I ask why you think that is necessary? I mean, one of my experienced officers can certainly fill that role on your behalf and save you the bother of being here. It's not as if it would be the first time we've had to tell prisoners bad news, you know.'

His snotty, patronising demeanour was pissing her off, but letting him know that would do her zero favours. So she said, 'Well, sir, the death of their father is currently being investigated as a murder. John Fitzpatrick Senior is suspected of having been involved in another murder – of a prostitute in Kings Cross – prior to his own demise. We believe that his sons have information about that crime, and—'

'That's all very well, Chief Inspector,' Creighton said, placing his glasses on the desk in front of him, 'but we already have both men in our custody, and I don't think they're going anywhere soon, do you? Besides, what more could they tell you about their involvement that you don't already know? They're not likely to give you anything else under these circumstances, not least if you give them bad news. It will just set them off, if you ask me, and potentially cause my officers a problem on the wing. No, I'm afraid this kind of news would be better coming from one of my trained officers and not some gung-ho policewoman trying to gain God knows what from them by informing them of their father's death.' He stood up. 'I'm going to refuse access to them. I don't think it's right that you undertake this task, but, moreover, I cannot take the risk of their lawyers accusing us of putting them under pressure to divulge information by way of coercion. We must entertain the proper protocol at all times. Good day, Chief Inspector.'

'Sir, if I may,' Sandra said, raising her voice just a little. 'I thought we had an agreement. My commanding officer,

Douglas Smithers, called you. He assured me you'd assist in this matter.'

Creighton frowned. 'That is incorrect, Chief Inspector. I simply told Douglas that I would see you, that is all. On reflection, I shouldn't have agreed even to that. Your guvnor is a good friend and ally of mine, but he's asked too much of me on this occasion. I'll address that with him in due course, but for now you have my decision. One of my officers will see you out.'

Sandra was lost for words and went to open the door.

A hand held it shut. Creighton's.

She sidestepped him, resenting the invasion of her personal space.

'Just one more thing, Chief Inspector,' he said. 'The circumstances would change if one of the prisoners offered up new information and requested to see you or another officer. Now *that* we could accommodate … legally. May I suggest you give me the particulars of your enquiry and then we'll see how things pan out, shall we?' He invited her to take her seat.

Sandra obliged.

And told him everything.

When she'd finished, she smiled and held out her hand. 'We can only hope that they'll cooperate, sir.'

She left the prison grounds hopeful. She and Smithers had underestimated Creighton, and his environs. After all, this wasn't the local nick where the desk sergeant would often turn a blind eye to unusual practices and give you access to vulnerable prisoners down at the cells.

She'd spilled her guts to Pentonville's guvnor.

The question now was: what would he do with that?

55

No Hidden Agenda

Jack drove towards Ronnie Fisher's place. Tommy was quiet, as if reluctant to strike up a conversation about what they were doing. To Jack, it all seemed quite surreal – Tommy retiring? Really? And did he actually want Jack to take over the business? The more Jack thought about it, the more it made sense he supposed. After all, he was family now. Tommy had said as much.

'You okay, son?' Tommy said at last.

'Well, now you mention it, I'm still struggling to get my head around this, wondering if all this is real. I mean why now, and why me? Surely you can't be serious about giving it all up and just pissing off to retirement in Spain. Is there something you're not telling me Tommy?'

Tommy laughed, but there was no condescension or malice in it. 'Fair play to you. I'd be thinking the same if the shoe was on the other foot. But there's no hidden agenda, son, I swear on my daughters' lives. You're family now and the only person I can really trust. And before you ask, I'm deadly serious about all this. Aside from the wedding and the expectance of a baby, the past few years have brought me and my family nothing but pain and misery. Being banged up and now this bloody stroke, it's made me rethink my life, Jack. None of us know what's round the corner, do we? The last couple of days have proven that. What if I'd been alone when that happened? Where would I be now? Either six feet under or a bloody vegetable, having to get my arse wiped and the dribble from my chin cleaned up by some stranger in a bloody hospice. No, I'm cutting out, mate, while I still can. While I still have my health and bloody sanity. That villa in Spain is my sanctuary and I intend to spend as much time there as I possibly can.'

Jack said nothing. What else could he say? Tommy had made his mind up.

'And you, son' – he prodded Jack's shoulder – 'you have everything it takes to make a mark in this business. You're courageous, clever and you have a way about you. Peggy sees it too, you know. She says you remind her of me back in the early days. Yes, you'll be more in the spotlight, on the front line – I'm not oblivious to that. But with my guidance and resources, you'll be fine, trust me.'

He was pleased that Tommy had that much faith in him but it still unnerved him a little. The world they operated in was fickle, he knew that, but the bigger question was: was he up to it? Stepping up was one thing, stepping into Tommy's shoes was another.

Tommy cut in as if he'd read Jack's mind. 'Listen to me – you have everything you need to make this a viable undertaking, but you must understand a few things. One, I've spent my entire adult life getting to where I am. I've done things that would make even the devil take a step back. I was making my bones among the criminal fraternity long before you were born, and respect doesn't come easily. And leads to number two: You have to earn it, and that takes time, but I know you have it in you. Three, don't take a step backwards under any circumstances. Ever. Take a good hiding if you have to, but come back stronger and with more menace. Be that scrapyard dog who never gives in but sees it through to the bitter end no matter what. Then, and only then, will people respect you. They'll fear you as well, which is my fourth point. Be feared, Jack. Want that fear. It's what separates you from the people who oppose you. And, yes, I'm including the filth in that. They're only as good as the next grass. So, five, be careful who you talk to and what you say. Stand up straight and look people in the eye, and like I said, don't ever take a backwards step. People are like wolves – even the Old Bill. One sign of weakness and they'll devour you. Always remember that and you'll be fine.'

Jack was speechless. He hadn't had a father figure since his own dad had passed away. The old niggles around intimacy, and his discomfort with it, returned, but it was tempered by a feeling of genuine warmth towards Tommy. Would his own father have given him the 'talk' when the time was right? Jack though so, at least from what his mother had told him about his dad.

An unexpected twinge of sadness hit him, a feeling he'd suppressed. Because he'd never really grieved for his father, had he? He'd just survived and tried to be strong for his mother in the face of their loss. He'd become the man about the house in an instant – until that animal Ritchie Powers had come along.

Jack reflected on that fateful night when he was just fifteen, and one side of his mouth twitched.

'What's on your mind, son? I won't pretend I haven't seen that crooked smile before. And since we're telling it how it is, I'll say that what I'm seeing there is menace. What I'm seeing would unnerve some people if they encountered it. And what I'm saying is that you should use that, harness it. Because in the coming months it might be useful, you hear me?'

'I hear you, Tommy,' Jack said, and let his mouth soften as he looked over at his father-in-law. 'I was just reflecting on a few things, that's all.'

They'd arrived. Jack punched the horn and Ronnie came out of his house and got straight into the car, without a word.

Silent but deadly.

Jack couldn't help it. He shuddered.

56

The Yard

'Cecil fucking Creighton. I'm telling you, there's a man you don't want to get on the wrong side to.' Sandra shook her head. 'I mean, he's a knight of the realm and all that, and doesn't he let you know it. The man practically threw me out of the bloody prison, and without so much as a how do you do. The bloody cheek of him. I felt like a schoolgirl being reprimanded by the headmaster.'

Stone's head was cocked at an angle, and she was trying not to laugh.

'It's not funny, Sergeant,' she said. But of course it was, and she grinned.

'It's not like he had much choice about things, ma'am. He has a duty of care when you think about it, and he needs to ensure that we don't gain an advantage over a susceptible or vulnerable prisoner. Imagine if one of the Fitzpatrick's said that that he'd felt intimidated or something. And you know what the bloody bleeding hearts would do with that information.'

Sandra nodded. 'It still rankled me. These are brutal killers and fucking gangsters we're talking about here. Would it have been so difficult just to let me have ten minutes with them?

Don't forget, we're talking about murder here and we still don't know where the poor woman's body is.'

'I totally agree with you but we have to follow protocol. The days of interrogating prisoners without their full rights being observed – solicitors, mentors, their mummies – are long gone. I suppose we just have to accept that and go about things in a different way.'

Sandra sighed. Those animals … they seemed to have more rights than the average Joe. How the fuck had that happened? She leaned back in her worn leather chair, and stared at the desk lamp. It cast shadows over the mess on her desk, reflecting her grim mood. She rubbed her temples, trying to erase the frustration. Her lot caught 'em red-handed, and ten minutes later they had to treat those bastards like royalty. They got their lawyers, their fair trials, their endless appeals. Meanwhile, the victims got a lifetime of nightmares at best, or in the case of the Maureens of this world, a death sentence. And they knew how to play the game, exploit every loophole, while she was stuck playing silly buggers with the system.

'And anyway,' Stone continued, 'without those rights, the innocent could suffer too.'

'A necessary evil, then. Maybe. But it doesn't make it any easier watching monsters get off the hook while good people suffer.'

Silence settled between them, thick with the weight of hard truths.

Still, maybe Creighton would come up with something. He'd seemed confident. All she could do was wait.

57

No Body, No Case

Liam Fitzpatrick lay on a single bunk in his sparce cell on A Wing, and wondered where the hell all this was going.

His father was dead – he knew that from his solicitor – but he didn't know why or how. Kingham had told him only that it had been confirmed by a coroner but had seemed unwilling to go any further, despite Liam's request for more information.

He'd been locked in his cell since he'd arrived. Which meant being kept away from his older brother too. He didn't have a clue where John was or even if he was on the same wing. Banging on the door hadn't helped either; that just seemed to infuriate the prisoners around him. Well, 'infuriate' was perhaps too polite a way of putting it. They'd made threats to his life. And so he'd stopped. Trouble with those guys was something he didn't need and didn't want. And didn't have the first idea how to handle, more to the point; this was only his second time in jail.

His first stint had been a remand that was over before it had started, or so it had seemed. He'd been released before it even went to trial because the witnesses had come over with a sudden and serious bout of amnesia.

This time things were different. Serious. Really fucking serious. Liam was shit scared. The police had a crap-ton of overwhelming evidence – enough to send him and his brother down for a very long time. The idea terrified him. He was no gangster. His father and brother? Yeah, they were the real deal, but Liam? Nah, he was just a follower, tagging along on the coattails of the Two Johnnies, as he'd sometimes called them, because it made him giggle at bit. And that relaxed him when everything felt like it was getting too much. He'd always relied on his family's reputation to help him navigate that world. He might have walked with a swagger at times, but it was all just face. Without them he was stumbling. Without them he was just another scared little wannabe who wouldn't last five minutes among hardcore criminals. And, fuck, didn't he know it.

John had told him to keep his mouth shut, said everything would be alright if he did. But that was just bravado. They'd been clumsy when they'd disposed of that prostitute, almost like they hadn't given a shit or as if they'd never be suspected. And then that copper had come along while they were in the middle of wrapping her up. That hadn't helped and it had made them rush it. Liam could recall his brother saying at the time, 'Don't worry about it. No body, no case.' Liam suspected that wasn't true but, as always, he'd followed his brother's instructions to the letter. He regretted that now – course he did. It was blindingly obvious that they should have been more diligent.

Liam had never actually killed anyone but that wasn't the first time he'd seen a dead body. The other time had been only a couple of years earlier, but they'd been more thorough with that disposal. They'd had to be they'd been acting on strict instructions issued by a very serious man, and had made sure there were no slip-up's, no traces.

The trip down Memory Lane was broken when his cell door opened. A giant of a man stood in the frame, blocking the view to beyond. Liam guessed him to be at least six four. Not quite as wide, but built like a brick shithouse, nonetheless.

'Get off your bunk, Fitzpatrick,' he barked, 'and stand over there facing the wall.'

Liam complied. 'What's going on, Officer? I haven't done anything.'

Maybe it had something to do with his banging on the cell door earlier. Perhaps it had pissed of the guards as well as the other inmates, and now he was going to get a punch or two to the back of the head. He'd heard about that sort of thing from talking with his brother and other guys on the outside. They'd almost bragged about it, like it was a badge of honour or something

He braced for the impact.

'Relax, Fitzpatrick,' the big screw said, patting him down from behind. 'We're not here to harm you. The guvnor wants a word, that's all. Now turn around and keep your back to the wall. And, son, do yourself a huge favour.' He leaned into Liam, so close that their noses were almost touching. 'Do not make any move forward towards the guvnor or you'll regret it, do you understand?'

'Yes, sir.' Shit, what the hell was going on? 'But what's this all about? I don't understand.'

'All will be revealed, young man,' a voice boomed from just beyond the door.

It was unfamiliar. Firm, no-nonsense, and posh as fuck.

'My name is Cecil Creighton and I am the guvnor of this establishment.' He stepped into the cell. 'I'm here to offer you help and advice. Are you're willing to listen and take it?'

'Do I have a choice, sir?' Liam said, a little more confidently than he actually felt.

'Why of course you do, young man,' Creighton said, turning as if about to walk away. 'This isn't a bloody gulag. You're free to do as you please. But if that's your position then I'll leave. Goodbye, Mr Fitzpatrick.'

Liam was dumbstruck for a moment. Was it that simple? Could you really just refuse a man like Creighton, even considering the position he was in? Maybe you could. But he was curious now.

'It's not that I don't want to cooperate, sir, or that don't want to hear what you have to say. It's just that I'm a bit worried where it will lead to, that's all.'

Creighton turned around in the doorway. 'Where will it lead to, Fitzpatrick?' He frowned, as if mystified. 'I've already informed you that I'm here on your behalf – to offer help and advice. So I'll say again: are you willing to talk to me?'

Liam nodded.

'Good, Fitzpatrick, good.' He produced a piece of paper from his jacket pocket. 'Now, I just need you to sign this first, and then we can begin.'

'What is it?' Liam asked, immediately suspicious.

'It's just a request form. It simply says that you wish to talk to me about a delicate matter and that you waive the right to a solicitor while doing so.'

Liam was dumbstruck again. He'd never heard of such a thing. But then again, what the hell did he know? All of this was new to him.

Creighton rolled his eyes and sighed. 'Come, come now, Fitzpatrick. I haven't got all day. And I'm not trying to trick you. I just need your signature on the request form for the record – it's as simple as that. Nothing more, nothing less. If you don't sign it, then I can't help you.'

Liam took a few moments to digest this information, then took the form and scanned it. It was exactly what the governor had described – just a request to see the man, printed on official prison paper. The big screw produced a pen and handed it to Liam.

Liam sighed.

'Excellent,' Creighton said, folding the form in two and placing back it into his pocket. 'Now, where shall I begin?'

58

A Level of Protection

It had been a long day. Jack, Tommy and Ronnie had visited nine establishments, and each time they were met with due reverence and understanding. The landlords were absent at two of the pubs, but the staff were advised that the landlord should call Tommy at their earliest opportunity and make themselves available within the next few days. Jack got the feeling that the bartenders had been left with very little doubt as to the importance of relaying this message.

They dropped Ronnie off and continued to Primrose Hill.

'Well?' Tommy said. 'What's your first thoughts on the day's activities?'

'Honestly? Seems pretty straightforward, if you ask me.'

Tommy laughed. 'It seems that way, doesn't it, son? But just wait until you get a call at midnight from one of those fuckers whose bouncers have left for the night, squealing that they need help or else everyone's going to die.'

'Does that happen often?'

'More than you might think, Jack, I can tell you. But I wouldn't take it too seriously. My advice is nearly always to call the police ... depending on the circumstances, of course. I mean that's what we pay our taxes for, right?'

Jack chuckled.

'In all seriousness though, you will be expected to provide some level of protection to these people. My way of doing that is very simple, so listen up.'

This was going to be interesting, Jack decided, and it struck him how much he was enjoying these little tête-à-têtes with Tommy, learning from his years of experience.

'Visit every single one of these boozers on a Friday or Saturday night, when business is as full flow. Take some 'friends' with you, in case there's real trouble, and just watch.' Tommy went silent.

'Is that it, Tommy? Just watch?'

It all seemed a bit lame to Jack.

'Yes, son. Just watch. Isn't that exactly what I just said? Didn't we agree that you'd listen to my words?'

Tommy shook his head. The movement was slight. Jack might have missed it if he hadn't glanced at his father-in-law. He was annoyed with Jack, that much was clear.

'What you're looking for isn't the troublemakers, son, but the local hardmen and their friends, who treat the place like it's their own. They're the ones who will go out of their way to protect what they see as *their* domain when the landlord's under pressure or there are some idiots making trouble. Trust me on this one, Jack. Most of the time they're your best doormen. And not only that – they're free.'

Jack considered that for a moment. Of course. Tommy was right. It made perfect sense. Every pub or club he'd ever visited had those types of men in them. Some were the real deal and really did think they owned the place. Others were just wannabes who wanted to impress the landlord and the locals with their fighting skills. Tommy's advice was sound.

'Absolute genius, Tommy. We use our eyes, while they do all the dirty work on our behalf.' He laughed.

'Just don't forget to buy them a drink or two,' Tommy said. 'And flatter their egos. Tell them how valued they are and that you owe them one. These guys just want an in, son. They'll brag to anyone who'll listen that they know who really owns the place – us – and that we're not to be messed with. Now don't get me wrong, these are usually hard men who love a scrap and who are sometimes the cause of the problem. And in that scenario, you'll have to sort that out yourself – just be aware of that.'

Jack smiled. He'd seen all this before. It went on in loads of boozers, but he'd never really considered what it all meant, what was going on behind the scenes. Now he did. And he'd learned something else too – he needed to stop second-guessing, to show him the respect he deserved. Because this man had probably forgotten more about protection and empire building than Jack would ever know.

Jack parked up outside Tommy's mansion, and both men got out of the car and walked towards the entrance. Halfway there, Tommy took Jack by the elbow and brought them both to a stop.

He looked up and nodded towards the grand house.

'This is yours now, my boy. I know you and Lorraine want your own place and Peggy and I agreed to help you out after the wedding. I want you and my daughter to live here. In this house. Permanently.'

Jack didn't say anything at first. He wasn't sure he'd heard right. But he had, hadn't he. Tommy had just given him a home. A palace.

'I can't accept that, Tommy. This is your place. Me and Lorraine need our own – somewhere we can bring up our child.'

'Exactly. And think about it. It's gated, a proper safe haven for you and your family. Things may get a little tricky, shall we say, once things start to change, and it would be doing me a huge service if I know that my daughter and grandchild are well protected.'

'I'll have to discuss it with Lorraine. But it doesn't seem right, Tommy. This is your place. And it's not like you won't be coming back home from time to time, is it?'

'In that case, just stay here for now. Please. Jack. At least until Peggy and I have settled in Spain. Then we can talk about it again. How does that sound?'

It was a reasonable request. And hadn't he just told himself not to second-guess Tommy?

He nodded. 'Fair enough, mate. Now, come on. I'm dying for a drink and I'm bloody starving.'

They went inside, and Peggy welcomed them. And an added bonus – even the dogs were pleased to see him for a change. Strange how dogs picked things up.

59

Nothing to Hide

Sandra and Stone were in the canteen, reviewing the case, when a familiar voice interrupted their conversation.

'Ah, there you are,' DCI Mike Peters snapped. 'I've been looking for you.'

'Oh, really? And why would you be doing that, Chief Inspector?' She was teasing him, and knew it was a bad call given the face like thunder he was wearing. But really, the man walked around like he had a stick shoved up his arse sometimes.

'You know damn well why, so don't go acting the bloody fool. I'm serious here. If you don't tell me what the fuck's going on, I'm going straight upstairs to the superintendent. I'll make a formal complaint, and I mean it, so don't bloody test me.'

'Oh, for God's sake, Mike, sit and calm down.' She offered him a smile. His own mouth didn't even twitch. 'I've got nothing to hide, and if you buy me and my sergeant a coffee, I'll tell you everything, I promise.'

Peters looked at them both for a moment, then walked off towards the counter, mumbling to himself.

'What are you going to tell him, ma'am?' Stone said.

'Everything, sergeant. Including the Creighton business. I'm sure he'll arrange something at the prison, and we need to be ready. Besides, it's only a matter of time until Peters finds out anyway.'

'But we still don't know if we'll get anything out of the Fitzpatricks, do we? At the moment, all we have is a suspicion that they were involved in the disposal of Maureen's body, and we still need prove that.'

'*We* don't need to prove anything. That's for Mike and his team to work on … although I think he has enough now anyway. What we need to focus on is finding out why John Senior was killed – and don't tell me it was about Maureen. Why would they torture him? Why would they kill him? She was just a prostitute to them, and these men are professionals. They wouldn't have killed him over that, even if there was a minor involved. No, something else is going on, and I intend to get to the bottom of it. My intuition's telling me that his sons may have some insight into that. And a reminder of how their father died might be just the nudge they need to provide it.'

Peters returned with the drinks, pulled up a chair, and said, 'Spill.'

And Sandra did, including her suspicion that Tommy Spillane had been involved in Darren Davies' disappearance and other murders. She also assured him that her only intention was to find evidence about Spillane and his North London firm, and that she wasn't interested in interfering with his current murder enquiries.

'I'm hoping for something that will put Spillane and his cohorts in the frame for Fitzpatrick's murder,' she said. 'Then, hopefully, you'll get your day in court with him. But remember that I have history with that worthless piece of shit, and I want a piece of the action, not just a conviction for the Fitzpatrick murder.'

'What makes you think it was him that killed Fitzpatrick?' Peters said.

'Oh come on, Mike, who else has that type of muscle? Who else can arrange that sort of thing at such short notice? And don't you think that it's a little too coincidental that one of Spillane's main enforcers let us know that he'd been killed and where the body was?'

'I suppose so, but you can't prove it. And why would he do that? It doesn't make any sense.'

'It makes perfect sense to me, and I'll tell you why. He's taunting me. He thinks he's untouchable. You know the story about his acquittal, don't you?'

Peters nodded. 'I'm afraid I do. The whole division knows what happened with that enquiry, or they think they do. It didn't look good for you then.' He shifted in his seat and looked down at his cup. 'Or with the Parkhurst fiasco down in Hythe last year either.'

'Thanks for reminding me. Really appreciated. But, look, I'm not going to let him wriggle through my fingers again. I know he's responsible for several murders. And, yes, I'm including John Fitzpatrick. His acquittal for the Anderson murder was just pure luck. We thought we had him with that video, but without any real hard evidence the jury weren't convinced and he walked. But he's living on borrowed time, and he knows it. He's just trying to stir things up in the hope that I make another mistake. But not this time. I intend to finish this off with hard evidence, and my intuition tells me that he's made a mistake somewhere. Killing Fitzpatrick wasn't his first error.'

'And you think the Fitzpatrick boys may have something else to divulge?'

'Yes, I do. It's a long shot, I know, but something tells me that they have something. It may be something so small they don't even know that it's important.'

Peters shook his head. 'Sorry, but I think you're clutching at straws here. Those boys are bit-part players and wouldn't have access to this kind of circle. John Senior would have had, perhaps, but not his sons.'

'But that's the key, Mike, don't you see?' Sandra leant forward. 'John Senior might have told them something about his involvement with Spillane, maybe in a drunken or drug-induced moment. Don't forget, he had a serious drink and drug problem towards the end. Once they're told exactly how their father died, and who we think is responsible, it may jog some memory that we can work with.'

Yes, she sounded desperate – the pitch of her voice gave her away; just a little too high, a little too excited – but it was worth a shot, wasn't it? Maybe she was dredging the bottom of the ocean, looking for buried treasure, but she needed this. She knew it. Stone knew it. Peters knew it. Everyone fucking knew it. She looked directly at him.

He sighed. 'Sandra, we go back a way, and I respect your tenacity and resolve, but I've got to say that this all sounds rather desperate. However—'

Sandra hung on to that however, like he'd thrown her a lifeline.

'—we've got nothing to lose by at least questioning the boys. So you have my blessing, I suppose'

Yes!

'But don't try to flog a dead horse with this. If the boys don't give you anything else, please just leave it to me and my team to wrap this up. I need your word on that. And you haven't got long to do it. My case against the boys in the matter of Maureen O'Brian is strong, and I'm confident of a conviction, despite not having a body. What I don't have is much in the way of evidence relating to their father's murder, so any help there would be greatly appreciated. And if you can get them to at least give up the location of O'Brian's body, that too would be most welcome.'

Sandra was about to respond with her gratitude but her phone was ringing.

And the caller was exactly the person she wanted to hear from right now.

'It's the prison guvnor.'

Peters raised his eyes to the ceiling, and said, 'Okay. Just keep me informed. Properly informed. Please.' He got up and left them to it.

Sandra listened, then hung up. 'On your feet, Stone. We're going to Pentonville.'

60

Continuing Professional Development

Jack and Tommy went straight to the den. This time, Jack resolved to keep his mouth shut. Just poured the drinks and sat opposite Tommy, determined not to spoil the mood by asking silly questions.

Tommy accepted his drink and sunk back into his chair. 'There's a few other things you should know about my business, son. And the first is this: I relied heavily on your uncle, may God rest his soul, and in a lot of ways I'm lost without him. He took care of the day-to-day stuff for me, you see. And with ruthless efficiency, I might add. Those people you met today respected him, as did Ronnie and most of our firm. But he's not here now, is he? And that's left me worried. Today, I felt a little uneasy, a little troubled. And that's the first time in my life that I've felt like that, talking to those people. I sensed something … but I just can't put my finger on it … It was almost like they were laughing at me, ridiculing me in some way.'

Jack had felt the same vibe with some of the landlords, and said so. 'Especially when we were talking to Stan Collins at the Old Red Lion. He didn't come across very well to me, like he was sneering. I didn't like him.'

Tommy nodded. 'You're very astute.'

'No one likes change, but they'd better get used to it. With you away, in semi-retirement, shall we say, there are some who might see that as an opportunity to take liberties with us. But I can assure you that me and the boys won't tolerate it.'

'You're a smart young fellow, Jack, and I'm glad that you felt it as I did. We need to keep these people in place by showing them your strength, or things will very quickly go to shit. These people don't go by words or reputation alone; they're serious businessmen who won't lie down for just anyone. Like I've said previously, it took me and your dear uncle years to make our bones and build this thing up to what it is. It wasn't always easy, I can tell you.'

'So what do you suggest?'

Tommy got up and walked towards the drinks cabinet. 'I'm not quite sure yet, but I think you need to make an example of someone. Collateral damage, shall we say. It's always worked for me and your uncle in the past. Another one, son?'

'Why not?' Jack smiled. 'It would be rude not to.'

A knock came at the door. 'Five minutes, boys,' Peggy barked.

'Be there in a minute, sweetheart' Tommy called back, then looked at Jack. 'We'll resume this conversation after dinner son, but here's another lesson for you in the meantime.'

Jack was all ears, ready for some extraordinary snippet of his wisdom.

'Never, and I mean never, upset the person who feeds you.'

61

Time Doesn't Fly

Liam paced his cell. Up and down, up and down. Trying to make sense of the mess in his head. What were the filth going to tell him? Did they have an agenda? Of course they did. That was their MO. Always. But what could he tell them? The coppers wanted to know where the prostitute's body was. That in itself wouldn't have been a big problem. The bigger problem was that revealing its location would almost certainly expose a dark secret. Because he and his brother had buried someone else there, in that exact same location, just over a year or so earlier. Liam had no clue about the identity of that particular corpse, just remembered his brother calling and telling him that they had a job to do. He'd just gone along with it, like he always did. But if they found that body, it would surely bring more shit down on their heads. And he'd be grassing up his own brother, who was far more resolute about giving the police nothing than he was. On the other hand, while neither of them had ever killed anyone, you didn't have to be a genius to work that that not giving up the prostitute's whereabouts would lead to a far longer sentence. For some, that wouldn't have been a problem. They vaunted their jail time at every opportunity, down the pub, in the clubs, like it made them better, stronger, more fearsome.

And it did.

Liam had hidden it, but inside he'd always been cowering, afraid that his weakness, his fear, his confusion, would be discovered. And jail terrified him. The codes and rules and culture were baffling. You needed a fucking PhD to work out how to survive in here. One mistake could finish you. And just these past few days had made him realise that this life wasn't for him. He wasn't like his brother. John had been there, seen it and done it several times before. John wasn't afraid of it, or so he'd said.

The doors out on the landing of the wing banged and crashed, snapping him out of his reverie, and before he could give any further thought to what he might say to the police, his door was opening and there stood the giant screw who'd accompanied the guvnor earlier.

'Follow me, Fitzpatrick,' he boomed. 'We're going to the guvnor's office. You have guests.'

Liam complied without a word.

'Just remember, son, that I'm right behind you,' the screw said, as they made their way along the walkway. 'One wrong move from you and I'll bring a shit storm down on you the likes of which you've never experienced before. Do you I make myself clear?'

'Yes, sir,' Liam said, hating the whimper that had erupted from his mouth as he'd spoken. He kept his chin down, his head low, imagining what years of dealing with crews like this would entail. Because time wouldn't fly in this place. It would drag, year upon year of hell, with Liam always looking over his shoulder, always cowering in the shadows.

And it was clear now.

He would do anything in his power to minimise the time he spent in this place.

He would sing loud and clear.

62

Assisting with Enquiries

Stone pulled into a space in the prison car park, and Sandra checked her watch. They had a few minutes. Time they could use to discuss their strategy for dealing with Liam Fitzpatrick.

'Creighton tells me that Liam's willing to talk with us, but he doesn't understand what we think he can tell us.'

'Well neither do we, do we? We don't know if he has anything that will help us either. And—'

'But at the very least we might be able to find out where Maureen's body is. He knows he's bang to rights on that front, and by helping us we can convince him that the judge will look favourably on that. I believe it's a third of the sentence for a guilty plea, but he'll get no credit without the body being given up. Don't forget that at this present time he and his brother are being treated as suspects in her murder – even if we both know that they didn't do it and only disposed of her. If we can convince him that he could be convicted of that if he doesn't cooperate, then he might just give us what we want.'

Stone sighed and opened her door. 'It's worth a shot, ma'am. Come on, let's go and see what he has to say.'

They were led to Creighton's office. The guvnor was absent. Again Sandra checked her watch. He'd kept them waiting a good ten minutes beyond the agreed appointment time.

And then the door opened.

'Ladies,' he boomed while stretching out his hand by way of a greeting.

Ladies? Jesus, what century was he living in?

'Glad you're here. I told you that I'd sort this out, didn't I, Chief Inspector?'

Sandra gave him her best smile, ignoring the smug look on his face.

'One of my officers is bringing Fitzpatrick up from the cells as we speak. Take a seat, please.'

He gestured towards two chairs just to the left of his. Sandra and Stone shook his hand and sat down.

'It is my wish that my officer and I keep an eye on proceedings, Chief Inspector. A guvnor's request is quite simply that, and doesn't extend to any other party. However, following our recent discussions' – he looked at Sandra – 'and a word or two with your own superior officer, it has been decided to allow you both some time, here in my office, to put forward your queries in this matter. I hope you understand that this is highly irregular, but God forbid that I would ever get in the way of justice. You must also understand that this fellow isn't under caution as the law requires, and is simply offering up information to assist in an enquiry. This must not turn into an interrogation. Are we clear on that?'

'Crystal clear, sir,' Sandra said.

Creighton took the seat behind his desk, and Sandra had just a moment to catch Stone's eye. Not that she could read the sergeant's mind, but she was pretty sure she could read in her expression what they'd be later be talking about on their way back to the station – how Creighton was a pompous twit, that his hands were clammy, that his entire demeanour disgusted them both, that he made their skin crawl a little, and how his obvious love of taking control of any given situation was clear for all to see.

And, probably most striking of all, that there was something distinctly odd about Mr Creighton, but that neither could quite put a finger on exactly what it was that made them feel that way.

There was a rap on the door.

'Enter,' Creighton boomed.

The door opened. And there was a very frightened-looking Liam Fitzpatrick. Behind him, a huge prison guard gripped him by the shoulders.

'Ah, Fitzpatrick,' Creighton said, 'sit down over there, lad, and take the weight off your feet. And for God's sake, stop looking so sorry for yourself. You'll give these two police officers the impression that we're mistreating you or something.'

Sandra had wondered, but kept the notion to herself. Even if they were mistreating him, he deserved it. He and his brother were responsible for disposing of a body, and who knew what else.

There were two additional chairs to the right of Creighton. The guard led Fitzpatrick to the one furthest away from the governor, and sat in the other.

'Mr Fitzpatrick,' Creighton said, starting the proceedings much to Sandra's surprise, 'you know who I am, of course, and I'm sure you're aware of the two police officers sitting opposite you.'

Liam Fitzpatrick nodded.

'As we discussed when you made your request to see me, these officers would like to talk to you about a person who is missing, presumed dead, and which you clearly have some knowledge about.'

Fitzpatrick seemed about to respond, but Creighton didn't give him the chance.

'Before you say anything, Mr Fitzpatrick, I'm not here to question you about your alleged involvement in this matter. However, this could be an opportunity for you to come clean about any part you may have played in this unfortunate business.'

'Mr Creighton,' Sandra said, 'with all due respect, this is a police matter, and although I'm extremely grateful for your input, and indeed for setting up this opportunity, I think you should leave me and my sergeant to conduct the rest of this interview. We have some specific information we wish to share and discuss with Mr Fitzpatrick, which could help us to locate Maureen O'Brian.'

She'd used Maureen's name deliberately. It was too easy in situations like this for sex workers to be dehumanised by virtue of their trade. Sandra wanted to remind Liam Fitzpatrick that the woman had been a real person, a human being, with hopes and dreams and worries just like everyone else, and not just a body that he and his brother had disposed of.

'I was merely trying to help you, Chief Inspector Bates,' Creighton said, his mouth drooping into a sulk. 'But the floor is yours.' He slumped back into his chair, arms folded like a petulant child.

Sandra nodded at the guvnor. 'Thank you, Mr Creighton. Now, Liam, I'm not going to beat around the bush with this – we know without a shadow of doubt that you and you brother had something to do with the disposal of Maureen's body. However, we also know that you didn't kill her. Your father did. And, yes, before you get all defensive, we have categorical and overwhelming evidence to prove that, so I'm not here to try and tie you in with the murder. I am simply here to offer you the chance to give up her location and save yourself a long prison sentence. Because, as you may already know, assisting us now – before any court case – and offering a guilty plea at your hearing in regard to the disposal matter, will guarantee you a third off your sentence. I'm also here to offer you an opportunity to provide information on your father's murder. And by the way, I want to offer you my sincere condolences, and I mean that. The horrific and dreadful way in which he was killed beggars belief, and we all want justice for him, in spite of his history.'

Liam Fitzpatrick looked shocked. 'How do you mean "horrific", Chief Inspector? What happened to him?'

Sandra paused for a moment. Making him wait, even for a few seconds, would ramp up the already frightened man's adrenalin levels. 'What we know, Liam – and it pains me to tell you this, especially while you're incarcerated like this – is that he'd been tortured and then burned alive.'

Liam buried his head in his hands and began to sob. His entire body seemed to shake with grief. Sandra almost felt sorry for him.

Stone seemed deeply affected. She wiped her eyes with a handkerchief and blew her nose as if she had a cold or something.

Sandra could imagine what was going through her sergeant's head, because she was a kinder person than Sandra. John Fitzpatrick may have been a suspected child rapist and drug user but his sons hadn't deserved to lose their father in that way. And she was right, to a degree, though it was a shame, Sandra thought, that the younger Fitzpatrick hadn't displayed the same empathy for Maureen O'Brian. Still, this was a godawful thing to for any kid to hear and so she redirected her hatred towards the man who was behind all of this shit. Tommy Spillane.

After a few minutes, Liam stopped crying and looked up at Sandra with bloodshot eyes. 'Who would do that to my dad, Chief Inspector, and why? I don't understand it.'

'We don't understand it either, Liam. I'm just relaying the facts to you. However, I strongly believe that Tommy Spillane had something to do with it, possibly with the help of Jack

Clay. Maybe others too. Do you know of any reason why they would want to harm your father?'

There was a shift in Liam – not just his expression but his deportment too. He straightened his back and stared at her hard, and she saw something new there. Pure, unadulterated anger.

'Oh, yes, I know exactly why they would do that to him, Chief Inspector Bates. Dad was nicked a few days ago, and accused of some nonsense about having sex with an underaged girl. But I know my dad; he wouldn't have done anything like that.'

Sandra exchanged a look with Stone, but neither said anything.

'Those fucking hypocrites,' Liam continued. 'Phonies and frauds the lot of them. They're involved in all sorts of things that make most people sick … including murdering people.'

Sandra leant forward, her interest piqued, and said gently, 'Who have they murdered, Liam?'

Liam ducked his head, as if he'd realised in that moment that he'd said too much.

Sandra pressed him. 'Liam, listen to me, anything you tell me about that accusation would help your position. I can make sure that you're protected, but, moreover, I can ensure you're treated as an asset to any enquiry that arises from that. You might not have to do any time in prison. I can't guarantee that, of course, but I'll make damn sure that the courts understand the importance of your help.'

Liam shrunk back into his seat. Fear seemed to overcome him and he started sobbing again.

'Come on now, lad,' Creighton said, 'stop that bloody crying. You obviously know something about these people who allegedly murdered your father. Just tell the chief inspector so she can bring them to justice. It's in your best interests, I can—'

'Mr Creighton, please. Let me handle this. This man has just been told about his father's brutal murder. We need to give him some time to mourn and make the right decision in this matter.'

Liam's head shot up. And now he seemed oddly excited, like a young boy who'd been told he was going to earn a scout badge. 'I don't need time to mourn or make the right decision, Chief Inspector. I'll show you where her body is. It's right next to the other one we buried last year.'

63

Plumage

'I think you need to pay Stan Collins a visit, son,' Tommy said.

They'd returned to Tommys den as soon as dinner was over. The beef wellington had been delicious, but Jack had nevertheless itched to continue the conversation with his father-in-law.

'He's a narky little prick,' Tommy continued. 'One who's gotten a little bit too big for his boots, I reckon. He's your collateral damage. A word of warning though –don't underestimate him. He's a proven fighter, and so are his boys. They've run the Old Red Lion for years now, and have caused me very little trouble. However, his pub is well known for drugs, which I've always told him to tone down. He hasn't. I think he needs to be told again, don't you, son?'

Jack nodded. 'Leave it with me. I'll make sure he understands.'

'Good, that's settled then. Get it done soon. I've decided I want to leave for Spain within a week.'

'So soon? There's still a lot I need to know and learn.'

Tommy laughed. 'I'm not emigrating to the other side of the world, Jack. Besides, you have everything you need right now. Trust me. Make an example of Collins and everything will fall into place, I guarantee it. Use Ronnie. You can trust him and he's a serious player.'

'Your shout, mate,' Jack said. 'Do the girls know what's going on?'

'Peggy does. We haven't told Lorraine or Amanda yet, but like I said, we're not going to the end of the world. Spain is a two-hour flight away, and there are such things as phones.'

Which reminded Jack – he had some calls of his own to make.

***

Less than an hour later, Jack, Ronnie and Callum were heading towards Kennington, where the Old Red Lion was located. Behind it sat the Cornwall housing estate, well known for its drug dealers and violence. Most sensible people kept away after dark.

During the day, the boozer was quiet, but at this time of the evening it was buzzing, exactly what Jack wanted. He needed to make a statement. And he was keen to get this little bit of business out of the way now so he could move it off his to-do list and make space in his head for other matters.

Tommy had filled him on the history. Stan Collins had been the landlord for the best part of twenty years and was well known for not taking any nonsense from anyone. The pub had previously been under the protection of the Parkhurst twins. This had been their turf, after all. However, there'd been that unfortunate business down in Hythe, after which Tommy had paid Stan a visit.

Stan had known all about the North London outfit, but had naively thought they were just chancers, trying to muscle in now that Jimmy was dead and Harry was serving a life sentence. Harry, it seemed, had even sent over a representative to the pub shortly after his arrest, to deliver a message: that the pub was still under Harry's protection. That had transpired to be bollocks. Just a no-mark trying to muscle his way in but with no real connections to Harry. So when Tommy had come calling, Stan had listened. Or at least pretended to. Now Tommy and Jack where thinking it had all just been lip service.

Tommy had told Jack to be careful. Ronnie's reputation would count for a lot, but Stan would be expecting the North London firm to assert their authority, especially after the recent visit.

Stan had his own boy – Charlie Banks – a well-known local thumper with his own team, and who was, according to the grapevine, still loyal to Harry Parkhurst.

Stan would think he was ready.

It would be up to Jack, Callum and Ronnie, to disprove him of that notion.

Jack appraised his passengers of the situation, and what was required of them. Neither had any issues. In fact, both seemed to relish the opportunity.

'Just follow the plan, boys' Jack said. 'This landlord and his cronies need to learn a lesson. There's a new boy in town, and they need to start listening. This is necessary. It's what Tommy and I want.'

They arrived at the pub, found a space in the car park, and went over the plan one more time.

Ronnie said nothing, merely nodded.

Callum said, 'Let's get on with it.'

Jack loved that attitude. He'd been in many a battle with his trusted friend and knew his capabilities. And while it was his first foray with Ronnie, if reputation was anything to go by, he should have no worries.

Jack stayed in the car. His two passengers got out and walked towards the pub.

***

Ronnie walked into the public bar through the front door and took a seat at the end of the bar. Stan came straight over.

'Ronnie, mate, what are you doing here, son?' He smiled and extended his hand. 'Did you miss me already?'

'What, a man can't come in and get a drink, Stan?' he said, not even trying to hide the animosity in his voice.

'Not at all, Ronnie. I didn't mean it like that. It's just that you were only here a few hours ago. I'm just surprised to see you, again, that's all. I meant nothing by it.'

'Good, then get me a fucking drink, son, and don't worry about why I'm here.'

Some of the nearby punters moved further away. Maybe Ronnie's menacing demeanour was palpable to them. If so, good. That was how he liked it. Always.

***

Callum walked into the snug through the side entrance. He bought a drink, then stood sipping it beside the toilet door, where he had an unobstructed view through to the public bar. No one knew him here. Just another punter having a late-evening drink and minding his own business. Besides, the atmosphere in the small-but-busy pub had changed in the past few minutes, all eyes were on Ronnie and the landlord.

Callum had watched Stan greet Ronnie. He hadn't needed to hear what was said. Ronnie's body language made it clear that trouble was coming.

All part of the plan.

Stan shuffled off , then returned a few minutes later with Ronnie's drink. That done, he went to a table in the far corner of the pub, where Ronnie wouldn't be able to see him.

No matter. Callum could see them.

Stan sat down and began an animated conversation with five men. All looked formidable.

Ronnie looked straight ahead, his eyes on Callum but showed no hint of recognition.

Callum nodded, finished his drink, and left.

***

Ronnie watched Callum exit. That was his signal. He strolled towards the toilets, passing a group of five men sitting just behind a glass divider. Didn't make eye contact with any of them. Didn't need to. Could feel the animosity radiating from them.

He almost laughed. He'd been in this kind of situation many times in his life, and for the most part, thugs like this lot were predictable and easy to manage. The big fella in the leather jacket looked like he might be a handful though. Ronnie suspected he was their ring leader. Charlie Banks.

He'd need to be taken out first.

Ronnie knew what he had to do. He'd had his orders from Jack. Callum walking out of the pub had confirmed the situation.

It was on.

Ronnie walked into a cubicle and began his routine. Tucked into his trousers was his favoured weapon – a telescopic truncheon he affectionately called Albert. He made sure Albert was operational. Nothing worse than your weapon of choice failing you at the last minute.

He was ready.

The boys should be in place about now.

He took a deep breath and walked back out into the pub.

***

After reporting to Jack, Callum went back through the side entrance. Closely followed by Jack. Ronnie was coming out of the toilets.

Charlie Banks was waiting for him.

The thumper stood four feet from the toilet. He had something in his hand.

Like lightning, Ronnie launched himself forward and swung a truncheon at Banks's head, knocking him to the ground.

Banks's cronies descended on Ronnie, drawing their own weapons.

Ronnie just kept on swinging.

Out of the corner of his eye, Callum noticed movement at the bar. The landlord, Stan, was holding a bat and was now making his way towards the chaos.

A figure flew past Callum.

Jack.

In less than a second, his friend was in the fray with Ronnie.

Callum focused on Stan. Raised his weapon. And fired directly into the stomach of the advancing landlord.

Stan looked down, then up again. He seemed almost confused. Fair play, Callum decided. It wasn't everyday you found plumage protruding from your midriff. Stan attempted to pull it out. His face creased in pain. His face became ashen, and he fell to his knees.

A few minutes later, it was over. Jack and Ronnie had finished off the group with extreme violence and consummate ease. Callum figured they'd never really gotten their heads around what had hit them. The speed and voracity of the assault had caught them all by surprise.

Callum stood stock still, crossbow in hand, challenging anyone who fancied it to get involved.

No one did.

They boys left. They were back in North London in less than thirty minutes.

They had made their point.

**

Stan Collins was interviewed at the hospital a few days later, but made no statement. The arrival of the filth almost made him laugh, though that hurt too much, so he put a lid on it. Still, did they think he was stupid?

Strangely, the coppers were struggling to find witnesses. Everyone had gone three wise monkeys on them.

The police investigation that followed went nowhere, and the case was closed. Just another bar brawl. The police had better things to do.

Which was fine and dandy as far as Stan was concerned. He'd learned over his twenty years as a publican that it wasn't about the beer or the gin or the wine, or whether you sold peanuts or crisps or pork scratching. It was about knowing your customers. Which ones counted. Who to listen to and pay your dues to.

Stan knew his customers, and who was in charge now.

His name was Jack Clay. Just like Tommy had advised.

64

Digging Up Dirt

Sandra felt like she'd won the lottery.

'Ma'am, may I politely suggest you take that smug look off your face? It doesn't become you.' Stone opened the car door. 'Yes, you were right, I'll grant you that. But you got lucky. I never thought in a million years that Liam Fitzpatrick would have anything on that firm, but it seems he does. Strange, though, that he didn't know who they buried last year.'

Sandra grinned. Couldn't help it. Couldn't stop it. 'Yes, that was rather strange, but we'll soon find out, won't we, sergeant? And that other body, whoever it is, might just have some evidence we can use against Spillane.'

According to Liam Fitzpatrick, the body had been picked up from a place Spillane had an interest in. Sandra had almost salivated when he'd let that little nugget out of the bag.

'The first thing I need you to do is obtain a search warrant for that lockup in Kings Cross. Make it a priority. In the meantime, I'll inform Mike about the latest developments. And I won't pretend I'm not really looking forward to that.'

Stone laughed and gunned the car into life. 'Let's hope Liam wasn't spinning us a yarn. I still can't get my head around the idea that he didn't know who they were burying.'

'Oh, leave it out, you big doom merchant. He has absolutely nothing to gain from telling us that, and everything to lose. Anyone would think you're jealous because I was right all along! Seriously though, you heard him yourself. He took orders, nothing more. He's just a frightened little boy who's been living off his family's reputation for far too long. And now he's been found out.'

Stone chuckled. 'Whatever, ma'am.'

Peters was waiting for them at the Yard. Sandra had already briefed him over the phone, and he'd been gracious enough to acknowledge that the news was unexpected but dynamite.

'I'll get the wheels in motion,' he said. 'But it could take a day or two. We need Home Office approval to remove Liam Fitzpatrick from custody and get him down to Sussex and show us where to start digging.' Mike scratched his chin. 'We're going to need help from the local constabulary with the necessary equipment. Can't be lugging all that down with us.'

'Leave that with us, Mike,' Sandra said. 'I know the chief inspector. I'll make the call and get things going.'

'Let's hope he's not got us on some wild goose chase. Operations like this are eye-wateringly expensive, as you know. I can't pretend I'm not twitchy.'

'I've got no reason to think that. As soon as he found out about the circumstances surrounding his father's death, his whole outlook changed. He was pretty adamant about helping us. And resolute about the location too. No, I think it's genuine. He's just a scared little rat that's been well and truly cornered, and now he's doing everything he can to survive. You want my opinion, I think he'd have given up his own grandmother to get a reduced sentence. That's the state he's in.'

'Fair enough,' Peters said, nodding. 'Let's go and solve some murders!'

***

It was all arranged for the following day.

Stone drove. Sandra was in the passenger seat. Liam Fitzpatrick was in the back. Their destination: Ashdown Forest, thirty miles from the capital, or thereabouts.

Again, Liam's behaviour was odd. Excited. Almost childlike. Like he was going on a camping trip or something. It made Sandra wonder if he was the full ticket. She was half-expecting him to come up with something like 'Are we there yet?' He fell short of that, thank goodness.

And then he didn't. He actually said it, or close enough.

'Are we nearly there yet?'

Jesus.

Stone drove them down a narrow lane and parked up by a group of police officers. Peters came over and peered through the window.

Liam just sat there, gawping. And then his face slackened. Peters and the other coppers seemed to hold no interest for him.

If anything, the stupid, arrogant twat actually looked bored.

**

Liam glanced around the familiar terrain. Saw the uniforms. Lots of people. Too many. Far too many. And the gravity of what he was actually doing hit him like a hammer.

He didn't want to do this. Not anymore. He was grassing on his big brother, and even if it was John who'd led him down this path, John was still blood. His only blood.

Somebody was peering through the window at him. Staring at him like he was some circus sideshow. It was no better than being in the cell. The police, the screws, the other inmates. They were all the same – all looking after themselves. Not Liam. John and his dad were the only ones who'd ever looked out for him. And his dad was gone. John was still here. Well, not here but somewhere. Alive.

'Come on, Liam,' Stone said. 'Time to get out of the car. I need to put some handcuffs on you.' She opened the door. 'Protocol, you understand – that's all. But don't worry. I'll cuff you from the front. You can lead the way.'

He climbed out. Turned to the sergeant, who seemed nicer than the other one. She'd even had a little tear back in the guvnor's office, when he'd got upset.

'I can't remember anything, Sergeant,' he blurted.

'What the hell do you mean?' a voice said.

It was the man who'd been staring at him through the car window. He came towards Liam and loomed over him. Menacing. Like that big screw in the prison.

'DCI Peters, please,' Stone said. 'Just give him a moment.'

'You have got to be kidding me,' Peters said, and rolled his eyes.

'It all looks different now,' Liam said. 'It was dark the last time I was here. I don't recognise anything.'

To the left was a farmhouse surrounded by a low-level stone wall that extended a few hundred yards or so. To the right was a field that stretched away into the distance. It looked to Liam like it had been ploughed only a few days ago. The soil looked soft and fresh.

'I really don't remember, sir. Honestly, I don't. My brother drove the van, and I don't know where we stopped.'

Peters glowered at him. 'See that lane, pal, the one that stretches way into the distance? The one that's at least a quarter of a mile long? If your memory doesn't improve sharpish, it'll be you digging the whole fucking thing up.'

He grabbed Liam by the arm and led him away from Seargeant Stone and the other officers. Then he leant in close and whispered in Liam's ear. His voice reminded Liam of a snake hissing.

'Now, you listen to me, you little cunt. If you don't tell me where those bodies are buried, I'm going to make sure that your stretch in prison is the most difficult time of your life.

Think about what it'll be like for you if the other prisoners suspect you of child molestation and rape. I can make that happen. You'll be a pariah. You know what they do to nonces? They'll pour boiling sugar water over you whenever the opportunity arises. Your visits to the showers and the latrines will be ones of pure survival. Even the screws won't be able to protect you once I've had my say. Believe me, son, I'll do it. No one makes a fucking mug of me or my team. Do I make myself clear?'

Liam felt lightheaded. Felt the blood drain out of his face. His lips felt cold, almost numb. Yeah, he believed him alright. The thought of it gave him the horrors.

Chief Inspector Bates and her sergeant, and all the others too, they were all looking over at Liam and this Peters guy. It didn't take a genius to work out that Peters was threatening him in some way, but were they doing anything? No. They were all turning a blind eye to it, or should that be a blind ear? All they all wanted was what he could offer them. None of them cared whether any wrongdoing was going on.

But what choice did he have? What choice had he ever had? Fuck his dad. Fuck John. Fuck everyone.

'Alright, alright,' he yelled. 'We took her – the prostitute, I mean – through those two trees just there, past that road marker. I recognise that from both evenings.'

It was a luminescent sign that warned cars at night of the upcoming bend in the road ahead. There was a layby of sorts, which allowed cars to pass each other.

'Are you sure, Fitzpatrick,' Peters hissed. 'If you're fucking with me, I promise you, you'll regret it.'

'As sure as I'll ever been, sir,' Liam said. His own voice disturbed him. He sounded meek, done in for. Resigned. Hopeless. 'We only came up a short distance and stopped right there both times.'

Peters marched him over to the gap in the hedge between the trees. 'Here? Is this where you entered the field?'

Liam nodded. 'Yes, sir.'

'And how far did you go in? Tell me first about the most recent time, when you buried Maureen O'Brian.'

Liam pointed to an area around six foot in. 'About there, sir.'

Peters snapped his fingers at two nearby uniformed officers. 'You, set up a perimeter around this area and close the road off at both ends.' He turned to the other. 'And you get yourself over to that farmhouse and inform the owners about our investigation. And find out if they saw or heard anything on the evening of the disposal. And I need to know when this field was ploughed and how deep the machine goes.'

He turned back to Liam. 'Now, Fitzpatrick, tell me about the other one you buried here.'

That was a bit of a blur. 'I don't remember exactly, sir. I really don't. Like I said, it was dark and it was a long time ago.'

'It was just over a fucking year ago,' Peters snapped. 'Hardly a long time, son. Now where the fuck did you bury it? Don't forget what—'

'I CANT FUCKING REMEMBER.' Liam took a few breaths, trying to quell the panic. Imagining boiling sugar water on his skin and being raped while he was trying to take a shit. 'I was pissed. All I know is it's there somewhere, I promise.'

Peters grunted and looked over his shoulder. 'Sandra, get this filth back to Pentonville. We don't need him anymore. He's fucking useless. Leave this to me and my team now. I'll update you when we have more information.'

Bates looked over at him. Maybe there was a flicker of pity there. But it was no more than that.

65

Too Old to Run

Tommy swore under his breath. He'd had it all mapped out, hadn't he? The flights to Spain had been booked for next Wednesday. The issue with Collins had been sorted beautifully. Old Stan wouldn't be playing up again any time soon. Ronnie had come up trumps and done what Ronnie did best. The man, Jack told him, had been a fucking beast. And Callum – well, he'd done the firm proud. Who have thought that the Legal and General firm would have William bloody Tell on its books? That had made Tommy laugh.

And then it had all gone to shit.

The discovery of bodies in Ashdown Forest was all over the fucking news. Their identities too – Maureen O'Brian and Darren Davies.

And then another blow the following day. The raid on his lockup. Just as he was about to leave the country.

He'd imagined this day, and how he might feel when the time came. Most involved in his world did at some point. He'd thought he might feel anger, or despair, maybe even fear. But none of that was happening right now. Instead, he was strangely philosophical about the situation. This was business.

He called Jack. Filled him in. How John Senior had used his own sons to dispose of the prostitute and that Judas, Darren Davies. Of course, it all made sense now. He'd not been able to get to the bottom of that issue, and it had niggled. Dear old Albie, God rest his soul, must have tried to use John Senior for the disposal of Darren, but then John had passed it on – subcontracted it to his boys.

'And there's a fucking lesson for you, son,' he said to Jack. 'Don't ever trust anyone who's on drugs. This is what it leads too.'

Jack asked him what he was going to do.

Again, Tommy found himself reacting rather stoically. 'Not much I can do now, is there? I can't run. I'm too old. And, besides, they'd catch up with me soon enough even if I scarpered. No, it's only a matter of time before the filth pick me up. I don't want to be staring at another TIA, thanks very much. Plus, son, it's not like it used to be over in Spain. The extradition treaties between our two countries are well established these days. I'm just going to wait for the knock on the door and fight them like I always have. You never know – they might not have enough to send me down the swanny. They didn't last time, did they?'

There was silence at the other end of the phone.

Tommy wondered if Jack was putting the pieces together. So he said it for him. 'They may want to speak to you as well Jack.'

More silence.

Then Jack said, 'Why would they want to question me? I had nothing to do with Maureen or Darren's deaths. I was inside when Darren went missing.'

'Because they've just finished searching the lockup. Which means they could have found something there that links you to the place. Can you be certain that you left nothing behind? No trace at all? None of us wanted to clean that pit properly, did we? With all the advances in DNA technology, we'd be stupid to assume they won't find something.'

The silence stretched between them. Tommy broke it. 'Just get your story straight, son. It's highly likely that you'll be lifted as well. See you on the other side, mate.'

66

It's a Wrap

Maureen O'Brian body was found wrapped in a carpet rug. It was clear she'd been beaten severely. Identification was immediate. Cause of death established the very same day: Murder.

Two days later, and by means of an excavator, the body of an unknown male was recovered. Half his head had been caved in. Cause of death: Murder.

Dental records revealed the identity of the cadaver. Darren Davies. The man had disappeared a year or so earlier and was well known to the police owing to his association with Tommy Spillane.

But what excited Sandra more was the substantial but as yet unidentified DNA recovered from the burial site by the investigative team.

A baseball bat.

And stuck on the end of one of Davies' shoes, a cigarette stub. Benson & Hedges Gold.

That evidence was with the laboratory team and their results weren't due for a few days.

Meanwhile, a search warrant for Tommy Spillane's lockup in Kings Cross was executed.

And that's where things had become really interesting. By Sunday morning, the forensic team were reporting human remains within a scorched car pit and substantial evidence of foul play. There were multiple DNA samples and numerous fingerprints all over the garage. Belonging to persons unknown as yet. Not enough to prove that they'd perpetrated an actual crime, but plenty to prove an association with the crime scene.

And that was the break Sandra had been itching for. It was enough to bring Spillane in. And that was a start. A warrant was issued. The first next step to justice.

She allowed herself a moment. Imagined wiping the smug look off his face when she snapped the handcuffs on him.

The others – his cronies? They were a bonus.

A short time later, Tommy Spillane, Jack Clay, and Ronnie Fisher were arrested. Spillane was charged with the murders of Darren Davies and John Fitzpatrick Senior. murders. Clay was charged with conspiracy to murder. Fisher was charged with conspiracy to murder and the unlawful disposal of a body.

None got bail.

And that, Detective Chief Inspector Sandra Bates decided, was a wrap.

Epilogue

Are We Nearly There Yet?

Tommy Spillane. Jack Clay. Ronnie Fisher. Liam Fitzpatrick.

All of them banged up.

My oh my. Marcus Kingham leant back in his chair and re-read the notes he'd made following his visit to Liam.

Because Liam was the link between them all. The one who'd spilled his guts to the police. The weak point.

Not weak for Marcus. Weak for the law.

DCI Peters, Liam had told him, had bullied and threatened him in the most appalling and shocking manner. Rape and torture had been mentioned. All anecdotal of course, but still.

He doubted Liam had the capacity to make that kind of thing up. And it wouldn't be the first time a police officer had done more than hint at what might be 'arranged' for a prisoner who wasn't prepared to play ball.

And Detective Chief Inspector Bates and Sergeant Stone had been more than happy to confirm that Liam's behaviour on the way down to Sussex had been odd and annoying. His jabbering. His excited childishness during the car journey. Asking whether they were nearly there yet; Stone had even giggled when Bates had relayed that. And then Liam's sudden disinterest when they'd arrived.

All of which had been interpreted by Bates as arrogance or some sort of sociopathic indifference. Stone had concurred.

Both officers had looked at Marcus with disdain as he'd asked about the car journey, as if the clients he worked for didn't deserve Marcus's support.

Wrong. Everyone had a right to representation. The Spillanes of this world. The Clays and Fishers too. But especially the likes of Liam Fitzpatrick.

Marcus's nephew – a sweet kid – had been diagnosed with a learning difficulty when he was seven. His parents had sought help after noticing that his reaction to stressful events wasn't what they'd expected. Most kids' behaviour in those situations was predictable. They'd cry or lash out or hide or sulk. Something like that. But not Evan. Evan would become excited, almost overly engaged. For a while at least. And then his mood would collapse and he'd stare into space, as if he was looking at everything and nothing.

It was a defence mechanism, the child psychologist had explained. A way of keeping it together under pressure. A way of managing trauma.

There was better support for kids with special needs these days. Not so much when Liam Fitzpatrick had been seven. Perhaps he'd slipped through the net. Or maybe his father had noticed it but been too busy with other 'business' to give a damn. Or maybe, just maybe, he'd thought it convenient – something to be exploited.

The police, especially custody officers, were trained to recognise learning difficulties and adapt their procedures accordingly. In theory anyway. And if Liam did have some sort of learning disability, even a mild one, and they'd not done their due diligence, that was a big problem for them.

One that Marcus could exploit.

People with disabilities were entitled to appropriate support that protected their rights and well-being. This included the presence of an Appropriate Adult, which could be a family member, a social worker, or some other kind of trained volunteer. AAs were supposed to assist with communication, ensure fair treatment, and help the individual understand the process.

Bates and Stone had experienced Liam's behaviour first-hand. Noticed it. Commented on it. Yet neither had questioned it. Hadn't thought to ensure that Liam was properly assessed and provided with the necessary legal and mental-health support.

Marcus could sympathise. Policing was a tough job. Maybe Bates had decided she needed to hold her nerve. The goal was the bodies and the possibility of key evidence she'd been hunting for. Maybe she'd figured that this was the way policing went sometimes – a little bend here, a little stretch there. All with the bigger end goal in mind. The wrong actions for the right reasons.

Perhaps she'd recognised that it wasn't ideal.

But decided it was necessary anyway.

But every decent defence lawyer had a job to do too. Find holes, weaknesses, gaps that would unravel a case fall at the seams one thread at a time. Focus attention on other spaces and places – like on the Met and the power they held, and the impact that might have on vulnerable others. Vulnerable others such as Liam Fitzpatrick.

No doubt Sandra Bates believed she had her perps bang to rights.

No doubt Mellissa Stone thought it amusing that Liam had asked if they were nearly there yet.

No doubt both thought their case was.

Marcus Kingham wasn't so sure. Not so sure at all.

Read on for a taste of

"THE RISE"

book 4 of the London crimeland series!

1

Knight of the Realm

Katie Finch had quickly established herself in her new surroundings. It wasn't all plain sailing, of course. She was still wanted for questioning by the Murder and Vice Squads in relation to a couple of matters over the water in Kings Cross. The attempted coercion of a minor no less and as a witness in the murder of Maureen O'Brian, a madam who'd fallen foul of the out and out wrongen John Fitzpatrick. She'd managed to slip away from the inquiry quickly once released from custody, and everyone believed she was back hiding in Manchester.

She wasn't.

And the brothel – what Katie preferred to call a working house – on Leigham Court Road in Streatham was doing rather well thanks to her adept running of the business. It had started when Rachel, an old acquaintance from her hometown of Oldham, had let her hide out in a flat just down the road from the brothel where she herself worked. Katie had needed work, and Rachel had seen a fresh nineteen-year-old girl able to do it.

Katie didn't fuck about. She'd quickly put her streetwise knowledge to work and offered to provide madam services at her new place of work. Good, reliable madams were hard to come by, mostly because the pay was shit – just a little retainer and a small cut from the day's business. That business end of things was usually undertaken by more experienced older women who'd either had enough of servicing men or were no longer in demand. It was usually the latter but in this case the madam had been

run out of town owing to her reluctance to work for the North London mob.

Katie had thrived. She'd always prided herself on what some had called a certain cunning and ruthlessness. Plus she sometimes earned a little extra, depended on the punter. And Big Steve had spotted it soon enough.

He was the security man. Katie, always one to keep her ear to the ground, had heard another role ascribed to him. Enforcer. For the Parkhurst twins. Well, one of them anyway. Recent and unfortunate events in Hythe had seen one brother killed in a police shootout and the other found guilty of double murder. He was still to be sentenced.

And then one evening a few months ago, a man called Jack Clay had come calling. It had been made clear that the establishment was now under new ownership. Big Steve had been told that if he wanted to, he could stay on – the choice was his. Katie, ever vigilant, had seen him treat it like just another day at the office. New ownership was nothing new in their business, he'd quickly agreed.

It hadn't surprised Katie. There was something about Jack Clay that you didn't refuse. He had a menace about him that commanded respect. She'd also heard about a "little" incident in a pub where the landlord and several of his customers had been brutally attacked by Jack Clay and other members of his firm. The landlord had been shot in the stomach with a crossbow and had barely survived the assault. While the others were left in pools of blood where they fought and lost. Steve had surely known that a refusal would not end well.

Jack Clay had offered him a shit ton of money, too, more than he'd been getting from Harry and Jimmy Parkhurst by all accounts, and Katie had seen her retainer increased as well. They'd both been assured that as long as they did their jobs there would be no issues.

Just as his nickname implied, Steve was a big fella and could handle himself. Any punters who played up in the brothel very quickly learned that to mess with the girls, was to mess with Big Steve. Very few did once they clapped eyes on him, standing in the lobby most evenings, looking like the nightclub bouncer, they behaved themselves. Steve, Katie had decided, was the real deal.

Now and then, a drunk might get too handsy with one of the girls or refuse to pay. Steve would step in and very quickly dispatch the offender. The outcome was typically a beating vicious enough to ensure that the idiot never came back for seconds or bothered the girls again.

It was the way of things in this world, and it meant that the girls always got their money, and he got a little something extra for his troubles.

One of their regular visitors was Cecil Creighton ... *Sir* Cecil Creighton no less. He was the guvnor of Pentonville prison in North London, but word had it he'd also been asked to stand in at Belmarsh because some MBE bloke, who'd been in charge since the early nineties, had popped his clogs.

Sir Cecil had a favourite, just as most punters did. Lovely Lucy Parsons was his go-to. At the tender age of twenty-two she'd been working at Leigham Court Road for just over three years. It was the usual story. Her crack and heroin addiction had taken her by the throat at the age of eighteen and dragged her down into a pit of despair. And just like so many of the girls Katie came across in her own short life, this had culminated in her having no other choice than to sell her precious body to the highest bidder in order to feed an out-of-control habit.

Just as Rachel had taken Katie in, so she'd offered refuge to Lucy. The girl had proved popular since she'd arrived a few years earlier, and her heroin habit was now mostly recreational. That had been essential. Katie had insisted. Lucy wouldn't have lasted a minute in the brothel otherwise. Jack frowned on it and his orders were made clear.. no drugs in this establishment.

Sir Cecil was Lucy's best customer and visited at least twice a week. She liked him, she said, because he paid extra. But Katie knew it wasn't just the money; from time to time, he'd bring her heroin confiscated from prisoners. Must be nice to have almost unlimited access, Katie often mused. And since Lucy's habit was under control, Katie was happy to let it slide. Plus, it made for a happy customer. By all accounts, Lucy was willing to please the guvnor in any way he wanted. A good job too because his appetite was ferocious, despite his age. Lovely Lucy obliged his every whim.

That did worry Katie a little. A girl who was out of it probably barely knew what was going on. If she was being abused, the heroin would for the most part take away the pain. And troubled girls tended to keep their private lives just that – private. Katie kept her nose out of it, as long as Lucy was bringing in the money, she really didn't give a shit. She was a good earner.

Today, Sir Cecil had had his hour, and yet there was no sign of him emerging from Lucy's room.

'What the hell is that girl doing?' she said to big Steve, standing just inside the main entrance. 'go and check on her, please mate? Clock's ticking and we have other customers to attend too.' She nodded towards the hallway where a lone man sat waiting patiently for his turn with Lucy.

Steve made his way down the corridor to her room. A minute later he was back at the desk. He leaned casually into Katie, his expression impassive, and whispered, 'You'd better come with me, love. There's a problem.'

She followed him, and looked through the open door to the scene beyond. Lying on the bed was their guest, Sir Cecil. He was breathing heavily and seemed dazed, almost out of it. To his left and curled up on the floor beside the bed was Lucy.

A foamlike substance mixed with blood and vomit trailed from her mouth. Her eyes were wide open, staring ahead into nothing.

Lucy was dead.

A terrible stench of faeces permeated the room. Katie would have preferred to turn around and leave; the urge to throw up was intense. But that wasn't an option, so she composed herself, tried not to breathe through her nose, and knelt down beside Lucy's lifeless body. The girl had soiled herself in her struggle to survive the deathly throws of her overdose.

Steve stood there silently. He told Katie about how he'd seen something like this in another establishment he looked after over in Brixton, although on that occasion the girl had been alone. It didn't stop a deep sigh rising from his throat.

Shit happened. Literally in this case.

There was movement, unfortunately not from Lucy. Lovely Lucy would never move again. Instead, it was the imposing prison guvnor on the bed who'd stirred.

Katie snapped into action. 'Steve, get rid of that punter in the hall. And after that, clear the building. I want all the girls gone and this place locked up tight, am I clear?'

Steve gave her a look, like he didn't quite understand why they weren't calling an ambulance, and said as much.

Katie rolled her eyes. 'Don't you know who that man lying there is?' she whispered.

Big Steve looked blankly at her.

'That's Sir Cecil Creighton, a knight of the realm, don't you know. He'll pay handsomely for us to keep this quiet. It could be a big payday for both of us, Steve –not just from him but Jack as well! This is dynamite, can't you see that?'

It was as if a light bulb had been switched on. Big Steve got to work. Before long, the man sitting in the hallway had been ushered out of the building and Steve was knocking on doors, citing an emergency that had arisen. There was nothing to be alarmed about, he told the girls and their customers, but that was all he could say.

'Please just leave and make your way home. Everything's okay but it's essential that we close the house for the evening.'

Any questions were brushed aside. Steve's imposing frame and professional attitude ensured that no one asked twice. Within five minutes, the building was pretty much deserted.

Katie nodded. 'Now get on the blower,' she said quietly. 'Call Jack and tell him what's happened here. He needs to know, than get back here, you need to make sure this fucker don't go anywhere'

Order yours now

www.davepalmerauthor.co.uk